"Erynn Mangum creates a warm, funny finish to her Maya Davis series with *Double Shot*. Poor Maya—she's marrying the man of her dreams, but making decisions for two is a lot harder than it seems! Erynn's characters keep me giggling through the night, and while I'm sorry to see this series end, I can't wait to see what's next!"

—LORI FOX, reviewer, TitleTrakk.com

"Refreshing prose, livable faith, and adorable characters are hallmarks of Erynn Mangum's novels, and all qualities are firmly in place in her final Maya Davis novel. More addictive than the caffeine Maya serves at *Cool Beans*, *Double Shot* has Maya and Jack negotiating over questionable wedding venues, debating hydrangeas versus roses, and choosing between zookeepers and baristas. Erynn provides a joyful, pure, and genuine glimpse into relationships, family, and faith, unsurpassed in this genre. As my daughters begin to investigate relationships, Erynn's books will be my first recommendation!"

—REL MOLLET, Relz Reviewz

"*Double Shot* is a fantastic ride through some of the most important times of a young woman's life. Hold on tight as Maya Davis finds out what wedding planning, marriage, and sacrifice really mean on a day-to-day basis. Erynn Mangum's writing is clever, funny, and, most of all, very real. She grabs the audience by the heart and gives them sustenance for their everyday routine that's wrapped in witty humor and precious heartwarming moments."

—LORI TWITCHELL, reviewer, Fiction Addict

a maya davis novel

book three

DOUBLE SHOT

erynn mangum

NAVPRESS
Discipleship Inside Out™

NAVPRESS
Discipleship Inside Out™

NavPress is the publishing ministry of The Navigators, an international Christian organization and leader in personal spiritual development. NavPress is committed to helping people grow spiritually and enjoy lives of meaning and hope through personal and group resources that are biblically rooted, culturally relevant, and highly practical.

For a free catalog go to www.NavPress.com
or call 1.800.366.7788 in the United States or 1.800.839.4769 in Canada.

© 2010 by Erynn Mangum O'Brien

ISBN-13: 978-1-61521-549-2

Cover design by Arvid Wallen
Cover image by Shutterstock

Some of the anecdotal illustrations in this book are true to life and are included with the permission of the persons involved. All other illustrations are composites of real situations, and any resemblance to people living or dead is coincidental.

Unless otherwise noted, all Scripture quotations in this publication are taken from the New American Standard Bible® (NASB), Copyright © 1960, 1962, 1963, 1968, 1971, 1972, 1973, 1975, 1977, 1995 by The Lockman Foundation. Used by permission. Other versions used include the Holy Bible, New International Version® (NIV®), Copyright © 1973, 1978, 1984 by International Bible Society, used by permission of Zondervan, all rights reserved.

Library of Congress Cataloging-in-Publication Data

Mangum, Erynn, 1985-
  Double shot / Erynn Mangum.
    p. cm. -- (A Maya Davis novel ; bk. 3)
  ISBN 978-1-61521-549-2
  1. Fiances--Fiction. 2. Fiancees--Fiction. I. Title.
  PS3613.A5373D68 2010
  813'.6--dc22

                              2010023151

Printed in the United States of America

1 2 3 4 5 6 7 8 / 14 13 12 11 10

Other Books by Erynn Mangum

For my husband —I can't imagine being happier than I am with you. You are my best friend and the person I love to hang out with the most. I love you!

ACKNOWLEDGMENTS

My Lord and Savior—Father, You have taught me so much in this last year! Please continue to draw me closer and closer to You.

My husband—Jon, thank you for giving me the opportunity to stay home and write. And for keeping me accountable to do it! I love you!

My son—Little Nathan, you were with me writing this story before I even knew it! I love you so much and pray for you continually, sweet boy!

My family—Mom, Dad, Bryant, Caleb, Cayce, and my grandmother, Nama. I'm so thankful I was born into such a fun family. I love you all!

My in-law family—Greg, Connie, Allen, Vicky, Tommy, and Ashlee. Thank you for all the encouragement, support, and understanding. I love you!

My sweet friends and family—Thank you for the phone calls, the e-mails, the Facebook messages, and the coffee and lunch dates!

Jen and Greg Fulkerson, Walt and Barb Kelly, Shannon Kay, Kaitlin Bar, Elisa Wingerd, Laura Wright, Shannon Harden, Eliya Kirby, and Sarah Chancey—Thank you for your wonderful friendship!

The fabulous people at NavPress—Rebekah Guzman, Kris Wallen, Amy Parker, and Tia Stauffer; my amazing agent, Steve Laube; and my "unofficial" official business manager, Susan Mangum—I'm so thankful to work with such a fabulous team!

CHAPTER ONE

I have always wondered why it is that when a couple decides to commit to each other forever in front of God and many witnesses, that those witnesses then pelt the happy couple with hard, stinging grains of rice.

I've heard it's for good luck. So here's my question: Does it matter what kind of rice you pelt them with? Should it be long grain? Short grain? White? Brown?

I'm standing halfway down Aisle 23 at Hudson's local grocery store. People are giving me weird looks as I stand there balancing white, brown, and Minute rice bags and boxes in my hands. But I think it's not so much because of the rice and more because I'm wearing a hunter green, floor-length evening gown made from a premium silk/fiber blend.

My best friend, Jen Mitchell, is going to become Jen Clayton in exactly one hour. Pictures of the bride have been taken, hair has been styled and sprayed, and people have been dressed, poked, and prodded.

We were "calmly" sitting there, waiting for the groom's pictures to be done so the wedding could start, when Jen popped off the stool we propped under her so she wouldn't wrinkle her gorgeous, silky white dress.

"The rice!" she screamed. "I forgot the rice!"

Which is why I'm here in Aisle 23. In a hunter green, floor-length, halter-top maid-of-honor gown.

Because a M-O-H does whatever the bride needs.

"Did you, uh, need some help, miss?" A nerdy-looking kid wearing the grocery store's red and white shirt is standing there, eyeing the dress and the five bags and boxes of rice in my hands.

"Which one is a lucky rice?" I ask, shoving the rice at him.

He fumbles the Minute rice but manages to hold on to the rest of it. "Lucky rice?"

You'd think my attire would explain this. "For a wedding," I say, trying to be nice.

"A wedding," he repeats again.

I don't have time to play the parroting game. "Brown, white, short grain, long grain, or Minute. Pick one," I say.

He stares at me, big eyed. "How about . . . white rice," he stutters.

"Plain?"

"Yeah . . ."

I grab the jumbo bag from his overladen arms and then give him a hug, rice and all. "Thank you!" I'm off to the checkout.

"Running in heels" should be a phrase with the same dire connotation as "running with scissors." So, I walk quickly instead. I hand the jumbo bag to the checkout lady, and she scans it. I hand her my card, and she swipes it. I grab the plastic grocery sack she hands me, and she stares as I leave.

I make it back to the park where the wedding is taking place with plenty of time to spare. The groom, aka Travis Clayton, is posing with his mom and grandma by a large grove of trees. I wave as I run through the doors to the tiny building across from where the ceremony will be, and he waves back.

Travis Clayton and I dated most of high school, so the fact that he's marrying my best friend is a little weird. But I have gotten over it. And so has Jen—and that is what's important.

Jen is pacing in the small room where we are waiting. Her mom, Mrs. Mitchell, her cousin, Lacey, and Travis's sister, Megan, are all just sitting there, obviously not knowing what to do.

"Here is the rice," I say grandly, lowering it in front of her like an offering.

She looks at it, looks at me, and tears start to well up in her eyes.

"What? Jen, oh no, don't cry!" I look at the others in the room. "What happened?"

Mrs. Mitchell is huffing. "We cannot just put the rice in front of the guests like that, now can we, Maya?" she asks me, arms crossed over her chest.

Crud. I didn't even think about that! I hurriedly look at the clock. "It's okay, Jen. It's okay. I'll run back to the store and get some little bags. We're fine. Do you hear me?"

She sniffles. "Everyone just looks so beautiful," she squeaks.

We all look at her. "What?" Lacey asks timidly. Not to be mean, but Lacey Mitchell is one of those girls who sort of reminds me of a mouse. She's incredibly tiny, has this quiet little voice, and rarely speaks.

Jen gulps a breath of air and starts waving her hands in front of her face, trying to dry her eyes. "I'm sorry. . . . I'm sorry. . . ." she mutters over and over.

I glance at Mrs. Mitchell, who still has her arms crossed over her chest. Mrs. Mitchell is slowly softening after living with Jen and me for the past three months, but she hasn't changed completely.

Travis's sister, Megan, is only nineteen, and she seems more interested in what her hair looks like than what is going on with Jen.

It's going to come down to me being the comforter.

Jen is still waving her hands. "I can't cry, I can't cry, I can't cry," she's saying over and over again.

"You won't, you won't." Apparently, the repetition is contagious. I let her calm down before I reach for her shoulder and start rubbing. "Jen? Do you want me to go get bags for the rice?"

She blinks at me. "The rice? We aren't allowed to throw rice here. Birds could choke on it and die."

I look at her. "What?"

"Yeah, they choke. It expands in their stomach or something and—"

I cut her off midsentence. "Why did you want me to go get rice then?"

Jen just closes her eyes. "Did I say rice? I meant bubbles. Oh dear . . ." She starts wringing her hands.

I look at Mrs. Mitchell, who just sighs. "Jennifer," she starts, but then I guess she sees my face and stops.

I squeeze Jen's arms. "Give me fifteen minutes." There is a Dollar Tree right down the street. If they don't have them, Jen isn't getting bubbles.

Mrs. Mitchell starts shaking her head, and I suddenly realize how similar Jen looks to her mom. "I will go get them, Maya," she says dramatically.

I nod, and Mrs. Mitchell leaves.

Lacey is sitting calmly in her chair, hands folded together, ankles crossed. She's serenely looking somewhere off in the distance, current crisis apparently of no concern to her. Megan, meanwhile, is hogging the one mirror in the room, curling her long brown hair for the third time.

I look at Jen. She's getting married in less than forty-five minutes.

We'd said our good-byes last night. I think we got about four hours of sleep altogether, because after we cried and talked for several hours, we decided to watch *Runaway Bride*, just for the fun of it.

I fell asleep on the sofa bed somewhere after Ike kissed Maggie and before she proposes. When my alarm buzzed at eight this morning, Jen was curled up around one of the couch pillows on the floor, snoozing away.

I look at Jen, and she takes my breath away. She is beautiful to begin with, but this is her wedding day and she looks ethereal. Her dress is stunning. It's fitted and simple in a way that makes it look extremely expensive. Her long blond hair is down in romantic, loose curls, and her makeup is flawless. The veil floats delicately over her hair.

I smile at her. "You're a bride."

The tears disappear. "I'm a bride," she whispers, and then she's grinning so wide, I worry about her makeup creasing. "I'm getting married!".

I laugh.

"Have you seen Travis?" she asks, voice hushed in respect for the sacred tradition of not seeing the groom before the grand entrance.

"I watched him take a picture with his grandma and his mom," I say.

"Well, how'd he look?"

I shrug. He actually looked a little uncomfortable, but it is August and he is wearing a tux.

Poor guy.

"He looked fine," I say when she gives me a look.

"Fine? It's his wedding day! Shouldn't he look exuberant?" Jen bursts.

"Okay, he looked exuberant," I say.

"Maya."

"Jen, relax. He looked fine. He looked happy. And hot," I say.

She raises her eyebrows, and now she's back to wringing her hands. "I thought you were over him!" She hisses this so Megan and Lacey can't hear.

There aren't very many absolutes in my life right now, but being over Travis Clayton is definitely one of them. I squinch my eyes at her. "I'm sorry?"

"He looked hot?"

I start giggling. "Warm, Jen. He looked warm."

"Oh." Now she's giggling. She covers her mouth and leans close, again so Megan and Lacey can't hear. "I was going to say that I know your timing is horrible, but really, Maya." She grins.

I take the opportunity to sneak in one more awkward don't-wrinkle-the-dresses hug. "Today is going to be perfect. Bubbles or no bubbles."

"Have you shown Jack your dress yet?" she asks.

And the real reason I'm 100 percent over Travis Clayton has arrived in our conversation. Jack Dominguez is one of my very best friends. I've known him since the second grade and worked with him for the last four years before he decided he wanted to shovel elephant dung for the rest of his life. He now works at the Hudson Zoo.

He's also the one who gave me the sparkling nearly-a-carat solitaire that is glittering on my left hand so much that it's over-whelming my dress.

That was three days ago. I'm still not used to the ring being there. Driving has become a hazardous experience for me because I get so distracted staring at the ring that I can't focus on the streets.

I haven't told Jack that.

Jen's waiting expectantly for me to answer. "Oh," I say, "no, he hasn't seen the dress yet."

Jen grins. "Well, you're going to knock his socks off. You look gorgeous, Maya."

"Thanks," I say.

The door opens and our pastor, Andrew, pokes his head in. "How's it going in here, ladies?" he asks, grinning.

Jen gasps. "Andrew, have you seen him?" She's back to wringing her hands and has that panicked look in her eyes again.

Andrew, though, is nothing short of difficult. Even when he's watching a bride have an anxiety attack. "Who?" he asks innocently.

I narrow my eyes at him, and Andrew winks at me. Maybe I don't want Andrew to officiate at my wedding.

My wedding.

Jack and I haven't talked about dates yet. The whole thought seems weird and strange. I'm going to be moving in with Jack. I'm going to be living with Jack forever.

Forever.

Long time.

I shake my head to make myself focus. Today is Jen's day, not mine.

And Jen is about to kill our pastor, and I'm thinking she needs to be reminded that without him, there is no second ring on that left hand, nor the opportunity to leave for her cruise honeymoon to Hawaii.

"Andrew," I say sternly, "have you seen Travis? Is he doing okay?" I grab Jen's shoulders and pull her back from the door and Andrew's head.

I guess he hears the unspoken warning in my voice, because he doesn't crack another joke. "Just finished with pictures. We've got about five minutes before we'll start changing the music and seating the grandparents."

Mrs. Mitchell runs in right then. "Here are all the bubbles they had," she says, panting. She shoves ten boxes at us, and in all, we now have two hundred bubble containers.

Sounds sticky.

Mrs. Mitchell dashes over to the mirror and not so subtly pushes Megan out of the way.

It seems like no time at all before Andrew is popping his head back in. "Time to line up, ladies. Mrs. Mitchell, I'm going to need you to come with me."

She walks over and gives Jen a short hug. "You look lovely," she says quietly and then leaves.

Mrs. Mitchell is not the emotional type.

I hear a squeal, and my mom appears in the doorway.

My mom, however, is the emotional type.

Mom is already brushing away tears, and the wedding hasn't even happened. "Oh, Jen, you look so beautiful!" she breathes, wrapping her arms around Jen's shoulders. "I'm so proud of you, darling. You will have a wonderful life."

Jen hugs Mom back, and then Mom looks to me. "You look gorgeous, Maya," Mom says, hugging me as well.

"Okay, ladies, time to go."

We all file out of the room. Mom hurries to her seat, and Mrs. Mitchell is already standing just behind Jen's grandma.

Mr. Mitchell, Jen's basically nonexistent father, is hanging up his cell phone and walking over. "Well, let's do it," he says, taking his spot by Jen.

Mr. Mitchell is never far from his phone, and he's only been out to Hudson once before. He never remembers Jen's birthday, so once a year he sends her a huge check as guilt money, I guess. It's helping to pay for the cushy apartment she and Travis got, but I think Jen would rather have a dad and live cheaply.

Travis's grandparents walk out, then Jen's grandma, then Travis's parents, then Jen's mom. Megan is up next.

I turn to Jen one last time. "Okay. I waited until now to tell you this, but I have a rubber bouncy ball, and I am not afraid to use it on your head if you start crying."

Jen laughs.

Lacey walks out. I give Jen a final hug.

I walk out, and my heels sink into the thick grass. Heels were not a good idea. There are about two hundred chairs filled with happy, smiling people and a center aisle that leads to a huge, lily-covered arbor in front of everyone. Travis is lightly bouncing on his toes, nervously smiling. Andrew is right behind him, giving me a smart-alecky smile.

I glance behind me and find Jack sitting next to my parents, my brother, Zach, and his pregnant wife, Kate. Jack winks, and I feel a blush start to rise on my cheeks.

"Everyone rise," Andrew says as I find my place in the grass.

The violinist and cellist that Jen found at our church start playing the "Wedding March," and everyone stands to their feet.

Jen appears, and she's just radiating. I can hear Travis take a deep breath, and I grin.

"Welcome, everyone," Andrew starts once Jen has taken Travis's hand.

And Jennifer Mitchell is no more.

CHAPTER TWO

"Weddings are messy," Zach says four hours later, stuffing a tablecloth into a trash bag to be taken to the cleaners.

My family volunteered to stay and clean. I've long since kicked off my heels, Jen and Travis are on their way to marital bliss, and Jack is flicking candy-coated almonds from another table at me.

One hits me on the arm, and I growl. "Stop it!"

"You guys have such a mature relationship," Zach says dryly. He stuffs another tablecloth in the too-full trash bag. "This must have been a kid table. Disaster."

"You forget that in a year or so, your table will be a disaster," I say.

"My kid is not going to act like that. We play Mozart and Beethoven every night, so they'll have a nice high IQ. And Kate reads medical journals and courtroom transcripts to them every day."

I keep waiting for Zach and Kate to slip and reveal the sex of the baby, but so far, they've been practiced. No slips, no Jennifer Garner on *Jay Leno* moments. Nothing.

It's annoying.

"Mozart, huh?" I ask. I try to hide the face I'm making

behind one of the centerpieces. I am not a fan of classical music. Some people claim it's soothing; I think it's grating. I like fifties music—Elvis, Sinatra, Dean Martin.

And medical journals and courtroom transcripts? What are they hoping for, a cross between McDreamy and John Cusack from *Runaway Jury*? I think they should be reading *Harry Potter* to the baby. J. K. Rowling is the richest person in England lately, if I remember right.

Apparently, I should have no hopes of having a smart child.

I put the centerpiece in a box filled with six other flower arrangements and frown. I'm not sure why Zach and Kate are so worried about having a child with a low IQ anyway. Zach is a doctor, and Kate is a lawyer. If any couple should feel secure about their children's genius, you'd think it would be them.

Me? I'm a barista. I majored in English because I didn't know what else to do, and I hate teaching. Jack? He's a zookeeper. He has chosen a career working with monkeys.

"Stop doing that to your lip," Jack says, coming up behind me and bouncing an almond off my head. "You're going to leave bruises."

I stop biting my lower lip and start rubbing my head. "Ow."

"What's wrong?"

"We're going to have kids with low IQs."

Jack shrugs. "I never liked smart people anyway," he whispers, nodding toward Zach.

I'm not sure whether or not I should be offended. "Are you saying I'm not smart?" I ask.

Jack winces. "No."

"So, if I'm smart, then now you're saying you don't like me?"

More wincing. "Am I going to need a shovel?" he asks in a small voice.

"To dig yourself out of the hole you're in? Probably." I stick another centerpiece in the box and turn to Jack, hands on hips. "Well?"

He comes over and wraps his arms around my stiff body. "Hi, baby."

I sigh. "Get away from me."

Zach walks by right then. "Sheesh, and you guys are barely in the engagement stage. You're supposed to be all syrupy right now, Maya. Not telling him to leave."

"He said our future child was not going to be very bright," I say, pointing fingers.

"She said it first," Jack says, pointing right back at me.

Zach sighs. "I'll copy the Beethoven playlist to your computer when the time comes, Maya."

Swell. I try to generate some enthusiasm, but I think I'd almost rather help my child with his or her homework than listen to Beethoven. "Great. Thanks, Zach."

Zach moves on to the last table, and Mom comes over, carrying the box for the archway.

"What a gorgeous wedding," she says, smiling and teary eyed.

"Mrs. Davis, I'll get the arch," Jack says, hastily grabbing the box from her. That's Jack for you. Avoiding confrontation while appearing to be a gentleman.

Mom is flattered. "What a sweet boy you have there," she says, all sickly sweet. "He's so polite! And so helpful!"

"And he just called your future Dominguez grandchildren not the sharpest knives in the drawer," I say.

Mom rolls her eyes. "Hush, Maya. Jack would never say something like that." She frowns at me. "Unless you provoked him."

I can already tell that my position as the favorite is slipping rather quickly. What is it about in-laws that causes some moms to forget their own children? Did Jack give my mother dandelions when he was four years old? Did Jack bring my mother complimentary bags of her favorite Cool Beans roasts? Does Jack call my mother every day to see how she's doing?

No, no, and no.

Kate comes by and wraps an arm around Mom's shoulders. She was never the huggy type until she got pregnant, so I'm curious to see if it's the hormones in her system causing her to be all touchy-feely or if she'll stay that way after the baby is born. She grins at my mom. "So, Soon-to-Be-Grandma, where can I put the lily and rose bouquets? I'm assuming Jen will want to keep them."

Mom turns from frowning at me and smiles all lovingly at Kate. "That's an excellent question, my dear. Let's go figure that out." She walks away with Kate, leaving me with the box of centerpieces.

Jack carries the archway, which has been disassembled and put back in the box, over to her. "Where should I take this, Mrs. Davis?" he asks cheerfully.

Brownnoser.

Zach comes up behind me, and we both watch as our mom chats excitedly with Kate and Jack and then gives them both hugs.

"Well, kid. I think we're officially not the preferred choice anymore." Zach squeezes my shoulder.

"How did this happen?" I ask, carefully packing another centerpiece. "I mean, we've known her the longest."

"It's very simple," Zach says. "Kate is carrying her grandchild, and Jack is nicer than you."

"Hey!" I protest. "I'm nice. I'm nicer than you are."

"I didn't say that you weren't." He leans against the table and watches me fight to fit one more centerpiece into the box. "Probably means I'm at the bottom of the food chain, but whatever. Wait until they are old enough to need medical care. Then we'll see who the favorite is."

I get the centerpiece to fit and then look up at Zach. "You're a pediatrician."

"So?"

"So, I'm not sure you'd be the first choice for good geriatric care."

He shrugs. "Medicine is medicine." Then he grins at me. "What are you guys going to offer them? A cappuccino and free admission to see the gorillas?"

Sometimes the differences between our careers are glaring.

I bite my tongue though. I never wanted to be a doctor. I'm not sure that I would have picked out a career in a coffeehouse as my lifelong profession, but for now, that's God's plan. And my boss, Alisha Kane, has mentioned the words *manager* and *raise* in the recent past, so I'm keeping my fingers crossed.

A raise will definitely help with the whole "one income paying the rent" problem I'm now facing. Jen and I shared a two-bedroom apartment for the last five years. I'm used to halving everything: half the rent, half the groceries, half the utilities.

I'm moving all my stuff out of the apartment today. My new place is a cute one-bedroom that is five minutes further from Cool Beans, but eight minutes closer to church. Jen's belongings are already over at her and Travis's new apartment.

Our old place looks sad and lonely.

I hate moving.

I pick up the box of centerpieces and carry it over to my

dad's Yukon. The back is open, and Dad is supervising the load-
ing. Dad is nothing if not a meticulous packer.

"Breakables?" he asks as I walk over.

"Flowers, vases, mirror things, and candles," I say, showing
him the box's contents.

"Top of the stack. I'll take it." He takes the box from me,
and I almost run into Kate as I turn.

"Whoa," she says. She hands Dad the box of lily and rose
bouquets and gives me an awkward pregnant hug. I can feel little
Davis Junior kicking against my lower rib cage. Kate is quite a
bit taller than me.

"Someone is active today," I say, giving her tummy a sim-
ilarly awkward pat. I never know the rules when it comes to
touching a pregnant woman's belly. Is it a yay or a nay? I know
I would feel incredibly uncomfortable if someone was rubbing
my abdomen and cooing.

Kate sighs and rubs her stomach. "Oh gosh, Maya. They
were skipping through the whole ceremony. I guess they're in
favor of Jen marrying Travis."

"Or, maybe they were just excited for cake." I'm holding out
this hope that, despite Beethoven and medical journals, their
little baby will be like his or her aunt and love coffee, sweets,
and SpongeBob.

Considering Zach and Kate are already hitting me up for free
babysitting, I think I'll have a good amount of corruptible time
with the baby. I'm already envisioning afternoons of bouncing
him or her on the couch and pointing out that SpongeBob wears
nice pants, a belt, a collared shirt, and a tie, while Patrick wears
nothing but board shorts. And yet, they are best friends and have
overcome the mismatched wardrobe obstacles.

And if Zach and Kate's child is a girl, I'll then explain that just because a guy decides on a career where he has to wear a safari hat and a shirt that has "We can ZOO it!" embroidered on it, it does not mean that they cannot be more than friends.

Even if the girl's favorite channel is the Style Network.

A thought-provoking lesson to learn.

Kate's hand is still on her extended tummy. "I think I'm going to have bruises on my spine from all the baby's trampoline jumps. Not to mention a shrunken bladder. Speaking of which, I'll be right back."

She disappears toward the little building where Jen got ready.

The park is almost back to being a park and looking less and less like a picturesque spot for a wedding ceremony. Boxes are packed, tables are folded, and chairs are stacked in the back of Zach's 4x4 truck.

I sigh. The boxes only remind me of all the work that has to happen at the apartment now.

Jack comes over and pulls me into a hug, and this time I hug him back. He doesn't ask any questions, but I know he saw my depressed look.

He kisses the top of my head and then my lips. "Cheer up, Nutkin," he says.

"I hate boxes."

"I know." He rubs his cheek on the top of my head. "You'll unpack soon enough."

I hate everything about boxes. I hate that they are constantly in the way. I hate that they contain a huge mishmash of things, some of which you didn't even know you owned. And I hate that they mean someone is moving.

Moving always equals sadness.

I sigh again.

Dad closes the back door of the Yukon. "Well, that's it!" he says, brushing off his hands. "Let's take this stuff by their new apartment and then move on to Maya's."

"One wedding down, one to go," Mom says, smiling at me. She's getting teary, and I'm thinking we need to have a very fast engagement.

Months and months of tears is not my favorite thing.

I nod at Mom and Dad and give Jack a final squeeze. "Let's go."

CHAPTER THREE

Sunday morning. Jack and I have been engaged for four whole days.

And we have yet to even mention setting a date.

I sit down in one of the chairs in my Sunday school class and set my Bible on the chair next to me, saving the seat for Jack. There are only a handful of people here so far; most are milling around the snack table.

I open my Bible and find a sticky note I'd written during my Bible reading last night. I just started reading through Luke, and I'm discovering a lot about myself.

> *Ways I Am and Am Not Like Mary:*
>
> *1. I do not trust God like she did*
>
> *(and sheesh —she was like thirteen!).*
>
> *2. I am engaged like she was.*
>
> *3. I worry. She worships.*
>
> *4. My biggest concern? Setting a wedding date.*
>
> *Her biggest concern? Being the mom of the son of God.*

The differences, needless to say, are glaring.

Andrew comes over as I close my Bible and rub my cheek.

"What's up, Maya?" He's munching on a muffin while he talks to me. It smells amazing, and I sniff the air appreciatively. He notices my look. "Liz made them. There's more if you want one. Wait a sec." He heads over to the snack table and tosses a muffin at me.

I catch it and peel off the wrapper. It's got cinnamon, cranberries, and walnuts. Amazing. I swallow. "What do you know about picking dates?" I ask Andrew.

He chews for a bit before answering. "Well. Obviously, the first thing to look for is a Christian. Then single. Then someone who has compatible interests—"

"A *wedding* date, dork."

He winks. "Oh." He settles in the chair next to my Bible and angles to look at me. "Well, what kind of a date did you have in mind?"

"I don't know. A good one? I mean, are there ones that are better than others?"

"I'm pretty sure it's not like picking out a good apple, Maya."

Jack comes in and nods at Andrew, then leans over and kisses my forehead lightly. "Morning, love."

He looks exhausted, but then again, he and my parents were helping me move and unpack and rebuild furniture that had to be broken down to fit through the doorways until almost midnight last night. Then, we were all so wound up from the wedding festivities that we popped a batch of popcorn and watched the first movie in my new place.

The Wedding Planner. I thought it would be appropriate. Maybe give me some ideas. Unfortunately, you need a wedding budget of about $25,000 to pull off anything in that movie, and that's just not happening for me.

Besides, I like simple. Simple and elegant is my thing.

"Having trouble picking a date, bro?" Andrew asks Jack.

Jack blinks. "A date for what?"

My life will be interesting being married to Jack. Repetitive, but interesting.

"For our wedding," I say, trying to be nice. He is tired, and he did help me move.

"Oh." He shrugs. "Soon as possible is fine with me."

Andrew looks at me. "Well, there you go."

I swallow another bite of muffin. "How many weddings have you done, Andrew?"

He thinks about it for a minute. "I don't know. Like ten or eleven."

"What was your least favorite date?"

He gets very serious. "Kevin and Ashley Wagner. February fourth. Two years ago."

Jack sits on the other side of me, ignoring the saved seat with the Bible. "What happened?" he asks Andrew. "Did the wedding get called off or something?"

"Sadly, no."

"Should it have gotten called off?" I ask. Maybe they weren't a good couple. I use my fork to push my muffin crumbs into a nice little stack while I worry. What if Jack and I aren't a good couple?

Jack puts an arm around my shoulders, and I stop worrying. We're a great couple. I have no doubts that God put us together.

Andrew is slowly shaking his head. "Worse. It was Super Bowl Sunday."

I look at Andrew for a long moment. "What?"

"Super Bowl Sunday. They got married right as the game started. I didn't make it back to my house until after the game was over."

I glance over at Jack, who is shaking his head sadly too.

"That was a great game."

"I know."

I look back at Andrew, and now I'm shaking my head. But it's not because of the football game—one that comes on every year, I might add—but for this poor couple who is only going to get married once.

"You two should be ashamed of yourselves," I say.

Andrew finishes his muffin and shrugs, standing. "You asked my opinion. I gave it." Most of our class is here by this point. "All right, everyone, grab a muffin and a seat!"

Jack stands to get a muffin and sits back down beside me a minute later. "These are amazing," he sighs.

Liz Chapman is the cook of this group. There was a period of time where all the girls here would rotate bringing a snack, but then one week we all woke up and realized that Liz was by far the most qualified and she loved to do it. And since Andrew likes her anyway, he appealed to the church staff and got her a weekly stipend to help pay for the ingredients.

I pick up my Bible since Jack is sitting on the other side of me, and Liz sits down there. "Still saving this?" She grins at Jack.

"Nope. Sit away. Those muffins are delicious, by the way."

She leans over and whispers in my ear. "Don't tell Andrew, but there are pureed carrots in them."

Pureed carrots. Read: baby food. I frown slightly. "Really?"

"Yeah, I wanted to get a little bit of nutrition into today's breakfast."

Here are my thoughts on adding healthy ingredients into muffins: It should be avoided at all costs. I think muffins are healthy enough on their own. They have eggs, which are protein. Flour, which is fiber. These even have cranberries, which are antioxidants or whatever.

No need for carrots.

I hold my tongue though, seeing how proud she is of herself. "Neat," I say.

"Thanks." She grins and faces forward, where Andrew is balancing himself on his tiny rickety stool.

Jack taps my shoulder. "What did she say?" he whispers. "She added what to the muffins?"

I shake my head slightly. Jack shrugs and finishes the muffin.

"Okay, everyone. Open up to Psalms. We're going to spend some time reading over King David's shoulder," Andrew says, flipping open his thick preacher's Bible.

I open my Bible, glancing around. There are about thirty people here. Everyone is finding the Psalms and looking expectantly at Andrew or finishing off secretly carroted muffins. And Jen is not here.

I blink and try to focus on the fact that next week she will be.

Last night was the first time ever for me to stay by myself. Which is probably why I had to cake the cover-up under my eyes this morning. Staying in an apartment by yourself is creepy.

Especially a new one. My new place has some weird noises.

Andrew is talking about David. "Tell me things you know about him," he says to the class.

"He was a shepherd boy," Liz says. Liz always knows the answers.

"He was anointed king as a kid, but didn't become king until many years later," another guy says.

"Yeah, thanks to Saul," one girl pipes up. "Didn't Saul try to kill him several times?"

Andrew nods. "We'll get into some of those stories. What else?"

One guy whose name I can never remember—Leon or Leonardo or something along those lines—stretches back. "How about the one about Bathsheba?"

"Or the stories of Solomon?"

Andrew is still nodding. "You guys know your King David," he says with this goofy, proud smile on his face, like a dad watching his son's first Little League game. "Okay. Turn to the first Psalm, and we'll start there."

We spend the next thirty minutes or so talking about David's early life and reading the first Psalm. Andrew closes in prayer, and the hum of people talking starts up.

"The wedding was gorgeous," Liz says, grinning at me. "I loved your dress! She did such a great job with those colors."

I nod. The hunter green looked perfect with a green park in the background.

"Where did they go for their honeymoon?" she asks.

"A cruise to Hawaii." They spent last night in a hotel and left this morning for the island. Before she left, Jen gave me the key to her and Travis's apartment so we could unload all of their gifts and decorations.

It was weird.

"Wow," Liz sighs. "I bet they are having a blast." She's not looking at me as she's talking, though. Her eyes follow Andrew as he makes the rounds.

Sheesh. These two have been flirting for a year. Time to just get married and be done with it. I don't see any sense in even dating at this point.

I pat her arm. "I think Andrew wanted to talk to you about next week's snack," I say, completely lying for the good of my two friends.

She blinks her gorgeous eyes at me. "Oh, thanks! I guess I'd better go ask him."

"Probably." She leaves, and I turn to Jack.

"What was in the muffins?" he asks.

I make a face as I whisper it, checking to make sure that Liz is on the other side of the room and not looking at me. "Pureed carrots."

Jack's mouth squinches up. "Okay then. Well, I guess I don't need to eat my vegetables tonight at dinner."

Sunday nights I have dinner with my parents. Lately, Jack's been coming too. Which is good, considering my mother now likes him best. She's always sending me text messages on Friday afternoons that go something like this: *Cld U plse aks J re: wht he wnts 4 dnnr?*

My mother is the worst text messager in the whole world. It kind of makes me wonder how she would have done with Morse code. Remember that movie about the dog that saved all the little kids who were dying in Alaska by racing to get medicine for them? And how they had to send a message over Morse code to bring more medicine?

If Mom were in charge of that message, the dog probably would have brought more medics.

"You can't skimp on the vegetables tonight. Mom's making corn on the cob especially for you," I tell him.

He grins. "Your mom likes me."

"Don't rub it in."

He laughs.

I get back to my apartment after first driving to the old one out of habit. Jack is going to change clothes and then come hang out until it's time to drive the hour from Hudson to San Diego, where my parents live.

My little beagle, Calvin, is sitting on the couch, quirking his head at me when I unlock the door. "What?" I ask him, stepping in slowly. "What's wrong?"

He just looks solemnly at me.

Poor dog. He's had too many changes lately. First, Jen's mom lived with us for three months, meaning Calvin and I were on the sofa bed because I didn't want Jen developing scoliosis or something before her wedding. I told Mom that, and she said, "Maya, you can't develop scoliosis."

Back problems, then.

"Cal?" I approach the couch slowly, hands held up in surrender. Lesson number one in owning a beagle is to realize you are the owned one, not the dog.

He sighs, hops off the couch, and nuzzles my leg.

I smile and reach down to rub his ears. "Hey, buddy. You're lonely, huh?"

I look around my cold, empty apartment. There are a few more boxes that didn't get unpacked last night and a couple that are half unpacked. Mostly dishes.

I didn't even realize I owned dishes. I thought everything in the kitchen was Jen's.

"Nope!" she said cheerfully when we were packing up the old apartment. "Everything in those two drawers is yours." Then she went whistling into the living room.

I pull a skillet from the box and look at it. I know I never owned a skillet. I don't even know what to do with one. Unless it's a saucepan to cook Bertolli instant dinners, I have no use for it.

I think Jen made me take all these mismatched, garage-sale-bought pans because she was getting married and registering for some nice, fancy, stainless steel ones.

My new apartment is tiny. The living room is half the size of the old one, there is a bedroom off one side of the living room, and the kitchen is on the other side. The closet-sized bathroom is off the bedroom. And the only seating I have in the kitchen is at the bar where my nonexistent bar stools are supposed to go.

Jen let me keep the couch we bought, probably because Travis's plush leather sectional sofa is way nicer than our faded, flowery cotton couch. I have that, a little coffee table, and my tiny TV balanced on a DVD storage cabinet in the living room.

My stomach rumbles, reminding me that it's time for lunch, and I dig through the box of pans to find the saucepan. It's buried near the bottom, and my new downstairs neighbors probably think I've got a little rat in here cooking Italian food with all this racket going on.

I finally yank it out of the box, fill it with water, set it on the stove, wait for it to boil, and grab the package of three-cheese tortellini from the fridge.

There's a knock on my door right as I dump marinara sauce over the freshly strained pasta. Calvin follows me to the door.

It's Jack. "Hey," he says. He leans down and gives me a kiss. Then he straightens and sniffs appreciatively. "Baking something with cinnamon?"

I step out onto the porch and inhale, too. "Oh," I say, shaking my head. "That's my new air freshener." I'd never gotten one of those plug-in things before, and now I'm wondering what took me so long. It smells like a bakery in here, and I am not opposed to living in a bakery.

Jack closes the door and follows me into the kitchen. "Wow, tortellini? What are the odds?" he says dryly.

I snap at him with the towel I have professionally placed over my shoulder like Emeril Live. "You offend the cook, you do not partake."

He comes over all contrite. "You're beautiful. I love you." He says it all singsongy, and I just roll my eyes up at him.

"You'd better get used to tortellini if you're marrying me," I say, stirring the pasta around in the sauce. It's lightly bubbling on the sides of the saucepan, which means it's almost done.

"I love tortellini," Jack says. He rubs Calvin on the head. "Hey, bud."

Calvin loves Jack. Loves him. He goes absolutely crazy whenever Jack shows even the slightest bit of attention to him.

"Roo!" Calvin says, weaving around Jack's legs like a cat. "Roo!"

I get two bowls from another box. "Time to eat," I announce. I spoon the tortellini into the bowls, and Jack carries them over to the couch. I grab two forks. And a stack of napkins.

"Let me pray real quick," Jack says when we sit down. "Lord, thank You for this delicious lunch and this beautiful girl. Be with us today. Amen."

I grin at him. "You can't use prayers to make up."

"I just did. Give me a fork."

I hand it over, and we dig in. "Great sauce. What jar?"

"I made this," I say, feigning offense.

Jack squints at me.

"Prego," I concede.

"Well, it's good."

"Thanks. I picked it out all by myself."

He laughs. "I'm very proud of you."

We eat for a few minutes, chewing in silence. Calvin is sitting in rapt attention right beside Jack's knee, waiting for the slightest spill.

"We need a date," he says, swallowing.

"It has been a while since we went out together." I wipe some sauce off my chin.

"Nutkin."

"How about November first?" I ask.

Jack quirks his head. "How come?"

I set my bowl on the coffee table and start ticking the points off on my fingers. "I love Christmastime, and we could celebrate our first Christmas together. Kate will have had the baby, and the baby will be old enough to go out in public. It would be before Thanksgiving and Christmas, so we wouldn't have to mess with getting married right by the holidays and in doing so ruin my mother's good opinion of you." I shrug. "And it's not too far away. I don't like the idea of a long engagement."

"Me either," Jack says. "November first," he mumbles it again, finishing off his tortellini. "Sounds good to me." He grins.

The relief is helping my shoulders. "Great!" I say. "Now. Where do you want to get married?"

He grins. "Alaska."

"Realistically."

"Hawaii?"

"Where in Hudson," I finish.

Jack smiles. "Totally up to you, Nutkin. This is your wedding; you plan it."

"You aren't going to help me?"

Jack slowly shakes his head from side to side. "I'd rather not."

"Well, thanks for nothing!" I yank his empty bowl over. "No more tortellini for you."

He laughs.

CHAPTER FOUR

We pull up to Mom and Dad's house at exactly five o'clock. Mom starts to panic that we've gotten in a wreck on the interstate if we're even a couple of minutes late.

I open my door and climb out and let Calvin jump out. He's so excited. He loves visiting Mom and Dad because they spoil him rotten. He runs for the front door, making little rooing sounds the whole way.

Jack comes around the car and weaves his fingers with mine as we walk up the front steps. Zach and Kate's car is already here, and I can smell something grilling.

Yum.

Mom opens the front door before we get there. "Hi!" she says, grabbing me in a hug. "Hi, Jack."

Jack grins at her. "Hi, Mary." I like that he's finally comfortable enough with my family to call my parents by their first names.

"Come on in. Dad's making steaks, and I'm making the fixings for potatoes," Mom says. Calvin is racing around the living room with a new toy that Dad left him, and Kate is leaning against the high counter, laughing at him and munching from a half-eaten bag of Chex Mix.

"What a goofy dog," she says, giving me a side hug. "I want a dog."

"You're getting a baby instead," I tell her.

Jack gives Kate a hug and then goes outside to talk with Dad and Zach over the smoking grill. Kate watches him go. "I like him," she declares.

"Me, too." I grin.

Mom is pouring a bag of grated cheddar cheese in a bowl. "Okay, girls, we've got cheese, sour cream, and chives. What am I forgetting?"

"Bacon bits," Kate says. Kate's first trimester queasiness has been replaced by a voracious appetite in her third trimester. She is always, always eating.

"Butter," I say, feeling like Paula Deen.

Mom rummages in the fridge and comes out with both. "Okay. Now for the salad . . ." she mumbles to herself, and she's back to digging in the fridge.

I stare at the fridge, thinking. It wasn't until I moved out that I consciously realized Mom went shopping for all the stuff in there. I mean, I knew she went to the store to buy everything, but suddenly I couldn't just ask Mom for yogurt and have it show up in the fridge two days later.

Nope, now I had to buy the yogurt. And considering how expensive dairy products are, I don't get yogurt too often.

Mom pulls a head of romaine lettuce, two tomatoes, an avocado, and a small bag of peeled baby carrots from the fridge. "So, Maya, how was your day?" she asks.

"Good. We decided on a wedding date," I tell her.

She perks up. I think Mom was secretly worried that Jack and I would be engaged forever. "Oh? When?"

"November first. No set location yet."

Kate rubs her tummy while crunching on another handful of Chex Mix. "You couldn't pick a date a little further away? I'm not going to have enough time to lose the baby weight." She scowls at me.

"Sorry. But I'll have a little niece or nephew." I grin. I'm going to be an aunt, and I can't wait.

"Yeah, and it will look like you're getting another one with how big I'll still be." Kate crunches on the Chex Mix. "I guess it's good to get married sooner rather than later," she concedes. "Temptation and all that." Now she's grinning, and I have no idea what to do with the roller coaster that is my sister-in-law's emotions these days.

Mom's thinking it over. "November first," she says slowly, chopping the veggies. Then she nods. "Sounds good! It's before all the holidays," she says.

"Which was exactly my point," I say. I glance at Kate. "Sorry, Kate. Will you be a bridesmaid?"

She sighs. "So now I'm fat, and you want me in front of hundreds of people. Great, Maya. This is great."

"Sorry," I say again.

"I'll do it. Only because I love you. And you'd better pick a dress that won't make me look goofy." She's grinning again.

"I'll do my best to."

"Not to, smart aleck."

I grin and help Mom shred the lettuce and toss the vegetables in. I set the bowl on the table, and Mom pulls a batch of homemade dinner rolls from the oven.

Dad comes in then with the steaks, followed by a drooling Zach and Jack. "All set?" he asks Mom.

She looks around the kitchen, hands on her hips. "I think so," she says, sounding doubtful.

"Well, it looks great, Mary," Kate says.

"Let's pray then." Dad takes Mom's hand. "Lord, bless this food and bless my wonderful wife who prepared it. And please keep Your hand on our precious grandchild and children. Amen."

I open my eyes and grin at my dad. "So the baby is not even born, and I'm already playing second fiddle in your prayer life," I tease him.

Dad winks at me. "The baby is quieter than you are."

I fake a sigh, but I smile.

Monday morning comes too soon.

I unlock the door to Cool Beans and pocket the key, creeping into the back so I can turn on the lights. Opening is my least favorite job.

But working normal full-time hours is nice.

I have the lights on and the dark roast grinding when Ethan Benson, my co-worker, walks in. "Hey, Maya," he says tiredly. I'm busy tying the strings of my cherry red apron around my waist.

"Morning, Ethan."

He disappears to the back and returns a few seconds later, pulling his apron over his head. "How was the wedding?" he asks, taking out a bag of Colombian medium roast beans.

"Beautiful," I say. "The weather was perfect for a wedding in the park. And everyone behaved." Even Jen's dad managed to stay off the phone until Jen and Travis had left. And he and Jen's mom didn't fight. Also a miracle. *Thank You, Lord.*

I pour the ground coffee into one of the huge coffee-makers and smash the *on* button. Ethan pours the beans into the now-empty grinder, and the sound of coffee beans hitting metal clangs through the whole store.

"Well, that's good to hear," he says. "Weddings are usually the cause of way too many ridiculous emotions anyhow."

I glance at him as I pull a light Breakfast Blend and a light cinnamon blend from under the counter. "Ridiculous emotions?" I question.

"Yeah. I mean, everyone's either crying too hard, celebrating too much, or doing both and getting completely wasted. You spend a zillion dollars on a dress and a tux that you'll wear once for six hours, and then you're expected to buy a bunch of people you hardly know and will never see again a huge buffet of food and a night of entertainment. Those people are the ones who end up drinking the open bar dry and then destroying your car. And then you have to write thank-you notes to all of those people."

Ethan's almost growling by the end of his speech. I wait for him to take the freshly ground medium roast out of the grinder.

Is it shocking that Ethan doesn't currently have a girlfriend?

"You sentimental fool," I say, dumping my beans in the grinder.

"I'm sentimental," Ethan protests. "I'm sentimental about things that count."

"And weddings don't? You're like the Scrooge of Matrimony." I grin at him, going into the back and pulling the tray of unbaked cinnamon rolls from the fridge. I stick them in the oven and go back out to the front where Ethan is running the cleaning cycle and shooting steam from the espresso machine.

"I'm not the Scrooge of Matrimony," he says, wiping off the wand with a clean dishrag. "I just don't like what a huge deal weddings have become."

He has a point. I open the cash register, make sure we have

the proper amount of cash, and turn to look at him. "Well, if it makes you feel any better, I'm not planning on spending a zillion dollars on my dress, I'm not buying a buffet or an open bar or any kind of alcohol for the reception, and I'm hoping that the night of entertainment is just dessert and dancing." I shrug. "So will you come?"

He smiles mockingly at me. "I don't know that I'll be able to if you guys don't ever set a date."

"Ha-ha," I say without enthusiasm. "For your information, we did set a date. November first. And it will be a wonderful fall day."

"Partly cloudy," Ethan says, eyes squinched closed, "with a chance of rain."

"And you don't have a girlfriend?"

It's a low blow, but it gets him off my case. "Easy now," he says, faking a stab wound to the heart. "Let's not injure the wounded."

"Be nice," I lecture.

"Yes, ma'am."

I go to the back to check on the cinnamon rolls, smiling. Ethan is a pain in the neck, but he's a nice guy all the same. He's not a Christian, and there isn't a week that goes by when I don't try to convince him that church is a good place to be, and there isn't a week that goes by when he doesn't tell me he doesn't believe in "that stuff," but he's a nice guy nonetheless.

Someday I'll get him to church. It might be my wedding day, but he will be in church and he will hear the gospel.

I peek at the cinnamon rolls, and they are rising nicely. It's almost nine o'clock, time to flip the sign on the door from closed to open.

Our cinnamon rolls are renowned, and we usually have to

make at least two batches during the morning. Our chef, Kendra Lee, swears that there is nothing special about them, but she lies. They are huge, melt-in-your-mouth doughiness smothered with sweet, creamy frosting.

They make my mouth water every single morning I'm working.

I try to avoid this place on the weekends. I think I gain pounds just smelling the rolls. Pounds are not the "something new" I want to have on my wedding day.

I go flip the sign on the door, and a few minutes later, our Monday Bible study group comes in. It's a bunch of the nicest, sweetest retired men in their seventies you've ever met.

"Well, good morning, Maya," Mr. Patterson says, ambling up to the counter. He's clutching his Bible and his notebook under his arm.

"Hi, Mr. Patterson." I grin.

He nods to Ethan over by the espresso machine. "How you doing, son?"

"Fine, sir. You?"

"Aside from a touch of arthritis, I'm just peachy." Mr. Patterson looks at me. "I guess I'll be boring," he says. Ethan already has a cup of decaf poured, and I exchange that with Mr. Patterson's dollar bills.

"The cinnamon rolls will be out in a minute," I tell him like I do every week. "I'll bring one over as soon as I frost them."

He nods, like he does every week. "Don't tell my wife I ordered another one," he says, winking. Then he goes to his favorite table to wait for the other men.

Like he does every week.

Technically, the Bible study isn't supposed to meet until nine thirty, but Mr. Patterson shows up at nine to save his favorite table, and everyone else is usually here by nine fifteen.

One time I asked them why they didn't just change the time of the Bible study to nine fifteen, and Mr. Patterson told me we didn't open early enough.

"We open at nine," I told him.

He shook his head. "But I need to save the table. And we like to visit before we start studying."

I just laughed. I've seen these men every week for the past year, so we've gotten to know each other fairly well.

The rest of the guys are, true to form, there by nine fifteen. Ethan and I get all eight of them decaf coffees, and we sell them eight cinnamon rolls.

A group of businesswomen come in around nine thirty, and they each order a latte and a roll and give us a hefty tip.

Ethan's eyebrows go up when he sees the tip jar. "Awesome!" he whispers.

I smile. God always provides. Here I am worrying about how I'm going to make it financially with only me paying for rent and groceries, and there God is pointing out that I don't need to worry.

I think I have an addiction to worry.

Maybe there's a twelve-step program for it? Or a club like Weight Watchers? Worrywarts Anonymous?

"Maya!" Ethan says sharply, and I look at him.

"What?"

"You're about to touch the burning-hot pan," he says, coming over and pushing the cinnamon roll pan away from me. "Snap out of the daze." He grins at me. "What were you thinking about? Wedding details? What color napkins you want?"

"You know, for being such a scrooge, you sure know a lot

about weddings," I say, wiping off the counter in front of the espresso machine.

"My sister got married last year," he says. "All she did was stress over the wedding for the entirety of the year they were engaged. And all she's done since is complain about how much the wedding cost and how useless it was."

"Well, they got married. That's useful," I say.

Ethan shrugs. "They were married in everything except name for the four years before that."

"Oh." I don't know what to say to that, so I keep wiping.

Napkins? I have to think about napkin colors?

I get home to my quiet, lonely apartment around five fifteen. Calvin is napping on his little doggy bed in the living room and barely cracks one eye open to acknowledge my presence.

"Nice to see you, too," I say, setting my purse on the counter. Jack is working until six, and then he talked about coming over to watch *17 Again* with me.

Or rather, I'd talked him into *17 Again*. He wanted to watch *Friday Night Lights*.

I am not a fan of sports movies unless they are the cute kid ones I grew up watching. I told him to find a guy friend.

I open my laptop and log onto the Internet. Napkin colors have been on my mind the whole afternoon, and I'm wondering what else I didn't know I needed in order to get married.

I find the Google search box and start typing: What do you need to have a wedding?

Several hundred sites pop up in .46 seconds, according to Google's time tracker.

I click on the first link, which lists fifty-four things you need to have a wedding.

The first one is *groom*, and I snort to myself, looking around for someone to laugh with. Calvin sighs since I interrupted his sleep.

I hate living alone.

Officiate? Check.

Location? Un-check.

Guests? Un-check.

Food? Un-check.

Tables? Un-check.

I get more and more depressed as I read, so I finally close my laptop and wander into the kitchen for some comfort food. I find the remote on my way into the kitchen and turn on the Food Network. Bobby Flay is on, and he's my dad's and Jen's favorite.

Which just makes me lonelier.

I turn off the TV.

My mom had handed me a book when she left on Saturday after helping me move. "Look at it," she told me.

It's still sitting on the kitchen counter. *The Art of Weddings*.

I pick it up and thumb through it. Apparently, it is not a book about drawings to hang in the church when you are getting married.

"Engagement is an extremely emotional time, second only to pregnancy," the book starts.

There are pictures of different people's decorations and other people's food choices and then a list in the back of things to double-check and a time line.

I skip down to three months away.

"Give final payment to location. Take dresses and tuxes to alterations. Finalize registry."

Finalize? How about begin?

I need Jen. It's only Monday. She won't be back for six more days.

And even then, she'll never be back completely.

I try not to give in to the tears and instead go pull one of those instant salad creations from the fridge. If I have to fit into a dress in the not-so-distant future, I probably should lay off all the Bertolli pasta.

Probably.

CHAPTER FIVE

It's now Friday, and my shift at Cool Beans is nearly over. Jen and Travis get back home Monday morning, and I'm so excited I can barely stand it.

I peek at the clock for the third time in ten minutes. Five more minutes, and I can leave and start my weekend. Jack and I are looking at locations today. Our church meets in an old YMCA building, so if you want anything classy, you have to go elsewhere.

Lisa and Peter, who have the shift after me and Ethan, walk in the door right then. Lisa is laughing, which is no surprise. Lisa is always laughing.

"I see you looking at that clock, Maya Davis, and we are not late," she says with a grin, coming behind the counter and giving me a hug. "Let me shove my purse in the back and you two can go."

Ethan already has his apron off and his time card marked. "Have a good weekend, Maya," he says.

I leave a few minutes later. I'm climbing in the car, a complimentary cinnamon caramel latte in my hand, when my cell phone rings.

"Hang on, hang on," I mutter, digging in my purse and

trying not to spill my coffee at the same time.

It's my mom. "Hey," I say, setting my cup in the cup holder.

"Maya?"

I frown. Mom doesn't sound like her normal self. Her voice is strained and catching.

"What's wrong?" I ask, hoping Mom just has a cold or something.

"Maya, Kate's in labor."

I let out my breath and squinch my eyes shut. "What?" My stomach has just sunk into my ankles.

She's only seven months! She has a good two months to go.

"Try not to panic," Mom says, though she sounds like she's panicking. "Dad and I are on the way to the hospital. I'll call you when I know more. Just start praying now, okay?"

I'm gripping the steering wheel so tightly my hand is cramping. "Okay."

"Love you." She hangs up.

I blink past the quick stinging tears and set my phone down. "God," I say out loud, "please be with Kate and my little niece or nephew right now."

I pick up the phone again and speed dial Jack.

"Nutkin?" I can hear safari-themed zoo music in the background. "You never call me at work. Are you okay?"

"Kate's in labor." Saying it makes it even worse.

"What?" We have the same reaction. I can hear the disbelief and shock in his voice.

"She's in labor. I don't know any details. Mom called and they're on their way to the hospital." I'm starting to cry as I talk.

"Where are you?" Jack asks.

"I'm in the parking lot at Cool Beans," I say, wiping my eyes.

"Stay there." He hangs up.

I lean my forehead against the steering wheel and let the tears come. *God, please don't let her be having a miscarriage. Please, God.* It's Zach and Kate's first baby.

I hear a knock on the window, and I look up to see Lisa standing there. I crack open the door, and she takes one look at my tear-stained face, walks around to the passenger side, and climbs in.

"What happened?" she asks, rubbing my back.

I tell her about Mom's call.

"Oh no," she says, meaning it. She keeps rubbing my back.

"I'm trying to just pray and not worry, but . . ." I wipe at my tears again.

Lisa squeezes my arm. "Don't worry, Maya. Isn't there something about that in the Bible? Didn't Andrew talk about that last Wednesday night?"

Lisa is not a Christian, but our weekly Bible study meets at Cool Beans when she's working the evening shift. And I've been hoping that at least a little bit is sinking in.

And apparently it has been.

I nod.

She nods as well. "It'll be okay, Maya. Try not to panic yet." She keeps rubbing my back.

A few minutes later, Jack's truck pulls up next to me. Lisa sees him climb out and smiles. "I'll leave you in good hands," she says, leaning over for one of those awkward car hugs. "You guys drive safely. And text me and let me know what's going on."

She waves at Jack and goes back inside Cool Beans.

Jack opens my door. "Come on, honey."

I climb out, and Jack reaches in and grabs my purse and latte and locks my car door. "We'll take my truck," he says.

He's still in his zoo uniform. He hugs me, and I smell hay.

"Sorry," he says when my nose wrinkles. "No time to shower."

He opens the passenger door. "Jack, wait," I say before I climb in. "You are supposed to be working for another hour. I can't let you miss work."

He shrugs and pushes me in. "It's not a problem. I told my boss what was going on. It was a slow day anyway. I'll stay late Monday to catch up."

We're on the highway in a few minutes. Traffic is mostly going the opposite direction from San Diego.

I call my mom once we're thirty minutes away. "What hospital are you at?" I ask.

"Memorial. Fourth floor," she says. "We're in the waiting area right outside the neonatal ICU."

"Have you heard anything yet?"

Mom starts to say something and stops. "We'll fill you in when you get here."

I hang up and stare out the windshield. Jack looks over at me. "Any news?"

"They're going to tell us when we get there."

"Oh." He says it quietly because he knows that my mom doesn't share bad news over the phone. One time, she drove all the way to Hudson and found me at Cal-Hudson, my alma mater, to let me know that my old dog Trevor, who was a nasty, mangy cocker spaniel, had died.

There's no way she's telling me what's going on now. This doesn't even compare.

Lord, please. Just wrap Your hands around my niece or nephew right now.

Jack reaches over and picks up my left hand. The diamond there catches the sunlight and sends rainbows dancing around the car.

My tears dried up a little bit ago, but now there's just this horrible ache in my chest.

"It'll be okay, Nutkin," Jack says, squeezing my hand. "Whatever happens, it will be okay. God is still God."

I nod.

Jack pulls into the parking lot in front of Memorial Hospital. I jump out and run for the door; Jack is close behind me.

I push open the front door and follow the signs to the elevator. Jack waits until the door dings and then hands me my purse. "Forgetful," he teases, trying to lighten the mood.

We get into the elevator. I push the button for the fourth floor.

The neonatal ICU is to the right. Dad is pacing the area in front of the chairs, and Mom is sitting, wringing her hands.

"Mom? Dad? What happened?" I run over.

Mom pulls me down in the chair next to her. Dad rubs my shoulder.

"They did an emergency C-section," Mom says quietly. "She started bleeding about two hours ago, and the baby was distressed."

I start crying again. "But she's only seven months," I whisper, rubbing at my cheek.

Mom is crying, too. "I know, honey." She smiles through her tears. "You have a little nephew, Aunt Maya."

I swallow. "He made it?"

"He did," Dad says, heaving a big sigh. "He's a tiny little guy, and he'll have to stay here for a long time, but last we heard, he made it."

"Thank God," Jack says quietly. He squeezes my hand. "Congratulations, Auntie." He looks at Dad and Mom. "Grandpa and Grandma."

Mom smiles at him, swiping at her cheeks with a Kleenex.

"Can we see him?" I ask. "And Kate?"

"Not right now," Dad says. "Kate's still in recovery. And they're working on the baby. So, we wait." He pulls Mom up off the chair and into a hug. "And pray."

We pray, pace, worry, sit, and doodle on a little pad of paper from Mom's purse for the next hour. Jack is playing me at hangman.

My little hangman has arms, hands, fingers, legs, feet, toes, eyes, ears, a nose, mouth, and hair. And I've correctly guessed only four letters.

"X?" I ask.

"You lose," Jack says.

"Nuh-huh. You forgot chest hair."

"You can't put chest hair on a hangman," Jack protests.

"Okay, well, you forgot clothes. My guy needs pants."

"No pants. You lose."

"A hat?"

"Maya!" Jack growls.

"Fine. I hate hangman."

"I hate playing it with you," Jack says.

"Kids," Mom warns from a few chairs away. "Enough."

Dad looks at us, then at Mom, then back at us, and just starts laughing. Mom shakes her head and giggles a little bit, too.

"This is ridiculous," she says. "I have to call down my daughter and her nearly husband."

I look at Jack and we shrug at each other.

Right then, the two swinging doors with the "DO NOT

ENTER" sign on them open, and Zach comes tiredly walking through.

"Zach!" I yell and run over to him. I grab my brother in a huge hug, and I don't let go.

"Hey, sister," he says, wrapping his arms around me, weariness lacing his voice. Everyone has crowded around us, and he looks at everyone. "So, Kate's awake. The baby is stable for now." He rubs his eyes, and I step back a few inches.

"Oh, honey," Mom says and starts crying again.

Zach hugs her and looks at Dad. "You guys can come see Kate if you want."

We all start nodding like a bobblehead contest. Zach waves at one of the nurses through the scary-looking doors and they open.

We follow him into a darkened room down the hall. Kate is lying on the bed, eyes closed. There are monitors and wires everywhere, some beeping at a constant pace.

"Katie? Honey, the family is here," Zach says, smoothing her hair away from her face.

She slowly opens her eyes and then even more slowly smiles at us. "Hey," she croaks.

"And I called your mom, and she's about four hours out," Zach tells her, kissing her forehead. Kate's parents live in northern California near San Francisco, so it takes them about eight hours to get here.

"Okay," she says, still all froggy sounding.

"Kate, you know, you're kind of taking this losing the baby weight in time for the wedding a little to the extreme," I tease softly, holding her hand, being careful of the IV in her arm.

She smiles tiredly. "Yeah. Well, you know how hard I try to stay thin."

I squeeze her hand and smile through my tears.

"Have you seen him?" Kate asks us.

Mom shakes her head. "I don't know that we'll be able to," she says. She strokes Kate's hair. "How are you, honey?"

"Groggy." Kate yawns.

"The nurse said two can go in to see the baby at a time," Zach says to Mom. "I'll take you over there after we're done here."

"Well, Maya, it's a boy." Kate squeezes my hand. "Don't you want to know his name?"

I blink. In all the worrying about his life, I'd completely spaced that I didn't know his name. "Yes! Yes, I do."

"Benjamin Zachary," Kate says, smiling.

"A big name for a little guy." Zach rubs his cheek.

Mom's tearing up again. "Benjamin." She looks at Dad. "Your middle name."

Dad has tears in his eyes now, too, and I can count on one hand the times I've seen my dad cry. "That means a lot," he manages.

Kate pats Mom's hand. "Go meet your grandson."

"Come on." Zach leads Mom and Dad out into the hallway.

"So, if Benjamin was in this big of a hurry to get out, imagine what he's going to be like as a two-year-old," Jack says, grinning.

Kate sighs. "I know. Crazy."

I can tell Kate is struggling to keep her eyes open, so I squeeze her hand again. "Go to sleep, Kate. You'll want to wake up again when your parents get here."

"Mmm. Okay . . ." She's out before she finishes talking.

Jack sits on the one chair in the room and pats his leg.

"Sorry I smell like hay," he whispers when I balance on his knee.

I shrug. "You could have apologized by leaving your safari hat on."

"I'm not that sorry."

I smile. Now that I've seen Kate, my nerves are slightly less frayed. I just need to see little Benjamin now, and I'll feel a lot better.

"So, you realize that you're going to be Uncle Jack," I say.

He nods, grinning. "Yeah. I'm so excited."

I'm chewing on my bottom lip again. Zach said that little Benjamin was very little. Scarily little?

"Stop doing that," Jack says, flicking my chin. He rubs my back. "Let's talk about places to get married."

He'd called all the places we had appointments with on our way over to the hospital and told them we would have to reschedule to tomorrow hopefully. As of right now, we have four possible locations: two churches, one community center, and some place called the Event Schloss that Jack found online.

I told Jack that I saw no purpose in going to a place called the Event Schloss; I thought it was a weird name anyway. Jack then told me *schloss* was German for *castle*.

I have lived in Hudson since my freshman year at Cal-Hudson—so more than six years—and I do not remember ever seeing a castle.

There's one church on the list that I'm excited about. It's tiny, but it has a really pretty sanctuary. Jack and I were there for my boss's son's baptism. There's lots of wood, lots of warm color tones.

Perfect for a November first wedding. November first pretty much screams fall colors.

"I'm excited to check out Bethany Church," I say.

Jack nods. "Yeah, they have a pretty building," he says. "I

like the landscaping there."

"Me too."

Mom and Dad come back into Kate's room then, and Mom is dashing away tears. "Zach is waiting for you guys by that sink we stopped at," Dad whispers, noticing that Kate is asleep. He gently takes my arm as I get up. "He's little," he says. "Just remember that he's okay for now."

I nod, feeling my chest tighten. For Dad to be warning me, it means the baby is far too little to be in this big, mean world.

Zach is wearily leaning against the wall by the sink. He's wearing a hospital gown, gloves, and a hat. I can't see any part of his skin except for his face. "Wash your hands again, and now you get to put on one of these lovely gowns," he says.

I blast my hands with the hot water and rub the soap in so hard that my hands sting. Zach gives me a backless gown, one of those elastic cafeteria-lady hats, mesh booties to cover my shoes, and gloves.

By the time I'm done getting dressed, I feel like I'm about to walk onto the set of *Grey's Anatomy*.

"Okay," Zach says once Jack and I are dressed. "Here's a mask." He gives us each a mask to tie over our mouths. "We can't touch him except for his little hand right now."

He pushes open a big door that again says "DO NOT ENTER," and we follow him down a long corridor and turn right into a large room with has lots of baby incubators. The room is dimly lit, and some babies are shining blue, thanks to what look like heat lamps above them.

Zach leads us over to an incubator near the back left corner of the room. "And here's your nephew," he says.

I peer into the plastic box. There are blankets and wires and machines, and looking so tiny and helpless in the midst of everything is the smallest baby I've ever seen. Proportionally, everything is how it should be. His head is nice and round, and there is blond peach fuzz covering it; his little eyes are open and blinking. His hands are perfect and flicking around. He's wrapped tightly in a blanket from the underarms down, but I can see his little feet kicking around.

He has a tube down his nose and wires attached to his chest and head. And there's a big air hose in his mouth.

"Hi, Benjamin," I say softly.

"You can touch his hand if you want," Zach says. He puts his hand through the hole in the plastic and holds Benjamin's fingers. Benjamin's palm is about the same size as Zach's fourth fingernail.

I reach in and gently clasp the baby's hand. It's so, so tiny; I feel like I'm going to break it.

"How much does he weigh?" Jack asks.

"Two pounds, nine ounces," Zach says. "He's not the smallest baby on record for being twelve weeks early, but he's also not the biggest."

The doctor in Zach is taking over, and I can see it. Zach is a pediatric doctor at this same hospital. Which is probably why there can be three of us crowded around Benjamin's bed when there are only one or two parents around the other babies.

"That's a ventilator," he answers our unasked question, pointing to the big tube coming out of Benjamin's mouth. "His lungs aren't quite up to speed yet. And we're monitoring his heart and blood pressure. He's already had blood drawn twice, and he's only been born for three hours."

"What's that?" Jack asks, pointing to the blue light over a baby next to us. Compared to Benjamin, that baby looks like the Hulk.

"It's to help with jaundice," Zach says. He walks over and checks the other baby's chart. "Benjamin so far isn't dealing with jaundice, but that might come later."

"Dr. Davis," the nurse says, coming over. "Time for vitals again." She smiles at us. "Aunt and uncle?"

"Yeah. Marcie, this is my sister, Maya, and her fiancé, Jack. Guys, this is Marcie."

"Hi," we say together.

Marcie smiles, tucking her stethoscope into her ears. "Well, your nephew is a fighter. I've never seen a baby this young be so active."

"He's Zach's kid," I say. "He's probably going to be a pig-headed perfectionist, too." I smile at Zach, even though he can't see it behind my mask. "Maybe that's why Benjamin wanted to be born so early. He wanted to be in charge."

Marcie laughs, and Zach knuckles my head. "Pig-headed?" he says. "You should check out a mirror sometime, Maya."

I pull my hand out of the incubator so Marcie can reach in with her stethoscope. Benjamin squirms when she touches him.

Marcie listens for a few minutes, twists her lips, and then pulls out her hand, making a notation on her clipboard. She hands the clipboard to Zach.

Zach's cheek muscle is twitching. "Keep him on the ventilator, and let's increase his oxygen a little bit."

"Is he okay?" I ask after Marcie leaves.

Zach nods. "He's holding steady, but his counts aren't where they should be. They'll get there." He reaches for his son again and rubs his tiny shoulder.

We leave the hospital about an hour later. Mom gives me a long hug in the parking lot. "Just pray, Maya. Don't worry."

I nod, but we both know I'll be praying and worrying.

"Drive safely."

"You guys too," Dad says.

Jack and I climb back into his truck for the long drive home. I look out the windows at the darkening sky and bite the inside of my cheek.

He's so tiny.

I've never seen a baby that small. Admittedly, my experience with preemies is pretty much nonexistent, but he just seems incredibly little.

"You're worrying." Jack says it matter-of-factly and reaches for my hand. "He's little, but he'll make it."

"He's on so many tubes and wires and machines," I say quietly.

Jack squeezes my hand.

I rub my face with my right hand. "He's got a long time ahead of him in the hospital."

"Taking after his dad at such a young age." Jack smiles.

I smile too.

"How about this, Nutkin?" Jack says. "We'll go by those locations for the wedding tomorrow morning, and then we'll head back up to the hospital. We can bring Zach and Kate something other than cafeteria food and bring a game to play to help them pass the time."

It's a sweet suggestion, and I can feel myself getting all gushy even thinking about it. "Really?"

"Really."

I nod and grip his hand tighter. "Let's do it."

I climb into bed that night completely, utterly, to-the-bones exhausted. My eyes are still stinging from the tears earlier, and I can't get the picture of my little nephew out of my mind.

I pull my Bible and my sticky notes over from my bedside table. I open to the Psalms, needing to hear from someone else who had some emotional days.

I start reading in Psalm 34: "I sought the LORD, and He answered me, and delivered me from all my fears. . . . The angel of the LORD encamps around those who fear Him, and rescues them" (verses 4,7).

Now instead of me seeing my little nephew lying in that incubator surrounded by wires yet all alone, I'm imagining an angel camping out right beside his plastic bed.

"Benjamin will be okay, right, God?" I whisper. "Please keep him safe. Help him to grow."

I start a new sticky note:

Evidence That Trusting God Is Good:

1. God has an angel watching over Benjamin.

2. God knows what I need before I even ask it
(such as wedding help).

3. God gave me a man like Jack.

4. Oreos were marked 30 percent off today.

CHAPTER SIX

I was so worried about what we'd find when we got to the hospital last night that I wasn't paying attention to which wedding location Jack scheduled first.

So, I have to groan when we pull into the parking lot of the Event Schloss at ten o'clock in the morning.

"Jaaack," I say.

"What? It's a great name! And it could be on your invitations," he says, putting the truck in park.

He comes around to open my door, and I hop out, looking at the front of the building. I have my camera in my purse so I can remember which location I liked the best and start coordinating with the décor, but I'm thinking I won't need the camera for this trip.

The front of the building is an ashy white stucco—like it's been fifty years since it's been redone. There are bars on all of the windows, and a huge billboard is perched above the flat-top roof with big scrolling letters on it: The Event Schloss—A Fairy-Tale Setting for All of Your Events.

Because "fairy tale" is exactly what pops into my mind when I see ashy white, old stucco.

Jack is grinning like a Cheshire cat. He shoves his hands into his jean pockets and rocks back on his heels. "Well," he says, "now this is just spectacular!"

"What exactly did this place look like online?" I ask, gaping. Right next to the building, there's a big drainage ditch with weeds and trash piled in it. The parking lot is crumbling around our feet.

Jack pulls a folded sheet of paper from his pocket. "It only showed the inside," he says, passing it to me.

Correction: The paper only showed one table in the inside. And even that was decorated a little weird.

"We'll be late for our appointment," Jack says, taking my arm and pulling me up to the glass door covered in bars.

I look at the bars—which scream, "We're scared of thieves!"—and wonder if the people who own the Event Schloss realize they are located in Hudson. Our crime rate is ridiculously low. The crime we do have usually occurs near the university, and this is nowhere near there.

Jack tries the door, and it's locked. So he knocks. And knocks again.

We've been knocking on the barred door for almost five minutes when he finally pulls out his phone and calls the number.

"Hello, we had an appointment this morning," he says to whomever is on the end of the line.

I cup my hands around my eyes and try to see into the dark building. It looks like a huge square room. No tables, no decorations on the walls. Just white walls and a white linoleum floor. Something shiny catches my eye on the floor, and I realize it's a big puddle of what I hope is water.

Ick.

Jack hangs up the phone, shaking his head. "They forgot about our appointment."

"Lucky us. Let's go."

"Too bad. I would have really liked seeing what my fairy-tale dreams coming true looked like," he says, mocking a sigh.

We get back in the truck, and I buckle my seat belt. "What's next?"

"The community center." Jack starts driving.

I smile over at him. "Thanks for rescheduling everything," I say, reaching for his hand.

He lifts my hand to his lips and kisses it. "No problem, love."

Hollman Community Center is the only community center in Hudson. There's a gym, a pool, a huge grassy field, and lots of trees. They also have a multi-purpose room, where several people Jack and I know have gotten married. It's not a big room, but we're not planning on a big wedding.

We walk into the community center, and the smell of chlorine mixed with sweat and rubber hits me. I try not to gag. "Ew," I say, making a face. "I don't remember it smelling like this at Stacy's wedding."

Jack's making a face, too. "Me neither. I don't remember it smelling like anything at all."

"Can I help you folks?" An older man in gym shorts that might have met the appropriate length requirement for men in the eighties but not in current times walks over. I try not to stare at his thighs.

I think there's a very good reason that men's shorts have gotten progressively longer: Men don't have nice-looking legs.

No offense to any men out there.

"Yeah, we have an appointment to look at the multi-purpose room," Jack says, keeping his eyes up.

The man nods. "Okay, let me show it to you. We have a wedding starting at two today, so it's a little crazy in there right now."

He leads the way down a long hall that ends at two double doors and pulls one open. "Ladies first."

I look down at the outfit I have on. It's August, and it's California, so I'm wearing a ruffly white T-shirt and brown Bermuda shorts. My shorts are much longer than this guy's. And not only am I female, I'm also probably a good thirty years younger than him.

I walk in the room, and six people are scurrying around like mice. "Mop?" one guy yells at me when I walk in.

I shake my head slightly. "Maya."

"What?" he says, grabbing a big bouquet of red roses.

"I'm sorry?"

"I asked you guys to get me a mop," the guy says.

I have problems with guilt, and this is very evident right now as I immediately feel bad. "Oh, I'm sorry," I say. "I can find you one."

"What?" Jack says, coming in behind me. "We don't work here," he says to the guy.

"Oh. Sorry about that, lady."

Short-Shorts nods at the guy. "You two look around; I'm going to go get that guy a mop." He leaves.

The floor is a white linoleum again. It looks like these people are creating a center aisle and adding roses at the front where they're constructing an archway. It's pretty, but not my style.

I glance at Jack, and I think he's feeling the same way.

"Nice, but not us," he says quietly.

Short-Shorts appears with a mop and hands it to the yelling man. "Well?" he says to us. "What do you guys think?"

"We'll keep you on our list," Jack says. We leave. And I even manage to keep my mouth shut about his shorts-length issues.

Our next stop is First Baptist Hudson. We walk in, and the

secretary tells us there's a $500 rental fee to use the church. So we turn around and walk out.

"Five hundred dollars," Jack gripes, climbing into the truck. "You and I can go on a four-day cruise for $500. Including meals and tips."

"Not if we're not married," I say, grinning at him.

"Bethany Church is next. Hopefully it's cheap and our style," he says.

"And hopefully they observe proper shorts lengths."

Jack grins.

We pull into the parking lot a few minutes later and climb out. Bethany Church has to be the prettiest church in Hudson. It's a dark red brick with white accents and has an honest-to-goodness steeple. There are two huge white doors at the entrance of the church.

The church itself is fairly small. I think it only has a sanctuary and a few classrooms. We walk in the front doors, and there's a little foyer before two more double doors.

"Welcome to Bethany." A man in khakis that fit him correctly and a button-down shirt smiles as we walk in. He's obviously just walking through the foyer, but he stops to talk to us. "I'm Pastor Mark. What can I do for you?"

"We have an appointment to look at the sanctuary for our wedding," Jack says.

"Oh wonderful," Pastor Mark says, very pastorally. "Well, let's go look at it." He opens one of the double doors, and we walk in.

There's a center aisle and pews. The carpeting is a neutral tan color, and the walls are a gorgeous chocolate-colored hardwood. There's a stage with steps leading up the front, and the steeple must be directly above the stage because the ceiling is ginormous there.

It's perfect.

"Would you be having the reception here as well?" Pastor Mark asks.

I nod.

"We have a multi-purpose room for that. Let's go check that out as well, shall we?" He opens a door on the right side of the sanctuary, and we walk into a surprisingly large room. It has laminate wood floors, and the walls are covered with long black curtains. Which sounds really weird but actually looks rather classy.

"We have a lot of receptions here," Pastor Mark says. "The lights will fully dim down, and we have special lights over the area that most people use for a dance floor."

Dancing. I try not to swallow loudly, but I'm not sure I pull it off.

Dancing is not my thing. When I was in the third grade, I was convinced I was going to be the lead in the *Nutcracker* when I grew up. I took ballet classes, I flitted around my whole house, and I wore my ballet flats whenever I had the chance.

And then I turned twelve, and whatever childhood grace I had left with the strong wind called Puberty. I turned into a clumsy, awkward preteen with braces, glasses, and too-curly hair that usually just looked frizzy.

"Oh?" Jack says, not looking at me. "Dancing?"

"It's very popular at weddings," Pastor Mark says, teetering very closely to a tone that says *uh, duh.*

Jack knows my stance on dancing. And yet Jack loves to dance. Swing dancing, ballroom, whatever. He thinks it's fun.

Heh.

"Well, I think this room is just perfect," I say, trying to pull the attention away from the dance issue.

I smile at Jack and he nods, smiling as well.

"I take it that you both like it." Pastor Mark grins. "That's great. We love having weddings here."

"Is there a fee?" Jack asks.

"One hundred dollars to help with the janitor's paycheck." Pastor Mark folds his fingers together as he looks at us. "There's also a fee to change out the curtains in here. Some brides don't like the black, although it does add to the ambience when the lights are lowered. We don't allow any alcohol. And there's a strict rule that if you use candles, they need to be tea lights only and in holders."

Jack and I are both nodding like little bobblehead dolls.

"Are you available November first?" I ask, praying that they are.

"I'm not sure. Why don't we go to the office and check?"

We file after him like ducks down a hallway, and he opens a door to a cute little room that has two chairs and a desk in it.

"Let's see," he says, flipping the huge pages of one of those calendars that lays flat on the desk. "November . . . ?"

"First," I tell him.

"Saturday. It looks like we're available then," he says, smiling at me.

"Yay!" I grin. Jack smiles at me.

"Do you know what time yet? And how long you're planning on being here?"

Time. Now there's a valid question.

"I thought we were doing good with a date," I say to Jack.

Pastor Mark laughs. "How about this? I'll put you down for the day, and when you figure out the time you need to be here and the time you want to leave, let me know. Someone needs to be here to unlock and lock the church. And we'll let you come in to rehearse and decorate the night before if you'd like." He scribbles our names on November first.

"Great," Jack says.

I'm about to kiss Pastor Mark's feet, but I don't for fear that he'll erase our names off the calendar.

"Just give us a call soon about what time you've decided. And if that's everything for you, I'll have our secretary call you about a month from the wedding and find out if there's anything you need," he says.

Jack writes a check for $100 and hands it to him. "Thanks."

"Thank you. God bless you both."

We leave.

As soon as we get into Jack's truck, I dissolve into relieved giggles. "We have a church! We have a church!"

Jack is grinning. "I can't believe you liked this place more than the Event Schloss."

"Panda Express?" I hear Kate in her room even before we get to the doorway. "Do I smell Panda Express?"

"Shh," I say, sneaking in all *NCIS*-like. "This is contraband." I have a huge bag stuffed full of those cute little Chinese take-out boxes tucked under a jacket that I definitely do not need in August.

Especially when there is hot, steamy food under there. I pat the sweat off my forehead with my forearm.

I set the bag on the little table that pulls up to and over Kate's bed like a TV tray. Jack is right behind me with another bag stuffed with Panda Express boxes.

Zach whistles. He's wearing his white coat today and looks all doctorly. "What did you do? Buy out Panda?"

"I wasn't sure what everyone liked," I say, pulling out the boxes and stacking them neatly. "And I wasn't sure how many people would be here." I look around and it's just the four of us in Kate's room. "Where are the parental units? Both ours and Kate's?"

"Ours are in with Benjamin," Zach says. "And Kate's are driving some poor nurse crazy."

I quirk a smile at her. "What?"

"They're pacing the hallways," Kate says, rolling her eyes. "My parents can't sit still."

"Oh."

"You realize that you snuck in contraband food to a doctor who works here," Zach says, inhaling the scent of orange chicken.

"You can thank me later," I say.

I help Kate shovel a few different choices onto her plate, since bending over after her C-section is probably painful and not allowed. "Thanks, Maya," Kate says. She lifts the plate up and jabs her fork into the food. Her hair is pulled back in a ponytail today, and she's wearing pink plaid pajama pants and a black cami. "They cut my ab muscles," she says around a mouthful of Beijing beef.

"What?" I'm in the middle of trying to spoon some chow mein onto my plate, and the noodles aren't cooperating. It's amazing how much they start to look like tiny strings of muscle.

"They cut it. Snipped it right in half." Kate swallows the beef and sighs. "All those years of workouts, all those months of dieting. All for nothing."

I can't decide if I liked her better on painkillers. Sleepy Kate was a lot easier to sit with than Mopey Kate.

"But it's all for a good cause," I say, trying to look on the bright side. Zach and Jack are chatting away about some baseball game that is muted on Kate's TV. I'm wishing for help here.

"Yeah," Kate says slowly. Then she starts tearing up. Tiny tear drops rain down on her Beijing beef. "He's so little, Maya."

"But he made it, Kate," I say, reaching for her hand and her plate simultaneously. No use in drowning the food. I set the plate on her TV tray and grip her hand. "He'll be okay. He's got God on his side."

She nods, tears streaming. "All I wanted was to be pregnant for nine months," she whispers.

"I know."

Zach finally notices that his wife is crying and turns from the baseball game. "Honey?" he says, coming over. He wraps an arm around her shoulders and nods at me. "Can you give us a second, guys?"

Jack and I slip out into the hallway. There are beeping monitors everywhere around us and nurses in scrubs walking up and down the hall.

"Thanks for getting the Panda Express," I say, giving Jack a long hug.

"No problem."

I see Mom and Dad coming down the hall. Dad sniffs appreciatively. "Panda?" he says.

I grin. My dad shares my taste for Chinese food. "Yeah. It's in Kate's room. But Zach and Kate are talking right now." I stop him from going in.

Mom is brushing away tears again. Being a grandma has not been easy so far for her. "The nurse said his vitals are still improving," she says.

Kate's parents are coming back down the hall with a nurse. "I just think she needs to be monitored more closely," her mother is saying to the nurse.

The nurse, who looks busy enough, picks up Kate's chart from the rack outside her closed door. "Kathryn Davis?" she says, plopping a set of bifocals on her nose. "This is Dr. Davis's wife?" she asks, looking at Kate's parents.

Kate's mom nods. "Yes."

I know the nurse is thinking, *I'm pretty sure she's being monitored*, but she is nice and doesn't say anything. Instead, she raps on the door twice and opens it.

"Dr. Davis?" she says, walking in; Kate's parents are trailing her. "I'm sorry, sir. I'm just going to check your wife's vitals again."

Zach sees Kate's parents and wisely doesn't remind the poor nurse that Kate was checked just twenty minutes ago.

I poke Jack. "Let's go hang out with our nephew."

He nods. "Sounds like a plan."

CHAPTER SEVEN

Tuesday morning starts out slowly at Cool Beans. By ten in the morning, Ethan and I have only made six lattes and five MixUps, our version of the Frappuccino.

The room is nearly empty. Two women are chatting on the sofa by the fireplace, and they are the only people in here.

Ethan leans tiredly against the counter, playing with a towel. "So, how's the nephew?" he asks.

I didn't get to go see him yesterday, but I probably will tomorrow. I called Kate last night, and the doctors are hoping to take Benjamin off his ventilator tomorrow. And he's back to his birth weight, which is a good sign.

Still tiny. But progress is progress.

"He's doing better," I say to Ethan. "He's gaining weight, and he's hopefully going to be breathing on his own tomorrow."

He nods. "Good. And the wedding plans?"

I sigh.

"Not so good, I take it."

We have the location. And Andrew to officiate. And nothing else. I don't have a dress. I don't have any invitations. We don't even have a honeymoon location.

We've got two months and two weeks to go. And my biggest

worry is if Benjamin will get to be there—nothing else.

Ethan snaps a towel at me. "Hey!" he says sharply.

I jump. "Ouch!" I rub my leg where the towel connected. "What was that for? I'll have a bruise now," I gripe.

Ethan grins. "Well, it got you out of your fog. Come on, Maya. You're always telling me to look at the bright side and whatever. So look at the bright side."

I glare at him, rubbing my leg. "The bright side is at least the bruise will be gone by my wedding day."

"Downer," he accuses lightly.

"Towel abuser."

He grins. Three men in business suits walk in then, each carrying a briefcase.

"Welcome to Cool Beans," Ethan says politely. "What can I get you?"

The first guy orders a very manly regular coffee, and the second guy follows suit, each dropping multiple bills in the tip jar. I get the two guys their coffees and head back over to the espresso machine.

The third guy winks at me. "I'd like a large hazelnut cinnamon soy latte, no whipped cream," he tells Ethan. Then he leans toward the espresso machine. "Baristas appreciate men who love lattes," he says flirtatiously.

Ethan rolls his eyes.

I block a fake yawn with my left hand. "Hmm," I say, letting the glittering diamond do all the talking.

The man tucks his hand against his heart and sighs. "It figures. All the beautiful ones are taken."

"That will be $4," Ethan tells him.

The guy hands Ethan $7 and tells him to keep the change. I make his soy latte and hand it to him a minute later.

"He's a lucky guy," the man says, nodding toward the ring.

"Thank you," I say.

The men take their drinks and go sit at one of the tables near the window, pulling out laptops and stacks of paper.

Ethan looks at me. "Jack needs to marry you quickly."

"Please. That's the first offer I've had in forever."

"Maybe the first one who was brave enough to say something," Ethan says.

"Sure." I shake my head and start making a cinnamon caramel mocha for me. "You want something?"

"No thanks."

I start foaming the milk and add the shot of espresso and the pumps of caramel and cinnamon flavoring a few minutes later. I lean back against the counter and sip the steaming beverage. This hits the spot.

Ahh. I need this.

I brush a hand back through my crazy curly ponytail. My hair has slowly been growing out since I chopped it off almost two years ago, and now it's about down to my bra strap. I had hoped the length would pull some of the curl out, but instead, it seems to make it even harder to keep in line.

"Layers!" my hairstylist shouted at me last time I went in three months ago. "You need layers!" Considering she was passionate enough to use exclamation points, I let her layer it.

Now I'm wondering if that was a bad decision. The layers looked pretty for the six hours after the haircut. Now they curl haphazardly and are always coming out of my ponytail.

I sip my mocha again and sigh at the espresso machine.

"Bad day?"

I look up, and there stands Jen, grinning and tanned.

"Jen!" I shout as I set my mocha down and jump over the

counter. I grab her in the hugest hug ever and don't let go.

She's hugging me back, and I finally push her back to arm's length so I can look at my best friend.

Marriage seems to suit her. She's grinning and glowing and wearing the cutest white skirt and red top I've ever seen. Her hair seems even blonder than before, and her blue eyes are sparkling.

"Hi, soon-to-be Mrs. Dominguez," she says, smiling.

"Hi, Mrs. Clayton." I hug her again. "You aren't working today?"

She shakes her head. "I start back tomorrow. So, I hoped it would be slow, and I could talk you into making me an English Breakfast tea."

I grin. Jen and her English Breakfast tea. "Done." I go back around the counter and pull down Jen's favorite mug, a huge pink one with daisies on it.

Jen sits at the counter and waves at Ethan. "Hi, Ethan."

"Hi, Jen. How's it going?"

She nods. "Good."

"Well, good. I'm glad you're back. Maya will be more cheerful," Ethan says.

I throw the towel he flicked at me on his head and hand Jen her steaming cup of steeping tea. I grab my mocha and lean over the counter so we can talk.

"So," Jen says, reaching for my hand. "Jack called me last night."

I take a deep breath. "Oh yeah?"

"How's Benjamin?" She squeezes my hand. "I'm so sorry, Maya. Are Zach and Kate doing okay?"

I tell her the whole story, how Kate started bleeding and how they had to do an emergency C-section. "Benjamin weighs just three pounds."

Jen nods. "Wow. Well, if it's okay with you, can I go with you guys to the hospital tomorrow night?"

"Please," I say.

"So, I'm going to assume you haven't gotten any wedding plans done," she says.

"We have a location." I tell her about Bethany Church, and she grins.

"That place is beautiful!"

"I know." I smile over my mocha.

"So, what else have you done?"

"Um. Nothing."

"And you're getting married when?"

"November first."

Jen blinks. "Wow."

"Yeah." I sigh.

Jen pulls the tea strainer from her cup and then wraps both hands around her mug. She takes a long sip. "Well, I'm back, so I'll help as much as I can."

"How was the honeymoon?" I ask, hoping she'll spare most of the details. I'm a firm believer that the secret life in a marriage needs to stay a secret.

"Oh, Maya." She sighs. "You should definitely consider going to Hawaii. It was gorgeous! The sea was so blue and the weather was so perfect!" She flips her hair over her shoulder. "All we did was lie on the deck of the boat and relax. So wonderful!"

"I noticed the tan," I say, trying to squelch the little jealous voice in my brain. I don't tan. I burn, then I peel, then I go back to stark winter white.

So, I'm thinking a cruise to Hawaii would be a disaster of a honeymoon for me and Jack. Between me being sunburned and cranky and Jack tending toward seasickness, I can see it becoming the honeymoon from way south of the border.

And not just in the physical location sense of that word.

But I'm glad that Jen and Travis had such a great time.

She's talking about the five-course dinners they had. "The steaks, Maya, were simply fabulous! And they have like fifteen dessert choices for each meal." She's using her hands now. "And if you can't decide? They bring you one of *everything*."

I grin. "So, how much time did you spend in the gym?"

Before they left, Jen told me all about the onboard gym, and I told her time and again to stay away from it and just enjoy her honeymoon.

But Jen can't eat dessert without working out.

She bats her eyes at me. "I'm avoiding the intimate details," she says.

"You went every day. Sheesh. Control freak."

"Wait until you're eating three desserts a night, and then you see how many times you go to the gym," Jen says.

She has a point. My mom, dad, and Zach are all tall and thin and blond. Me? I'm short, have to run to stay thin, and brunette. I look exactly like my grandmother.

I ignore her, but Jen knows she just won. "Mm-hmm," she grins, sipping her tea.

A few high school girls walk in then, and I help Ethan make three MixUps. They sit at one of the tables near the counter so they can giggle over Ethan, and I grin as I wipe up the counter.

Jen raises her eyebrows at the girls and then looks at Ethan, who is rolling his eyes. "Fans of yours?"

He sighs.

"You could do what I did," I say, passing him a small cup of extra caramel MixUp. "Get engaged and flash a big diamond at them."

He rolls his eyes again—this time at me.

Jen grins. "Don't you love how she hands you the sugar before she insults you?"

"Yeah. It's great," Ethan says dryly.

"Seriously, though," I say, once I've moved back over to Jen's counter. I cup my mocha and lean over again. "Where is a good place to go on a honeymoon if one of you gets seasick and the other one sunburns badly?"

Jen sips her tea again, thinking. "Have you thought about a beach? And just dumping on the sunscreen?"

I nod. "It doesn't help. The only thing that works is SPF 70."

"SPF 70?" Jen gasps. "That's like wearing a shirt!"

"I'm cursed," I say.

She lets out her breath. "Well, have you thought about going in the other direction?"

"Like north?" I question.

"Like up. You could go to the mountains and go skiing or something."

Skiing. Now there's a good activity for someone who can barely walk without tripping over something invisible.

Jen obviously thinks about what she just said. "Oh wait. Not a good idea for you. Hmm. What are other snow activities?"

Thinking about snow makes four things come to mind: cold, mocha, book, blanket.

Reading is not a good honeymoon venture. Or so I've heard.

"Well." Jen waves her hand. "You'll come up with something. Maybe you can go overseas and do some touristy thing. Like Italy!"

"Why Italy?" I ask.

She shrugs. "I don't know. They have that canal place where someone can sing while you float down the street." She makes a face. "Although I've heard that they don't have the best voices. And you never know what they're singing over you because it's all in Italian."

"Sounds like fun," I say, raising my eyebrows.

"You could just go to Vegas. They have the same thing in the Venetian hotel. And they sing in English there," Ethan says, popping in on our conversation.

Jen makes a face. "You can't go to Vegas for your honeymoon," she says.

"Why not?" Ethan says.

"Because. It's *Vegas*. It's got weird people there."

Ethan laughs. "And Italy doesn't?"

"Probably not as many," she defends her choice.

"A friend of mine went to Italy and got his wallet stolen in Rome," Ethan says.

"Maybe your friend wasn't being careful."

"Or maybe Italy is just like every other place and has its own share of crooks and thieves and weird people," Ethan says.

"A cruise," Jen says, changing back to her original idea. "A cruise is the best way to go. Everything is on the boat, everything is safe, and the people who are there with you are all nice older couples."

"Seasick," I remind her, trying to get back into the conversation. Considering it is my honeymoon and all.

They ignore me. "I never disagreed with a cruise," Ethan says.

"Right. I did," I say.

"A cruise is such a great way to see the world without having to risk your wallet getting stolen," Jen sighs.

"And I've heard the dinners are amazing, too," Ethan says.

"Oh, the dinners!" Jen says. "And the desserts. And there's

a restaurant that is open twenty-four hours a day, so if you get hungry right before bed, you just run down there and get a complimentary snack."

"So it's like my mom's house on the water." Ethan grins.

"Except with views of ocean so blue and so clear you can see the fish swimming in it." Jen smiles.

"You can't see that from my mom's house," Ethan agrees.

I finish off my mocha and help a customer who walks in. Jen and Ethan don't even notice that I've left.

"I'd like a small americano to go," the man says. He hands me a five, and I give him back his change. He waits by the counter for his drink, and I hand him the espresso a minute later.

"Hey," he says, stopping by Jen and Ethan. "If you guys are trying to decide on a good honeymoon spot, you should consider going to Quebec. We stayed at this little bed and breakfast, and it feels like you're in Europe." He shrugs. "Just a thought. You two make a nice couple." He smiles and then leaves.

I have to laugh. Jen and Ethan frown at each other first and then at the man.

"He thought we were getting married?" Ethan asks, shocked.

"He suggested Quebec?" Jen asks, also shocked.

I close the cash register and help myself to a cinnamon roll, sticking three dollars from my purse in the cash register. I'm talking Calvin for a walk later, and I need the sugar now.

I climb into bed that night and pull the covers up to my chin. Jack and I met at a local hamburger place to talk about honeymoon locations. After listening to Jen and Ethan go on for an hour about it, I started stressing out.

"Relax," Jack had said over dinner.

"But we need passports if we go out of the country, and there are customs forms and reservations and trip-planning services." I rubbed my cheek. "Maybe a wedding in less than three months isn't possible."

"It's possible," Jack said all soothingly. "We just need to remember why we're doing this."

Trust Jack to always have the answer.

I pick up my Bible from the bedside table. Maybe there's some wisdom about planning a wedding in it. I flip to the concordance and look up *wedding*.

There are a few references listed for John 2, so I turn there. It's the story of how Jesus changes the water to wine as His first miracle. And it takes place at a wedding.

The story ends with this: "This beginning of His signs Jesus did in Cana of Galilee, and manifested His glory, and His disciples believed in Him" (verse 11).

I read that line again. "Manifested His glory . . . disciples believed in Him."

What a way to end a wedding.

I take a deep breath. Maybe I've been looking at our wedding the wrong way this whole time.

CHAPTER EIGHT

It's Wednesday night around six, and we are finally headed to the hospital. Jack told me he would not go to the hospital again without showering, so Jen, Travis, and I waited a whole ten minutes in his living room while he showered and messed some gel in his hair.

In his defense, he does smell better this time. Which is nice, since I'm in the front seat next to him.

Jen is holding the softest little teddy bear I've ever seen. "I bought it for their baby shower before I left," she says.

I nod slowly. Kate's shower was supposed to be in two weeks. And it was supposed to be in plenty of time for little Benjamin's birth.

But God knows best. Maybe little Benjamin is going to be one of those annoying people who is early everywhere he goes.

Travis taps me on the shoulder. "So, no one has picked him up yet?" he asks.

I shake my head. "No. They can't yet. I guess the doctors are worried about too much stimulation. We can touch his hand. That's about it."

I texted Zach earlier today, and he said that Benjamin has gained a little more weight, which brings him up to a respectable three pounds and two ounces.

Jen and Travis tell Jack all about their honeymoon on the drive. "It was such a gorgeous place," Jen says.

"Yeah. It was nice. Really quiet. The ship wasn't too crowded, and we got to do a lot of things on land, too," Travis adds.

"Sounds like fun for you guys," Jack says.

I peek in the back and see Jen's grin. "But not for you?" she giggles.

"I don't like boats," Jack says. "They rock. And tilt. And do all kinds of things that just don't sit too well."

"Guess you aren't a big fisherman either," Travis says.

"Not really, no."

I grin. This does not bother me in the least. He's not big on camping either. Again, I'm a-okay with that. Jack doesn't like a place where he can't put gel in his hair. I don't like a place that requires me to sleep amidst the insects and vermin. So, we will stay in hotels. And get our omega-3s from Joe's Crab Shack instead of the local lake.

This doesn't keep Jen and Travis from sharing more though. They go on about the food and the room and the views for almost half an hour. They're just wrapping up the flight home when we get to the outskirts of San Diego.

"Let's stop and pick up a pizza," Jack says, glancing at the dashboard clock. It's nearly seven.

I'm thinking Kate and Zach will have already eaten, because they're one of those couples who eats at five thirty.

But none of us has had dinner, and I'm starving.

"Sounds good to me," I say. "How does that sound to you?" I ask Travis and Jen.

"Pizza." Jen sighs.

"That means yes," I translate for Jack.

He grins and drives to Pizzoré, a local San Diego favorite. And it's only a few miles from the hospital, so it works out nicely.

By the time we get to Zach and Kate's room with the pizza, we're all drooling so much that it's soaking through the collars of our shirts. The pepperoni and pineapple pizza smells so good.

We knock on the closed door, and there's no answer. I bite my lip. Enter and catch them sleeping? Don't enter and eat our pizza in the hallway?

A nurse solves our problem. "Are you here for Dr. and Mrs. Davis?" she asks, pausing her walk down the hall.

"Yes," I say.

"They're with the baby right now. I can take you down there if you'd like."

Jack steps into their empty room to drop off the pizza, and we follow the nurse to the NICU.

"One minute," she says, going inside.

Jen frowns her question at me.

"There can only be two people in there at one time," I tell her. "NICU rules."

"Oh," she says.

Zach comes out a minute later, and he looks like he's been crying.

I've never seen my brother cry. I immediately assume the worst. I can't even speak; my throat is suddenly as dry as dust. I just wrap him in a hug. A thousand different thoughts are running through my head at the same time.

"We got to hold him," Zach chokes into my hair.

My heart rate slows, which is good, because I'm thinking it was pounding so hard that a heart attack was imminent.

"What?" I ask, pulling back a little bit.

He's tearing up again. "We got to hold him. Kate's holding him right now."

Suddenly there are tears slipping down my cheeks, too. "Really?"

Zach pushes me completely away. "Go wash. Go hold him."

"No, you need to go in there for a while. We'll go eat our dinner and come back in a little bit," I say, shaking my head. I grab for Jack's hand. "We'll be back soon."

We all walk back to the room, and I sniffle away the tears.

"Today was a good day," Jack says, grinning.

He prays quickly over the pizza, and we dig in. It tastes just as good as it smells. I see a nurse hovering near the doorway, and I wave her in. "Quick, grab a slice," I whisper to her.

She clasps her hands at her chest. "Oh, thank you, thank you!" She grabs a piece of pizza and takes a huge bite. "They're serving some kind of grayish meatloaf in the cafeteria," she says.

I glance at the others, who are all making faces. I think we can safely say we have a new appreciation for the medical profession.

The nurse says thank you six more times and then leaves, wiping her hands on a paper towel she stole from Kate's bathroom.

Jen licks off her thumb. "So, Maya, I never got a chance to ask you how the new apartment is working out," she says.

Aka, The Lonely Pad.

I shrug. "It's fine."

Jen looks at Travis. "Told you. She hates it."

"I don't hate it. It's just . . ."—I roll my shoulders, looking for the word—"different," I finish weakly. My seventh-grade English teacher always said that *different* was the worst adjective in the whole world and *fine* was a close second.

"Use your words!" she would lecture us. "There are so many, many wonderful, unique, fabulous words—use them!"

Well, I apologize, Mrs. McKimwick. I don't know how else to explain it.

Travis gives Jen a conceding look. "You're right."

"I'm fine," I say, wincing. If Mrs. McKimwick were here, I'd be getting extra credit work to last me until Halloween.

Being out of junior high does have its many benefits. Fewer acne breakouts, no more sad feuds started by notes that went something like this:

You are my new BFF, and don't tell Stacy because she used to be my BFF, but I took my friendship necklace back from her when she wasn't looking.

And no more Mrs. McKimwick.

Jack polishes off his third slice and wipes his hands on a napkin. "Well, she won't have to live alone for too much longer," he says, grinning at me.

I smile back.

Marriage is weird. Not only am I about to live with a *man* for the rest of my life, but I am about to *live* with a man for the rest of my life.

And it will all be legal. In both the state's eyes and in God's eyes.

It's sort of like being offered that Forbidden Apple and being told to peel it, core it, and make a cobbler with it.

Jen's smirking at me like she's reading my thoughts, and my traitorous cheeks start to turn pink. "So," I say brightly, trying to change the subject, "are you two all settled in?" Shift the focus. That's all I need to do.

Jen exchanges glances with Travis. "Almost," she hedges.

"Sort of," he nods.

Then they both just sit there and look at us.

"Okay, what?" I ask.

"Well. Maya, we have a proposition for you," Travis says slowly, folding his hands together all lawyer-style.

"I am not going to move in with you two," I say.

"Good," he says. "No, we would like to offer you a trade."

"You can't have Calvin." I shake my head. "Or the cheese grater."

"Your couch for a new couch," Travis finishes.

"I'm sorry?" I ask.

Jen sighs. "You can say no if you want," she says. "But I just love that couch. I love it so much, and I fit like perfect on it, and I can't find another couch that I love quite as much."

I just look at them. "You have to be kidding," I say.

"We're not. She's set on it," Travis says, coming this close to rolling his eyes. "We've been to tons of furniture stores, and she only likes your couch."

"I think I bought that couch at a Goodwill," I tell Jen.

"I know. But I love it. You can have a completely new couch. Please?" She bats her sad-looking blue eyes at me.

"Are you sure? I feel like you're getting the worse deal."

"I'm sure." She nods. "I love that couch. You go pick out whatever couch you want, and we'll cover the cost."

I look at Jack, and he's shrugging. "Sounds fine to me."

"Okay. Thanks, guys."

"No, thank you!" Jen grabs me in a hug. "Yay!"

"You're weird."

We go back to the NICU about an hour later after playing a couple of games with the deck of cards that Jack brought.

We can peek through the window, and I cup my hands over my eyes, trying to see in through the mess of wires and machines everywhere.

There's Kate. She's sitting in a rocking chair next to an empty incubator, and there's the tiniest little bundle cuddled against her chest. Zach is kneeling beside her, talking to the bundle.

It makes tears start to swim in my eyes all over again.

"Can you see them?" Jack asks, leaning against the window next to me.

"Yeah." I sniff. "Right there. See them?"

"Oh, that's sweet," Jack says.

"What?" Jen asks, leaning on the window next to Jack. Travis cups his hands over his eyes next to her.

We all just watch. It's such a sweet scene. Kate is slowly, almost imperceptively, rocking and gently kissing her son's forehead beneath the blanket.

A nurse comes over and talks to Zach and Kate and then points toward the window. They look up at all of us, and we immediately jump off the window.

"I think we got caught," Jack says, grinning as we all try to act nonchalant.

The nurse comes out and laughs at all of us standing in the hallway. "Nice try," she says, smiling. "There's no one else in the NICU right now. And seeing how Dr. Davis is one of our best pediatricians . . ." She shrugs. "Scrub up and come on in. Don't forget your hats and gloves." She points to the sink and the gear neatly stacked in cubbies next to it.

I run for the sink, and five minutes later, I'm tiptoeing into the NICU and over toward Kate, Zach, and tiny Benjamin.

"Well, look who's here," Zach says, grinning at me. "It's my super subtle sister." He stands and gives me another hug.

I could get used to all the hugs I've gotten from Zach and Kate lately.

"Well," I say, shrugging and blushing.

Kate smiles up at me. "Would you like to hold your nephew, Aunt Maya?"

I nod, holding my hands out.

She stands carefully, being wary of the wires and tubes that are still attached to little Benjamin and nods toward the chair. "Sit down first. He's hard to hold with all these things attached to him."

I sit and hold up my arms, and Kate sets him carefully in the crook of my arm.

He's so tiny and so light.

I hold him tenderly, feeling like I might break him at any point. His little face is half hidden by the blanket, and I smooth the tiny hairs dotting the top of his head.

"What do you think?" Zach asks, acting like the proud daddy.

"I think he's a keeper," I say. I lean over carefully and lightly kiss his soft little head. "He smells like a baby."

"Probably a good thing," Kate says, smiling tiredly.

"When did you guys get to come hold him?" I ask. Jack, Jen, and Travis come in then.

"Around noon," Kate says. She and Zach greet Jen and Travis and welcome them home from their honeymoon.

I look down at Benjamin's little face. It's so perfectly formed, just so small. His little lips are moving up and down like he's dreaming about eating.

All of us get a chance to hold him. Jack takes him from me and gently kisses his head. He just rocks and murmurs to Benjamin about when he's bigger and his Uncle Jack will play baseball with him and let him go on elephant rides at the zoo.

It makes me fall in love with Jack just a little bit more.

We head home from the hospital around nine thirty. All of us have work in the morning. Jen falls asleep on Travis's shoulder.

Jack drops me off last, walking me up to my door. "Goodnight, sweetheart," he says sleepily. He gives me a kiss and holds me in a long hug. "See you tomorrow."

"Drive safely."

"I will. Love you."

"I love you, too." I unlock my door and wait for him to get back to his truck before I close it and go inside.

Calvin is waiting for me when I walk in. "Hi, buddy," I say, tiredly leaning down and rubbing his ears. "I got to hold Benjamin tonight."

"Roo!" Calvin says excitedly.

"Need to go out?"

By the time I get back inside, I'm fighting sleep. I lock my door, stumble to my bedroom, change into my pajamas, and fall onto the bed. Too many emotions in too short of a time frame.

I grab my Bible and flip it open, staring at the words swimming on the page through bleary eyes.

Half of a sentence stands out: "He grants sleep to those he loves" (Psalm 127:2, NIV).

I close my Bible, turn off my bedside lamp, and am asleep before my head even touches the pillow.

CHAPTER NINE

"So, guess who missed Bible study last night?"

I look up and see Andrew standing on the other side of the counter. It's ten thirty on Thursday, and I've already made sixteen lattes.

Sixteen.

I smile at Andrew and shrug, wiping the counter. "I got to hold my nephew."

Andrew immediately snaps out of lecture mode. "And how's he doing?"

"So far, so good."

"That is great to hear." He grins. "I hoped that was where you were. Can I get a large cinnamon latte, please? To go," he says hastily when he sees me reach for a huge yellow mug with smiley faces all over it.

"Fine. Be that way."

"Fine. I will," he says.

I write Andrew's order on his cup. Ethan is in the back, icing our second tray of cinnamon rolls for the day.

Yes. Our second.

"So," Andrew starts again, leaning against the counter, "we need to schedule some premarital sessions pretty quickly here, I think."

I foam the milk. "Oh boy."

"You could be more excited."

I finish foaming the milk and sigh. "Sorry, Andrew. It's just that I barely have time to plan the wedding, much less actually make myself dinner." Jack and I have been eating instant dinners or grabbing food on our way to the hospital.

It's getting expensive. Tips have been very appreciated lately.

Andrew twists his mouth sympathetically. "Okay. We'll wait another couple of weeks. But we're going to have to cram it in then."

"Thanks." I snap a lid on the cup and slide it across the counter to him. "How's Liz?"

He pretends to be busy sipping his latte, but I smirk at the telltale blush sliding up his cheekbones.

"I'll take that as 'Just fine, thanks,'" I say, grinning.

"You are too nosy for your own good."

"What can I say?" I shrug. There's another group about to walk in the door, and Ethan comes out from the back carrying the tray of freshly baked and iced cinnamon rolls, filling the whole room with the sweet, cinnamony scent.

Three people get up from their tables and follow their noses toward the counter.

Andrew looks at the small crowd gathering around him and smiles. "I need to go anyway. We've got a meeting at the church."

"You mean you really do work sometimes?"

"Funny, Maya." He winks and leaves right as ten people get in line.

Ethan looks at me and takes a deep breath.

"Next!" I call.

The next fifteen minutes are filled to the brim with lattes and cinnamon rolls. By the time we're done with that mini rush, both Ethan and I have burned fingers, and we have to make another pan of rolls.

Again.

Alisha, our boss, is going to be very excited about today. I sneak a peek at the tip jar, and I get excited about today, too.

At least I'll get to eat dinner tonight.

Ethan collapses against the counter, a towel over his shoulder. "Wow."

"You can say that again."

"Wow."

I roll my eyes at him. "I'm going to stick another pan in the oven." I go in the back and pull the last pan of cinnamon rolls from the fridge. Our chef, Kendra Lee, is going to be busy tonight.

I leave her a note.

Kendra—The cinnamon rolls were a HUGE hit today! You are a culinary genius!

I slide the rolls into the oven and set the timer, wiping off my hands on my cherry red apron.

Ethan pops his head in the back. "Might as well take advantage of the break and grab a bite to eat," he says. "Go ahead and take your lunch break."

I nod and reach for the sack I stuck on one of the shelves in the back earlier that morning. Sitting at the table, I open my bag and frown at the contents. I think it's time to make a trip to the grocery store. I pull out an expired trail-mix bar, a squishy tomato, and a multivitamin.

Ethan pops his head back in. "Hey, Alisha called and she needs . . ." He looks at my feast and stops talking. "What is *that*?"

"Lunch." I poke the tomato with a fork, which makes a sad

little wrinkle. I'm thinking it's bad that it didn't pop open.

"Ugh," Ethan says, making a face. "That's gross, Maya." He glances behind him, and I guess no one is in line. "Here." He comes in and hands me a Healthy Choice meal from the freezer.

"I'm not taking your lunch, Ethan."

"It's not my lunch today. I left it last week and forgot about it." He nods to a mini pizza in the freezer. "That's my lunch today."

"Are you sure?" I feel bad taking his lunch, but my tomato does look pretty nasty. And I packed the multivitamin to ward off whatever disease I would catch from the tomato and the expired trail-mix bar. I'm thinking that's bad.

"Positive." He's making another face at the sad little veg-etable—or is it a fruit?—sitting in front of me.

"Thanks, Ethan." I grin. Ethan gets nicer every day.

There's definitely hope for him.

"Please. It's the least I could do." He shakes his head and leaves.

I unwrap the Healthy Choice meal and pop it into the microwave, looking at the box while it's heating. Mexican rice something or another.

Sounds much less fattening than my Bertolli instant pasta dinners. I glance down at my hips. Maybe if I switch to these, I won't have to work out as much.

Not like I've been working out at all lately with everything that's going on.

The microwave beeps, and I pull out the steaming plastic tray. It smells edible. So far, so much better than my nearly rotten tomato and my hard trail-mix bar.

I eat my lunch quickly and lick the fork when I finish. Not too bad, not too bad. It had rice and a cheese and red pepper quesadilla in it, and I'm imagining that now I don't need to feel guilty tonight when I get home and don't feel like going for a run.

"Thanks again," I say to Ethan as I join him in the front.

"Good?"

"Great."

"Did you throw the tomato away?" he asks, finishing a MixUp for a freckly redhead who has a braces-laced smile. She's waiting eagerly for her drink; her mom is already sipping her latte.

"Yes, I threw it away."

Ethan slides the drink across the counter. "Good."

"Go take your lunch break. I got it."

He nods and heads toward the back, right as the oven starts beeping that the final tray of cinnamon rolls is done.

"I got it," I say again, grabbing some oven mitts and carrying the steaming tray to the front counter to ice them so I can watch for customers.

"Thanks, Maya."

"Eat. And thank you again for the lunch."

I mix up our cream cheese frosting and quickly spread it over the rolls so it melts into the cracks a little bit.

"Wow," the mom of the redhead sighs, staring at the cinnamon rolls. "Those have to taste amazing."

"Yes, they do," I say, grinning. "Would you like one?"

"They also have to have about ten million calories," she says mournfully.

"Not quite ten million," I say, finishing up the frosting.

The redhead looks at her mom. "You should get a roll, Mom. You got a nonfat latte. And I'll split it with you if you want."

I grin as the daughter works her persuasive magic on her

mom.

"Fine," the mom grumbles, but she's grinning. She hands me a $5 bill and tells me to keep the change. "Oh, that looks so good," she says, almost whimpering as I slide the hot roll onto a plate.

I just smile. Another day, another convert to our cinnamon rolls.

I get home and kick off my shoes. Calvin barely looks at me as I walk in. "Thanks for the hi and hello," I say.

He groans, stretches, and goes back to sleep right smack in the middle of the hallway to my bedroom.

Calvin likes to lie in places that put me at high risk for sprained ankles.

I sit down in front of my laptop and start searching wedding flowers in Hudson, California.

Google comes up with a list a few seconds later.

Nothing. All of the results are in San Diego.

I sigh. Jen had her flowers brought in from San Diego for a hefty price, and I thought she'd done it because she has more expensive taste than I do.

Apparently not.

I rub my forehead. Okay, so I'll wait to look at flowers. What else was I supposed to do?

Someone knocks on my door, and I frown. It's after five, and I'm not expecting anyone. While I'm normally not a worrying person, living alone has made me a little more wary.

I look through the peephole, and Calvin trots over from where he was napping.

It's Jen.

I open the door, and she grins at me. "Surprise!"

"Where's your husband, newlywed? Are you allowed to leave at night yet?"

She rolls her eyes. "Please. Am I allowed." She leans down and pushes a big box filled to the brim with books and magazines into my living room while Calvin goes crazy around her.

He won't greet me, but he'll fall all over himself trying to say hi to her.

What a loyal dog.

"Travis is working late tonight," she says.

"What's all this?" I point to the box.

"Wedding stuff." She squints her eyes at me. "You need help. And you need help fast."

I pick up the magazine on the top. *Bridal Elegance* is the name of it, and the girl on the cover looks more like a Barbie doll than a human. "Swell."

"You can thank me later." She shoves the box one more time and closes my door behind her. "Okay. You sit there." She points to the couch and then pulls her purse off her shoulder and sets it on the floor. "Hello, love," she purrs to my old crappy sofa.

"You're weird."

"I'm weird? You're the one who thinks it's perfectly normal to have only one pan in the entire kitchen." Jen walks into my tiny kitchen, and I sit as I was told.

"What are you doing?"

"None of your business."

"Well, it's kind of my business. You're in my kitchen."

"Let me tell you a secret from being married," Jen calls from the kitchen. I can hear cabinets opening and closing. "It's never going to be your kitchen again. So just get used to sharing."

"Such amazing advice after only two weeks of matrimony."

"I learn quick."

I pick up another magazine, and I'm on page 10 when Jen finally reappears holding two mugs filled with something steaming and cinnamon scented. She hands me one of them.

"Chai tea?" I ask excitedly. Chai is one of those drinks that I never realize I'm craving until someone makes it for me.

"Yep." Jen sits next to me, cradling her own mug. She takes a long sip and then grabs a stack of books and magazines. "Okay. You take these," she says, handing me most of the magazines. "Anything you like, fold over the corner of the page."

"Okay."

"And once you've figured out what kind of dress you want, we can move on to invitations and decorations."

I nod, trying not to get overwhelmed.

Jen reaches for my wrist. "Take a sip and a deep breath. And don't worry. It will be beautiful."

I'm not even worried about whether or not it will be beautiful. I'm worried about if I will make it there without forgetting anything and whether or not Benjamin is going to be able to make it.

But I don't tell Jen this. I just sip my tea, take a deep breath, and open the first magazine.

Thirty minutes go by, and I haven't folded over one corner. Jen is oohing and aahing over everything she sees. But all the dresses I've found look like a cross between *The Little Mermaid* and something Stephen King would have designed.

I'm not a fan of mermaid gowns. To me, walking is too important. And I really don't like drawing that much attention to my Bertolli-crafted hips.

Not so much.

Jen points to a dress in one of her magazines. "Oh, Maya,

look at this one!"

I glance over, prepared to mutter an "Mmm, that's pretty" for the thirty-second time, but then I see the dress and I stop.

It's lacy. Covered in lace, actually. And it's more of a blush white than a true white. It's strapless and form fitting, and it flutters away from the hips and falls gracefully to the floor with a medium-length train. It's not poofy or cupcake-ish but simple, graceful, and flowing.

It's beautiful.

Jen grins at me. "Perfect, right?"

"It's really nice." I'm still staring at it. And the girl in the picture even looks happy, not all depressed and freaked out like the brides in my magazine.

"So. Lace." Jen's still grinning at me. "I never would have figured you for a lace girl."

"Me either." I smile back at her. "But it's beautiful."

"Corner is being creased," Jen says, making a big deal about it. "Okay. If we go with a lace dress, you are going to have to step it up a little bit on the formality of your wedding. Are you okay with that?"

I shrug at her. "Um. Sure." I wasn't even aware that *formality* was a word, much less a wedding category.

Jen hefts a huge book up from the box and sets it in my lap. "Here," she says. "This is the invitation catalog I used. You don't have to order from them, but I'll get a 20 percent off discount that you can use if you want." She grabs another huge book and sets it on top of the invitation catalog. "And this is the florist I used. If you want to keep the cost down, don't use roses or exotic flowers."

I'm understanding more why Jen's wedding was so expensive. Her flowers were all roses.

My lap is hurting from the weight of the books, and I push the flower book to the side so I can look at invitations.

I get through three pages before I start yawning.

"You're tired?" Jen says it like it's a cardinal sin.

I cover the bottom half of my face with both hands. "No, ma'am."

"How can you be tired when we're looking at wedding stuff?" Now Jen is ranting. "We are looking at things for your wedding! You should be excited! Wedding planning should be giving you a high!"

I nod. "I'm excited." I rub my cheek and look back at the page with five different variations of the same invite on it. One is white, one is off-white, one is eggshell white, one is peach, and one is taupe.

Who knew there were so many different shades of white?

Jen watches me for a minute and then pats my leg. "You know what? We're going to finish this tomorrow." She stands and puts her mug in the sink. "You're tired, and rightfully so. So go to bed."

"Thanks, Jenny."

"Night, Maya." She gets her purse and leaves.

CHAPTER TEN

"So then I said, 'Not without my long johns!'"

It's Sunday after church, and Jack and I are at Olive Garden for lunch with Jen, Travis, Liz, and a very animated Andrew, who is in the middle of telling his story. And while I imagine there's a place for stories about long johns, I'm thinking your first group date with the girl of your dreams is not the right place.

It's definitely not the right place.

We were all dawdling around the empty Sunday school class—the girls were reliving Jen's wedding, and the guys were complaining about being hungry. So, everyone decided to go to lunch together, after Jen and I convinced Liz to come.

Liz is sipping a glass of bubbling Diet Coke like she belongs in a commercial, and she smiles politely. "That's a funny story, Andrew."

Most definitely not the right place.

Thankfully, Andrew then shuts up and downs his Cherry Coke in one gulp.

"So," Jack says, reacting to the well-placed elbow I just shoved into his ribs, "what does everyone have planned for this fall?"

"Your wedding," Jen says, grinning.

Should the planning ever finish. I hold in my sigh, which doesn't go well as I take a drink of Dr Pepper at the same time and end up spitting it all over Jack's leg.

"Auuugh!" he yells. Without a word, everyone passes Jack their napkins. He grabs them and looks at me. "What happened?"

"Sorry," I say, still choking. "My swallower wasn't working."

Jack starts mopping himself off, giving me weird looks. I take another drink, showing everyone else at the table that yes, I do know how to consume a beverage like a normal human adult.

They aren't too impressed.

"That was talented." Jen grins.

"Shhh," I say.

"Jen said she moved the Debt Box to your house," Travis says cheerfully, almost gleefully. "How's that going?"

"The Debt Box?" Liz parrots. "What's that?"

Jen is giving Travis the evil eye. "It's my box of wedding books and magazines, and we did not go into debt, so I don't know why you insist on calling it that."

Travis shrugs. "It's funny."

Andrew squints at me. "You've got what? About two months left?"

"Around there."

"You'll be fine," he says. "I think people make too big a deal of a wedding." Then he clamps his mouth shut and takes a side-long glance at Liz. "Not that it's a bad thing if people make a big deal. I mean, it is a big deal."

I grin. It is kind of cute seeing my normally sure and steady pastor bumbling around like a caterpillar who is missing all of his legs on one side.

Liz doesn't even seem to notice what Andrew is saying. "I love weddings," she says, sighing into her Diet Coke. And she doesn't choke on it.

Liz lives a charmed life. She's gorgeous, she sings like an angel, she's brilliant, and she cooks.

I chew on the inside of my cheek and look at Jack, who is still dabbing the coughed-up Dr Pepper off his jeans with an already-soaked wad of napkins.

I'm thinking that Jack should have paid more attention to Liz. He wouldn't be sticky and wet right now if he were dating her. And their kids would be those tall, beautiful kids who everyone is insanely jealous of but can't say so because they would also be like the sweetest people on the planet.

Our kids will probably be some confused mishmash of a family with so many differing heights and personalities that everyone will think they're cousins instead of siblings.

Jack finishes with the napkins and sets the wad on the table; then he reaches for his water and douses his hands quickly to get the stickiness off. He dries them on his clean pant leg and then grins at me.

I smile back. What the heck. There aren't words to say how glad I am that he decided he could live with a short, frizzy-haired klutz for the rest of his life.

"Why do you love weddings?" Andrew is asking Liz without making eye contact.

She sighs again. "I love the symbolism. And I love that everyone is happy and excited, and it's just this huge celebration. It reminds you of what's really important in life, you know?"

"Like those little crab cakes?" Travis grins.

Liz laughs. "Like love."

I'm pretty sure that only Jen and I catch the look she ever-so-quickly sends toward Andrew. And I know that Jen saw it too, because she swiftly kicks Jack's shin.

"Ouch!" Jack groans, reaching for his leg. And, yes, the wet leg.

Jack's leg is not having a good afternoon.

"Oh. Sorry, Jack. Spasm." Jen pats her thigh like that explains it.

The server appears right then with our food. "Okay," he says, setting the heavy tray down on one of those little tray-holder thingies. He hands each person his or her entrée and sets our second humongous bowl of salad in the middle of the table. Then he adds my favorite finishing touch: two baskets of breadsticks.

I love this man now.

"I'll bring more napkins," he says, noticing the wad in front of Jack. "Everyone set?" he asks and barely waits to see if, yes, we're all set before he grabs his tray and tray holder and gets out of there as quickly as he can, taking Andrew's empty Cherry Coke glass with the promise of a refill.

"Shall we pray?" Pastoral Andrew is back.

I try to push the wicked grin off my face and reach my hands out for Jack and Jen's. Anytime someone starts the hand-holding during a prayer, everyone feels the awkward call of duty to do likewise.

As a general rule, I hate hand-holding during prayers. I think it's weird and unnecessary. I have yet to see a verse in the Bible that dictates that we as Christians are supposed to be holding each other's hands while we pray silently that we don't contract whatever illness the person has that we're holding hands with.

So, I avoid it whenever I can. But today I have different motives. And I'm about 90 percent sure that both Jack and Jen are not sick with anything contagious.

Jack reaches a hand over to Liz, Jen grabs Travis's hand, and Travis holds his open for Andrew.

Which leaves Andrew to grasp Liz's hand.

I smirk. Especially when I see Pastoral Andrew disappear in front of me and Bumbling Andrew return, complete with the blush and stammer.

"Uh. Okay. Um, Lord, we just, uh, ask You to bless this, uh, food and this, um, afternoon and that, uh, we'll, um, live for You in all we, um, do. Amen."

Jack squeezes my hand gently; Jen squeezes my hand so hard my knuckles pop. And Andrew slowly lets go of Liz's hand.

"Here are some extra napkins and your drink," the server says, stacking the napkins on the table and handing the icy glass to Andrew, who manages to hold it against his cheek while everyone except me is distracted with checking their food in case the server needs to get them something.

I smile at his blush, and he catches my eye and glowers at me.

I grin wider and use my fork to saw off an edge of my lasagna. The cheese is all melty and perfect. I decide that we should serve lasagna at the wedding.

Then I drop a bite on my lap—which, thank goodness, is covered with a napkin—and decide that maybe lasagna and a white dress are not the best match.

I bite into a breadstick and almost moan with pleasure. "These aw so gwood!" I say, shoving the rest in my mouth. I swallow and realize everyone is watching me. "I think that when Jesus fed the five thousand, the breadsticks tasted like this," I say.

Andrew just laughs then. "You don't think it could have possibly tasted even better?"

"I don't know how it could have. Hot? Check. Buttery? Check. Parmesan cheese?" I tick the points off on my now-butter-greased fingers. "Check."

Jack grins at me. "What about the fish?"

"Definitely shrimp," I nod. "Like the popcorn shrimp at Red Lobster."

Jen sets her fork down, frowning. "Wouldn't it have said *shrimp* in the Bible then instead of *fish*? I mean, they were all fishermen; they knew what shrimp were."

I shrug. "I'm no theologian. I just have my beliefs."

Jack grins again. "Like your belief that God's favorite color is pink?"

Andrew about loses his mouthful of ravioli. "Pink?" he sputters. "Why pink?"

I have very good reasons for this. "Sunsets and sunrises are always at least a little bit pink," I say. "Since God takes so much time to create those, I figure it has to be a favorite color of His."

Liz is smiling. "I like your logic, Maya Davis."

"Thanks. I like your cooking."

She laughs.

Jack drops me off at my apartment a little while later. He picked me up for church this morning with the excuse that it was silly for us to both drive, even though he had to come a good five minutes out of his way to get to my apartment.

"I'm going to run home to change, and I'll be right back," he says, giving me a kiss. I feel bad, knowing that the reason he has to change is because of my spitting incident.

"Sorry," I say again.

He grins. "You keep life interesting, Nutkin. I'll give you that. Be right back." Then he drives away, and I climb the metal staircase to my apartment.

Calvin is bouncing off the sofa when I get inside. "Roo!" he howls. "Roo! Roo!"

"Calm down, buddy," I say, rubbing his ears. Calvin loves Sundays because it means we're going to Mom and Dad's.

Only tonight, we're going back to the hospital. So Calvin can't come. I've heard of dogs that go to the hospital and cheer up all the sick kids, but (1) Calvin is too hyper; (2) Benjamin is too little to appreciate his canine cousin; and (3) Zach would freak out.

So, Calvin is going to stay at home. I pull my wriggling dog onto my lap to try to break the news to him.

"Calvin," I say, using the exact same tone that my mother did the day she told me that Santa Claus wasn't real.

This is a side note, but I cried like a water fountain when she told me. And I was probably around eight years old. Mom felt awful.

"Calvin," I begin, "you don't get to go to Mom and Dad's today."

He just cocks his little head at me.

"I'm sorry. I'm not going there either, if it makes you feel better."

He sighs and lays his head down on my lap, and I feel the appropriate amount of sadness for him. "But . . ." I say, and he looks up at me.

I reach for my purse and pull out one of those huge beef-basted rawhide bones that he loves.

He goes berserk. "Roo! Roo! Roo!"

"You can have this instead. Happy again?"

He's doing circles around the coffee table, so I'm going to assume he's a lot happier. I make him sit and then give him the bone.

The bone is nearly twice as long as he is, so it looks pretty funny to see him struggling to carry it around. I grin.

I love my dog.

I decide that it will be cheaper than stopping for a snack if I make Jack and I sandwiches to eat on the drive, and I go to the kitchen to find out what amazing culinary masterpieces I can whip up in ten minutes.

But watching the Food Network and having the same ingredients in your kitchen are not the same thing.

I went grocery shopping yesterday, but I'm shocked at how empty my fridge still is. I bought about ten Healthy Choice frozen meals and another ten Bertolli because supposedly real women have curves. I wouldn't want to become a stick figure like those anorexic brides in the magazines Jen brought over.

On one girl, I could see every bone in her back. Obviously, I'm not a guy, but I just don't see how that could be very sexy.

So, I got the Bertollis. And I bought some apples because my mom told me that there was a girl at Dad's work who got scurvy because she never ate fruit.

I told Mom I eat canned peaches and that should count and I thought scurvy had gone the way of the Oregon Trail, and she told me there are new studies being done about some chemical they put in canned foods that causes all kinds of awful diseases.

Thus the apples.

I peer at the bag in the fridge. I wish I liked apples.

I bought some bread and a multi-cheese pack that looked yummy, because as a Bertolli fan, I love all things cheese.

I guess we'll have cheese sandwiches. And Capri Suns from two years ago that Jen moved over here without my knowledge. And Jack can have an apple if he wants one.

I'm just sticking the sandwiches into plastic baggies when Jack knocks once and then tries the door. It's open, and he frowns at me.

"What happened to being more careful and locking your door?"

"I forgot," I say. "But it's okay because even if someone came to steal something, there's nothing worth stealing here."

He comes into the kitchen and watches me shove his sandwich in a bag. "I still don't like you leaving doors unlocked. Someone could steal *you*." He points. "What's that?"

"Lunch," I say, smiling all housewifey. "And here is an apple to ward off the scurvy."

"Scurvy?" Jack snorts, taking the apple. "I thought that's why you take vitamin C."

"Mom told me we should be eating more fresh fruit."

"There's only one apple here," Mr. Observant says.

"I don't like apples."

"You bought apples, and you don't like them?"

"They were on sale."

He just looks at me for a minute and then takes a bite of the apple. "Life is going to be interesting."

"So, we have sandwiches and Capri Suns and Oreos for a snack," I say, putting everything in a big plastic grocery bag and stuffing some napkins in there. I'm feeling very frugal.

Jack just grins at me and swallows another bite of apple. "You're cute when you're proud of yourself." He gives me a hug and picks up the bag. "I'm assuming by the size of that bone and the lack of even a polite welcome that Calvin is staying here?"

I nod. "Let me grab a jacket, and I'm ready."

It's not nearly cold enough for a jacket during the day, but sometimes the nights can get a little nippy. I grab a brown jacket, find my purse, pat Calvin on the head, and lock the door behind us.

"Hospital?" Jack asks when we climb into his truck.

"Yeah. You know, we could take my car and put the miles on that." The cost of gas is almost a non-issue because in two months, we'll be merging our bank accounts anyway.

He shrugs. "It's the same either way. And my truck is bigger. We're fine." He starts driving.

"I don't think Andrew made much headway with Liz today," I say a few minutes later.

Jack snorts again. "You can say that again. What's with him telling stories about his long underwear?"

"I don't know that I'll ever understand him."

"He just needs to relax." Jack settles in as we merge onto the highway. "He's trying too hard, and that's just going to make her wonder who the heck he is."

"Maybe we can do a double date with just the two of them," I suggest.

"I'm not sure it's kosher to do a double date with a couple that isn't technically dating," Jack says. "I think that's called a blind date."

"Well, what was today then?"

"A bunch of friends hanging out."

I give him a look. "There were two couples and then Andrew and Liz. Isn't that considered a triple date?"

"I've never heard of a triple date." He reaches for the radio and tunes it to one of those talk shows where all the host does is argue with the guests on the show.

I've always wondered why anyone goes on this guy's show as a guest. It's more like willingly going there to be roadkill.

We listen to it for half an hour before I've finally had enough. I'm halfway through my excellent cheese sandwich, if I do say so myself. I'm almost growling under my breath now.

Jack looks over at me. "What?"

"Seriously? This guy isn't driving you insane? He hasn't let that lady get more than three words in at a time!"

Jack shrugs. "I think he has some good points."

"I bet the lady does, too."

"Mmm. Maybe." Jack shrugs. "I don't mean to be cruel, but I doubt she's very bright. I mean, she did ask to be on his show."

I just shake my head as the talk-show host cuts her off again. "She needs to do something so that he'll let her finish a sentence or two."

"Like what? Bite his arm?"

I giggle at that mental picture. "I don't know. Something, though. She could start screaming."

"Or growling." Jack grins over at me. He takes a bite of his sandwich and raises his eyebrows in appreciation. "These are good."

"Thanks." I wait for him to ask, but he just keeps chewing. "Well?" I say.

"Well what?"

"Don't you want to know my secret?"

He looks briefly at the sandwich. "There's a secret?"

"Yes, Jack. All chefs have secrets."

His mouth tips. "Okay, Chef Maya. What is your secret?"

"Well, I actually put the tiniest smidgen of Dijon mustard on the bread," I say proudly.

"Hmm. Well, it tastes good. Good work."

"Thanks."

He stabs his Capri Sun with the tiny plastic straw that comes with it and sucks some out. Next thing I know, he's hacking away and grasping the steering wheel so tightly that his knuckles are turning white. "Ack!" he gasps.

"What? What?" I shout.

"That does not taste right," he says, coughing. "Where did you buy those?"

I squint at the dashboard. "Um. I don't remember."

"You don't remember?" he parrots.

I hedge. "Well, it was a while ago."

"How long?"

"Two years."

"Two years?" Jack gasps. "Ugh. No wonder it tasted all fermented. That's disgusting. Do not drink that."

We're passing signs that say one of the little suburbs of San Diego is coming up, and Jack gets in the right-hand lane. "We're stopping at Sonic and getting something that is actually potable," he says.

We're back on the highway ten minutes later, cherry limeades in hand.

"So, the snack was halfway good," I say sadly.

"More than halfway, Nutkin. You forgot about the Oreos. And I know those are fresh because Oreos don't last too long in your house." Jack grins at me.

We get to the hospital all hyped up on Oreos and limeades, and when we get to Kate's room, we're both still giggling over something we heard on the radio.

"What's with you two?" Mom says, giving us both a quizzical look.

"Nothing," I say, giving her a hug. "Hi, Mom."

"Hi, guys."

It's just Mom and Dad in Kate's room. "Are they holding Benjamin again?" I ask.

Dad nods. "He's doing so great. They got to dial his oxygen levels down a little bit, and he seems to be staying steady."

"That's great," Jack says, pumping my dad's hand in a

welcome. Guys have weird ways of saying hello.

"And Kate is going to be released tomorrow," Mom says, straightening Kate's covers. "I think her mother is going to stay with her for a few days just to help her get things done and drive her back and forth over here."

I nod. Knowing Kate, she'll be here every day, all day. Benjamin is not going to be one of those babies in the NICU who is there by himself.

Those babies make me sad. I wish I lived closer so I could volunteer to be one of those cuddlers who holds the babies and loves on the kids who are sick and alone. There's a tiny hospital in Hudson, but it's not big enough for a children's hospital or a NICU. If kids need special attention, they are airlifted here.

"Have they said how much longer Benjamin will need to stay here?" I ask Mom.

She shrugs. "I've heard three weeks and I've heard three months. It just depends on when he's completely off oxygen and stable."

Dad turns on a football game, and he and Jack make themselves comfortable in the chairs in front of it. Mom is still messing with Kate's covers.

"I just hate that they are going through this," Mom says, brushing tears from her eyes.

"But they live in the same town as the hospital, Zach is a doctor here, and there's family close by." I smile. "It's really about the best situation it could be, considering the circumstances."

"True," Mom concedes. "Anyway. Enough tears. How's the wedding planning?"

"Probably worthy of tears." I sigh. "It's frustrating, Mom."

"You know, honey, I have planned a wedding before, and I can help you if you'd like me to," she says, squeezing my shoulder.

I nod. "Please." It's hard because Mom lives an hour away, but maybe we can do things over the phone.

And we already know that all my flower options are here anyway.

Mom finishes making up Kate's bed and sits on the edge of it, patting a spot beside her. "Sit. Okay, what have you done so far?"

"We set a date."

Mom looks at me. "Please tell me you've done more than that."

"And we found a church that has a reception place attached to it."

She lets out her breath. "Thank goodness. I was worried there for a minute. Okay. So you need a dress?"

I nod. I'd spent last night cuddled on my couch with Calvin, watching TLC's *Say Yes to the Dress*. Women fly in from all over the country to buy their wedding dress at that store for outrageous prices. I'm aiming for an entire wedding that costs less than one of those dresses. Spending thousands of dollars on something you'll wear once doesn't seem smart for someone who is marrying a zookeeper and works at a coffee shop.

Mom pats my hand. "Which reminds me. All this stuff with Benjamin has overshadowed your wedding plans, but your dad and I have a savings account set up for your wedding."

I'm touched. I honestly wasn't sure if my parents would be able to pay for the wedding or not, since I know my dad's retirement has been partially washed away by the bad economy.

"Oh, Mom," I say, squeezing her hand. "Really?"

"It's not much," she warns me. "And I would recommend that you spend as little as you can so you can start living on the rest of it after you get married."

I nod. Good thought.

She gives me a hug. "We'll talk about the numbers later. But for now, have you looked at any dresses yet?"

"Just in magazines. I was hoping you'd go with me."

"Of course! I wouldn't miss it. Do you want to look here in San Diego or in Hudson?"

"Definitely San Diego."

"Let's see," Mom says. "If you come back on Saturday, we'll plan a whole day of going to different bridal stores here." She smiles at me. "You can bring Jen with you if you'd like."

I nod. "Maybe Kate will want to come, too."

"Maybe, if she's feeling up to it." Mom reaches for her purse and pulls out the small notebook and pen she keeps in there for grocery lists.

My mother is so much more organized than I am.

"So. I'll set up a few appointments for you. And I remember that Jen had to get her flowers here in town, right?" Mom is scribbling on the notebook already.

"Yeah," I say.

"Okay. So bridal salons and florists." Mom taps the notebook with her pen. "Have you thought about what you want for centerpieces yet?"

"Centerpieces?"

"And where you're going to register? And where you're going to get your invitations?"

I'm rubbing my forehead before Mom's done talking, and when she looks up and sees me, she stops. "Well. One thing at a time," she says, patting my leg, obviously sensing the impending panic attack.

Zach and Kate walk in right then. Jack and Dad immediately turn off the TV.

"Hi, Maya. Hi, Jack," Kate says wearily. Her eyes are red and puffy, and she's leaning heavily on Zach.

I'm not sure she's ready to be discharged from the hospital.

Mom and I scoot off the bed so she can stumble over to it. Zach helps her climb under the sheets and kisses her forehead before turning to me. "Hey, Sis," he says, giving me a hug.

"How's Ben?" I ask.

Kate sighs and lies back on the pillows. "Oh, he's doing so well," she says, getting teary. She swipes under her eyes. "So good," she says again.

Mom squeezes Kate's shoulder. "You need to rest, honey," she says, loud enough for everyone to hear.

We all take our cue, grab our stuff, and head into the hallway. Kate's eyes are drooping even as we leave. Mom snatches Zach's sleeve and pulls him into the hallway with us.

"What happened?" she demands as soon as Kate's door is closed.

Zach looks frustrated. "She won't let herself rest," he gripes. "Watch, she'll sleep for an hour and then want to go back in with Benjamin for the next six. She's been doing this for the last three days, and she's killing herself." He rakes his fingers through his hair. "I don't know what to do. I know she wants to be with Benjamin, but Ben needs his mom to get well."

Mom nods. "She does need to sleep. Maybe this time she'll stay in bed."

"Maybe." Zach doesn't sound too convinced. He sighs. "Anyway. Thanks for coming here, guys."

Mom glances at Dad and then pats Zach's arm. "We're going to take off now. You need your rest just as much as Kate does. Go lie down in one of the on-call rooms. A nurse can page you when Kate gets up."

My mother is such a mom.

Zach tiredly nods. "Good idea. And thanks. Thanks, guys."

"Bye, Zach," I say. A short visit this time.

Zach heads down the hall toward the on-call room, and we all look at each other. "Well," Dad says.

"Well. Let's go buzz by Ben real quick, and then we can do some wedding planning and get an early dinner. Anyone feel like The Cheesecake Factory tonight?" Mom asks, grinning at me.

I love my mom.

CHAPTER ELEVEN

It's Monday morning, and I'm at Cool Beans.

Alone.

There's a note stuck to the cash register when I walk over, and I pull it off, squinting at Alisha's scribbled handwriting.

Ethan is sick with the flu. If it gets to be too much here, call me and I'll send a sub over from the café. I'd come, but I've got meetings scheduled all day. I'm paying you time and a half for today. So sorry!

I put my purse and jacket in the back and pull on my cherry red apron.

Today is going to be a very long day. Working alone means that (1) it's boring, and (2) it's very difficult to get a lunch break. I pop the cinnamon rolls into the oven and go back out to the front.

Our first customer comes in right as I'm finishing up the medium roast for the day, a sweet and smoky mix of cinnamon and Colombian blends.

It's Mr. Patterson, early again for his weekly Bible study.

"Morning, Maya," he says, ambling over. His Bible and the

book they are going through are tucked under his arm, and he's digging out his wallet from his back pocket.

"Hi, Mr. Patterson." I grin at him. I started the decaf first because I knew he'd only be a few minutes. "Decaf should be done in about five minutes, cinnamon rolls in about ten."

"No worries." He's peeking around me. "No Ethan today?"

"I guess he has the flu," I say, shaking my head and pulling out some beans to grind for the dark roast. The roasts of the day always reflect the mood of the barista, and today's dark roast is a deep, thick French blend with a few shakes of dark cocoa.

Like I said, it's going to be a long day. Chocolate is always appreciated.

Mr. Patterson makes a face. "That's too bad. You know, he's not as chipper as you are, Maya, but he's okay just the same."

I grin. "I'm working on him."

"I know." Mr. Patterson taps his Bible. "He'll get there. Salvation is just one of those things that can't be rushed for some people."

"Frustrating for the people around them, though."

"Well, yes." He pulls a $5 bill out of his wallet as I tap in his order on the computer.

"Three dollars and fifty-three cents," I say.

"You didn't even ask what I want," he says, pretending to gripe.

"Sorry. What did you want?"

"Small decaf and a cinnamon roll," he says.

"Okay. Three dollars and fifty-three cents." I'm grinning unrepentantly at him.

Mr. Patterson sighs. "I need to be more unpredictable."

I laugh.

By lunchtime, I'm exhausted. I have huge stains all over my apron and my jeans from when the espresso machine decided it hated me and dispensed three shots of espresso three separate times without me pressing the button. And I'm starving.

The place is packed. Almost every table is full, and I can see yet another car pulling into the parking lot. I wipe my hands on a towel and sigh, half wanting to pick up the phone and call Alisha for help.

But she is paying me time and a half. And that will be nice as far as rent and grocery bills go. And while I miss having someone to talk to, I really don't want someone who has never worked at Cool Beans to come try to help me—I think that would be more of a hassle than a help.

I glance at the door and run to the back to shove my Healthy Choice meal in the microwave really quick before the next people come in. I'll just have to grab bites in between making drinks.

I run back out to the front, and the people are just getting to the counter. It's a mom and two junior high kids, both wearing braces. The girl has tear-streaked cheeks, and the boy is wincing in pain as he touches his jaw.

"Hi," I say, looking curiously at the teary girl.

The mom notices my glance. "Orthodontist appointment," she says quietly.

"Oh." Ouch. I wince in sympathy pain. I look at the kids. "So sorry to hear that. Want something cold? That might help."

The mom nods. "That's what we came for." She motions to the kids to order.

The girl goes first, sniffling. "A medium caramel MixUp, please," she says.

"And I want a medium chocolate MixUp," the boy says. The chocolate MixUps are caffeine and coffee free. So basically, it's a milkshake.

The mom is glancing at the menu. "And I would like a small caramel latte with fat-free milk and no whipped cream, please."

I nod, punching the order into the cash register. She's obviously one of those women who worries about her weight and doesn't need to. "For here or to go?"

"To go," she says, pulling out her wallet.

I can hear my lunch beeping in the microwave, and I try to hurry it up. I swipe her card, put the MixUps in the blenders, and froth her fat-free latte.

Even though I race as fast as I can, lunch is already cooling off when I get back to the microwave. I scarf down four bites, and then I see another person coming in.

I need to call Alisha.

I wash my hands and run out to the front to help the next customer. It's Jen. She's frowning at me as I stumble over.

"What's wrong with you?"

"Ethan's sick today."

She squinches her mouth. "You're by yourself?"

I nod sadly.

"Well, this explains why you weren't answering your cell," Jen says, unlooping her purse off her shoulder. "Isn't this the normal time for your lunch break?"

"Yeah. I'm trying to eat between customers."

She nods. "Go eat. I'll stall any customers."

I'm curious how she's planning on stalling them, but I don't question. "Thanks!" I run for the back, my stomach growling in protest of the late lunch.

Five minutes later, I'm back out front, and it's still just Jen. "No customers," she says. "And can I have an English Breakfast tea?"

I start making it for her. "So what's up?" I ask.

"Well," she starts, sitting down on one of the stools at the bar, "I was thinking about that church where you are going to have your wedding. What colors do you think would go best with that church?"

I slide her mug of steeping tea over. "Colors?" I parrot.

"Yeah. Like for the bridesmaids."

I shrug. "I don't know." The church has rich dark wood everywhere. I'm thinking deeper colors. Maybe hunter green, but I don't want to copy Jen's wedding.

"What are you thinking?" Jen asks.

"I'm thinking that I don't know. What goes with brown?"

"Red, burgundy, teal, gold, green, blue, pink . . ." Jen starts rattling off the colors and stops. "Actually, those are the colors I'm painting my future nursery. Blue and brown or pink and brown."

I just look at her. She's already thinking about painting a baby room, and she's only been married for three weeks.

Jack and I have discussed the Kid Topic. We want to wait. Approximately three years. Then we'll have two kids.

I'd prefer a boy and a girl.

But, then again, God is God. And He does have a way of changing my plans. After all, I'm marrying Jack Dominguez instead of Justin Timberlake.

Seventh grade was interesting.

"Is there something you're forgetting to tell me?" I ask, watching yet another car pull into the crowded parking lot.

Jen looks at me. "Um. I don't think so. Why?"

"Baby rooms. Just curious."

"Oh," Jen says, waving her hand dismissively. "No, I'm just planning ahead."

Well, she is Jen.

"Teal is the color of gangrene," I say, quoting from *The Wedding Planner*. "Not a good choice. And I look gross in teal."

"No, you don't."

"Yes, I do. Remember those pictures of my sixth-grade dance when I wore the teal dress?"

Jen rolls her eyes. "It wasn't a pretty dress to start out with, Maya. The color was not the problem."

"Well, thanks." It wasn't a pretty dress, but she doesn't have to point that out.

A man in a business suit walks in, talking loudly on his Bluetooth. "No, I said fax pages 11 through 16, not 7 through 16," he says, frustration in his voice. He stops at the counter and doesn't even glance at the menu. "Americano. Hot," he barks.

I blink. Wow! I am glad I do not work for this person. Working alone is not fun, but working for him would be even worse. I punch in his order and start to make his americano.

I hate Bluetooths. I never know when the person is talking to me or not.

"No, *no!*" he shouts.

I freeze halfway through pouring the espresso into the hot water. "I'm sorry?" I ask as politely as I can.

He's still yelling in my direction. "I told you to stop faxing it now!"

Bluetooth. I finish his americano, pop a lid on his to-go cup, and hope he catches the hint that he needs to move this conversation outside.

"Two sixty-eight," I say.

He hands me exact change and leaves, still yelling.

Jen looks over at me, eyebrows raised. "Well. He seems like a nice guy." She sips her tea while I wipe off the counter. "Hey, who is performing the ceremony?"

I'm going to assume we're back on the wedding topic. "Andrew."

She nods. "He's getting his fair share of weddings in lately."

"It's wedding season."

She finishes her tea and glances at her watch. "Lunch break is over. I'll give you a call tomorrow, okay? Hope the rest of your day goes smoothly."

"Thanks. See you, Jen."

She leaves, and I look at my not-quite-as-crowded store. I can do this alone.

I think I can anyway.

I'm like the Little Engine That Could of the mocha variety.

I get home that night exhausted.

Ethan texted me at one thirty: *I am SO sorry. I have been sleeping and throwing up all day. Sorry to leave you in the lurch.*

Ugh. I'm glad he left me in the lurch. I don't handle throw up well.

I texted him back: *Don't worry about it. Get well soon. And please don't come in until you feel better.*

The last thing I need is to get the flu—especially if I still want to see Ben, Kate, and Zach.

It's almost six o'clock, and I'm getting hungry. As healthy as Healthy Choice meals are, they just aren't that filling.

Calvin is doing happy-doggy dances around my feet as I pull out his food, and I rub his silky ears. "Let's go on a walk to the park after dinner," I tell him.

He perks up at the word *walk* and barks. "Roo!"

I pull out—what else?—a Bertolli instant meal and an apple so I can stare at it and feel guilty about maybe contracting scurvy.

Jack calls while I'm spooning the garlic shrimp and asparagus into a bowl. See? There are vegetables in my dinner.

"Hey, love," he says, and I can tell he's hiding a yawn.

"Long day for you, too?"

"Mmm. Trouble with the giraffe exhibit."

I will never get used to what a zookeeper's "hard day" is like.
"Did one of them escape or something?" I'm picturing Geoffrey
from the Toys "R" Us commercials wandering around the zoo,
stealing little kids' cotton candy.

"No, no." Jack gives a short staccato laugh. "Just a slight
feeding error. Nothing quite that dramatic. How was your day?"

I tell him about being alone at work and how Jen thinks I
should have the bridesmaids wear teal.

Jack's quiet for a minute. "Okay. I'm a guy."

"Teal is like a mix between blue and green," I say, rolling my
eyes. I sit down on the couch and grab my fork. My stomach is
growling loudly now that I can smell the shrimp.

"Oh. I'm not really a fan of baby colors in weddings."

I'm chewing, so I don't answer right away, but I guess that
green and blue mixed together equals baby colors for my fiancé.

He's a strange one.

"It's not a baby color," I start, then stop. I don't want teal
in the wedding, so I'm not sure why I'm defending it. "Never
mind. What do you think of blues?"

"I think they can be depressing, but sometimes they have a
good beat. Particularly if there's a saxophone."

Insert big sigh by me here. No wonder we haven't gotten
anything planned.

"Sorry, Nutkin." Jack's laughing. "I think they are fine.
Why?"

"Maybe we could have a blue wedding."

"How about orange?" Jack suggests.

I am careful to finish swallowing my shrimp before I react. I'm picturing Jen's reaction if I told her I want her to wear orange to my wedding.

It wouldn't be pretty.

"I don't think so," I say.

"Why not? We're getting married in the fall. Orange is a fall color."

"So is that tannish-brown color of dead leaves, but I'm not going to use that color in my wedding."

Jack is still half-laughing; I can tell. "Look. How about you decide, and I'll just be happy with whatever you come up with?"

That's probably for the best, but I really need input. "Fine," I say, sulking. I spear an asparagus with my fork and chomp on it.

"What are you doing tonight?" he asks me, cleverly changing the subject.

"Eating. Taking Calvin for a walk. And then I'm going to look at wedding magazines while I watch *What Not to Wear.*" It's a fun evening except for the wedding magazines part. Now, they're starting to get depressing. I keep seeing all the beautiful brides on the pages shaking their heads at me like, "Sheesh, Maya, I was so much more organized than you. I had my whole wedding planned out when I was eight years old."

I had a friend who had her entire wedding planned by the time she was in the eighth grade. She knew everything: napkins, invitations, bridesmaid dresses, her dress, the ceremony site. Everything but the groom. I always thought she was a little weird.

Now, I'm wishing I were more like her. Pulling off a wedding in less than three months would be way easier if I were one of those girls.

As it is, I hadn't really thought about my future wedding except once when I went to a wedding when I was twenty-one. They had mini chocolate fountains and these gorgeous strawberries to dip in them. I decided that was the best way to get married ever.

"We should get chocolate fountains," I tell Jack.

"As a souvenir?"

"For the reception. We can have strawberries and stuff with it."

I can almost picture him nodding. "That sounds good, Nutkin. How about those little mini hot dogs things, too?"

I make a face at Calvin. "Mini hot dogs? You don't mean Vienna sausages, do you?" My gag reflex is starting to kick into gear. Surely, surely, surely the love of my life and the man I'm going to spend the rest of forever with doesn't like those.

"What are Vienna sausages?"

"They come in a can, and they're the color of death."

"Oh. No, no. These come in a bag thing. They're like mini smoked sausages and you roll them up in biscuits."

"Oh!" I'm so relieved to hear this. My future will be Vienna sausage–free. "Little smokies?" I ask.

"Sure," Jack says. "I don't remember what they are called. My dad made them a lot. We used to put barbecue sauce on them and eat them with toothpicks every New Year's Eve."

Odd tradition, but okay.

Jack's getting all nostalgic. "And we would play Phase 10 until it was fifteen minutes until midnight, and then we'd watch the ball drop in New York. And my mom made enchiladas, and all of my cousins would come over." He pauses. "What did you do for New Year's Eve?"

Up until this past year, Zach and I didn't get along very well at all. Call it sibling rivalry, call it differing personalities, but we couldn't talk to each other without bickering.

"Well," I start, "none of my extended family lives near us, you know, so it was usually just the four of us. Zach and Dad would play Scrabble or something 'educational,' and Mom and I would watch some sappy Lifetime movie until the ball dropped. Then we would try to go to bed without fighting so we'd at least have twelve hours in the New Year that were fight-free."

"I'm sorry, Maya."

"It's better now." God does change and soften hearts; I'm probably the poster child for that one. I love my brother now. I never thought I'd be able to say that without rolling my eyes.

"I know. But still. So, you want company on this walk?"

"Maybe. What did you have planned for tonight?"

"Well, tonight is a big night. I'm having corn dogs and hoping to eat all of them before Canis steals one. And then I didn't have anything else planned."

I grin. "If you want to come, that would be great. Bring Canis."

"I'll do that. Let me eat, and I'll be over soon."

We hang up, and I finish my garlic shrimp pasta. It's amazing, and I'm so grateful that God created a man named Bertolli to make it. Or maybe Bertolli is just a company. Either way, stuff this good is not made only by human hands.

Canis is Jack's Labrador pointer cross. And *canis* is the Latin name for dog. Jack was meant to be a zookeeper. Canis is a good dog, but he's a little too big for Calvin's taste. Calvin can only stand playing with him for about ten minutes before I think he starts feeling short and they get in a tiff. And since I know what that feels like, I let Calvin be all huffy and standoffish for a little while.

We short ones have to stick together.

Calvin's napping on the floor by my feet, and I nudge him with my shoe. "Hey."

He cracks open one eye and looks at me.

"Want to go on a walk?"

The *w* word is barely out of my mouth before he hops up, does three quick circles, and starts making noise. "Roo! Roo!"

"Okay, okay!" I say, grinning. I set my bowl in the sink and go get Calvin's collar and leash from the hook by the door. I don't usually leave his collar on during the day just because the tags clanging together drives me crazy, so I figure it has to make him a mental case.

I only make him wear his collar when we're going for a walk or driving to Mom and Dad's.

I buckle the collar, clip on his leash, and let him run excitedly around the living room in circles while I change into my ratty jeans and a T-shirt that says "Wheaties. It's What's for Breakfast." I got the shirt free in a cereal box.

And yes. It was a Wheaties cereal box.

By the time Jack pulls into the parking lot, Calvin and I are sitting on the bottom step of the stairs leading up to my apartment. Calvin sees Canis jump out of the car and starts barking at him.

Probably warning him not to make fun of his height again.

Jack grabs Canis's leash and walks over. Jack's wearing worn khaki carpenter shorts and a black T-shirt.

"Hey, honey," he says, bending down to give me a kiss. "Hi, Calvin." He rubs my ecstatic beagle's head.

Canis is sniffing all over Calvin and then turns to give me a bunch of sloppy kisses all over my arms. "Hi, Canis," I say, standing, making a face.

"Easy, boy," Jack tells him. "She's taken."

"Ready for a walk?" I reach for Jack's hand, and he switches Canis's leash to his right hand.

We start off toward the park and see that we aren't the only ones taking advantage of the beautiful evening. Kids are playing wiffle ball with their dads, moms are pushing strollers next to each other and walking the sidewalk that winds around the park, and couples are cuddling on blankets on the grass.

Calvin, being an attention hog, immediately aims for the couples on their blankets, but I grab his leash tighter. Last time I let him run without his leash, he wagged over to one poor couple and stood right in between them, waiting for one of them to pet him.

It was embarrassing for me.

"So," Jack says, "looked at any magazines yet tonight?"

I shake my head. "Nope. Not yet." I let go of his hand and pull my cell phone out of my back pocket to check the time. "I've still got an hour before *What Not to Wear* starts."

"And then the magazines come out of hiding?" He's grinning.

"They aren't hiding. They were put in the hall closet behind my coats very purposefully." Then it's harder for those smug brides to look mockingly at me.

Jack is sighing, reading my mind. "It's not like they are real people, Nutkin. They're just pictures."

"Still."

He laughs. "You are ridiculous."

"Do you think we should serve a dinner at the reception?" I ask. We haven't officially nailed down a wedding time yet. Maybe if we decide yes or no to a meal, it will make it easier to figure out a time frame.

Jack is squinching up his mouth as he thinks. "I think it

would be expensive."

"I think you're right."

"Maybe just cake. And finger foods. Like those little hot dogs."

Brain translates: "Not Vienna sausages" just so my stomach doesn't get grossed out. "Don't forget the chocolate fountain," I remind him.

"And the chocolate fountain." He squeezes my hand as he smiles. "I think that would be enough."

"So we could do one o'clock in the afternoon or something. That way there's no dinner and no lunch."

He's nodding. "Sounds good to me. And we don't have to get up at the crack of dawn."

I grin. That's my fiancé.

CHAPTER TWELVE

By Wednesday, Ethan is back and feeling much better. "I guess it was just a twenty-four-hour thing," he says after our morning rush is over.

I nod. "That's good."

"Yeah. Sorry to leave you in the lurch yesterday and Monday, though."

"Eh . . ." I wave my hand and succeed in knocking over a cup of tea I didn't know was sitting on the counter.

It hits the floor with a *sploosh!* as the lid on the paper cup pops off and tea floods the floor.

I sigh. Ethan sighs. Then we both grab paper towels and start soaking it up.

By the time I'm done mopping the floor, I've forgotten what we were talking about. Ethan is making another cup of tea, and that reminds me.

"Was that yours?"

"The one you bulldozed? Yes, it was mine."

I ignore the meanness. "Since when did you start drinking hot tea?" Normally, Ethan is an iced-coffee guy. No frills, no dressings. Black coffee and ice.

I think it's nasty, but I do work in a coffeehouse and I'm paid to sell everything. So if you ask me, I say, "It's not my favorite, but I know people who love it." I guess that sounds better than "It reminds me of roadside sludge the day after a snowfall."

"Since I got the flu," Ethan says. He sips the tea, gagging. "Someone told me the antioxidants ward off germs."

I look at him. "It was a girl, huh." It's not a question. I just know.

Ethan shrugs. "So what if it was?"

"And you listened to her?" Now I'm trying my best not to smile.

"Don't go getting any ideas, Maya Davis. It made sense, so I decided to try it. She didn't tell me how awful tea tastes, though." He takes another sip and gags again.

"So stop drinking it," I say, knowing full well he won't. Whatever Ethan says about getting ideas, he doesn't do anything that anyone suggests unless he can prove to himself that it really does work.

Obviously, he likes this girl.

He shrugs. "Eh. I'll try it."

Told ya.

I just grin at him. I look around the coffee shop, and today is quite a bit slower than the last two days.

Of course.

About two-thirds of the tables are filled, it's almost eleven, and we have yet to sell all of our first pan of cinnamon rolls.

I think that's a new record for August. Usually, I only see this in January when everyone is sticking to their New Year's resolutions of no carbs, no sugar, and definitely no more cinnamon rolls.

I do not make New Year's resolutions. I think they are a waste of time. Why would I write down a bunch of things that I know I need to change but never will?

Plus, I think God works on me all year long, not just in January.

But enough about resolutions.

Ethan's still gagging on his tea, and I've about heard enough. "Look, at least put some honey or something in it so you can get it down," I tell him. I grab for one of the mini honey bears under the counter that we have for customers who like their tea sweet. Although, I did have one girl ask for honey for her coffee.

That one was weird.

Ethan holds out his mug, and I squirt a healthy dose of honey in there and tell him to stir it in.

He takes another sip, half wincing. Then he makes a surprised face. "Wow! That does make a difference."

"I told you." Not that I know anything about tea, but Jen swears that honey is the ruiner of all things tea, so I figured for those of us who don't like tea to begin with, honey has to be the answer.

Ethan finishes the rest of his tea without sounding like he's working his esophagus loose.

"Healthy Choice, huh?" he says with a grin while I sit down with my freshly microwaved meal.

I nod. "They're pretty good." I point to the freezer. "I brought you one to replace the one I ate," I tell him.

"You didn't need to do that."

"Well, I did." I dig in to today's choice, some kind of chicken quesadilla thing. I take a bite and chew. It's not too bad. It's obviously low fat, but it's not too bad.

Ethan's on his second cup of tea. I'm wondering how long

this phase is going to last. One day? One week?

"So," Ethan says, loitering by the doorway. I guess we don't have customers needing his attention right now.

"So."

"What, uh, what time is your meeting tonight?" He stumbles over the words.

I have to focus on the fact that I have a half-chewed piece of quesadilla in my mouth as I stare at Ethan in shock. "You mean Bible study? You might come?"

"Um. Yeah." He looks uncomfortable and awkward, and I don't want to make a huge deal about it, but . . . this is a huge deal!

I swallow my bite and try to take a deep breath. *Lord, help me not to scare him away!* "Wow, that's great," I say, nice and calmly. "It starts at eight."

He nods. "Okay. Good to know." Then he disappears back out to the front.

I stare at the empty doorframe, eyes wide.

Sometimes, God just totally surprises me.

And I love it.

At seven fifteen, I'm grabbing dinner, changing clothes, and feeding Calvin all at the same time. I'd gotten distracted after looking at a new bridal magazine Jen had left on my doorstep.

There was a sticky note on the front of it: *Look at page 57!!!*

Page 57 had a centerpiece display that was just gorgeous. Hydrangeas were piled into a clear glass vase and set on a light blue lacy doily on a white tablecloth. Little tea-light candles were scattered over the rest of the table.

It looked beautiful. And simple.

So, I immediately started looking up hydrangea prices on the Internet. It looks like they're a lot cheaper than roses.

Good by me!

I rub Calvin on the ears really quickly and grab my Bible. Dinner is a corn dog that I'm going to eat in the car on the way back to Cool Beans. A shower took the place of nutrition tonight.

I think that Jack and whoever else is sitting next to me will appreciate that I don't smell like work. Even though we'll be at Cool Beans, there's a big difference between what you smell sitting out in the store and how you smell working behind the counter. I always come home smelling like a mix of stale coffee, burnt milk, and sweat.

It's gross.

I'm meeting Jack at Cool Beans since he got off late tonight. I pull into the parking lot, and I'm actually a few minutes early, which is great because I wanted to be here when Ethan arrived.

But Ethan is already inside. He's leaning against the counter, chatting with Lisa. Andrew's muscling the tables out of the way so he can set up a bunch of chairs.

He sees me come in and starts humming "Here Comes the Bride."

"Hi, Andrew." I grin.

He shoves a chair over and smiles at me. "Wedding planning?"

"Ugh."

"Work?"

"Good."

"Jack?"

"Great." I grin again.

Andrew nods. "Good to hear."

"Your turn. Work?"

"Great."

"Church?"

"Good."

"Liz?"

He sighs.

I grin and pat his arm. "It's okay, Andrew. She'll come around."

He changes the subject. "Hey, isn't that the guy you work with during the day?" he asks, voice lowered, nodding toward Ethan.

I nod. I glance over at him, and Ethan is still talking with Lisa.

And smiling.

I share a look with Andrew and then look back over at Ethan. Now Ethan is laughing, and his cheeks are getting a little pink. Lisa goes to make a drink, and Ethan just watches her.

"Looks like Ethan's got his eye on someone," Andrew says, again under his breath.

I just stare. Ethan and Lisa?

Andrew makes a *hmm* sound and leaves to get another chair, muttering, "Whatever gets them here," as he goes.

I'm still staring at Ethan. So was it Lisa who told him to drink the tea?

I watch her smile at him, and I grin.

Yep. I think we've found the tea encourager.

"You know, some people find it a little weird when a person is standing there by herself grinning," Jack says, walking up to me. He's got on his nice jeans and a brown polo shirt, and he's carrying his Bible. He leans over and kisses me. "What's so funny?"

"Ethan's got a crush on Lisa," I whisper.

Jack looks over at the counter, notices the flirtation going on, and shrugs. "Huh. Cool. Hey, where do you want to sit?"

I sigh. Boys are so unromantic.

A crowd has steadily gathered, and Andrew finally claps his hands. "All right, everyone, grab your coffee and a seat!" he yells.

Jack points to an empty row in the back, and I wave at Ethan, pointing at the chairs. He nods, says something to Lisa, and walks over.

"Hi, Ethan," I say, grinning at him.

"That's not ever a good look on you," he says, squinting at me.

"Hey, Ethan," Jack says, reaching his hand over for the customary guy handshake. Again, something I don't understand. It's not like they are just now meeting.

Of course, this only scratches the surface of things I don't understand about boys. I don't understand why they feel the need to hit each other when they've made some accomplishment. Or that scene in *Remember the Titans* where they decide they all need to jump around howling like monkeys. Or why they can have multiple holes in the bottom of a sock and not only not throw it out but keep wearing it.

Zach was the worst at that one. It completely grossed me out the entire time we were growing up. Mom finally had to sneak into his bedroom while he was on a date and steal all of his socks and replace them with new ones.

He swore that our high school football team, the Wallabees, would never win another game.

Considering it had been at least six years since the Wallabees had won a game, and considering the name of our team was the Wallabees, I don't think Zach's holey socks really made a difference.

But I digress.

Ethan sits in the chair next to me, and I'm stuck between the guys. I hand Ethan my Bible, since I can share with Jack.

"Oh," Ethan says, holding it like it's the Holy Grail. "Thanks."

"It's a Bible, Ethan, not a newborn. You can use it."

"Oh," he says again. "Okay."

Andrew is standing in front of everyone while Lisa and Peter frantically finish making all the drinks, and about five minutes later, everyone is sitting down. I look around. There are probably twenty-five to thirty people here.

Anytime you combine a coffee shop with a Bible study, you get a good turnout.

"Okay," Andrew says loudly, and everyone stops talking. "Open your Bibles. We're doing a short study on different character qualities every Christian should have."

Lisa drops into the empty chair beside Ethan. "Is anyone sitting here?" she whispers.

"You are." Ethan smiles. Then he blushes, clears his throat, and looks at Andrew, trying to be all cool.

Awww. I try my very best to hide a grin as I open Jack's Bible.

I called Kate this morning before work since I knew she'd be up. Kate is one of those people who wakes up at six whether it's a weekday, weekend, or holiday. And without an alarm. She said they were able to dial Ben's oxygen back yet again, and it doesn't look like he'll need any kind of surgery at this point. Then she had to go because she was getting ready to go see him.

I told her that Ben needed a mom who was all better, and she just said, "Mm-hmm, thanks for calling, Maya!"

I don't think she heard me.

Andrew clears his throat, and I shake my head slightly, trying to pay attention. "In the last three weeks," he starts, "we have covered faith, love, and peace. Tonight, we're going to cover justice."

I'm mentally reciting the fruit of the Spirit, and I don't remember justice being on that list.

"I hope you guys are catching on that this list, like most things related to God's Word, is a direct reflection of God's attributes. As Christians, we are to reflect the One who made us. Which is why qualities we need to possess are simply characteristics of God."

I guess I'd never thought about it like that before.

"Flip to James 2, if you have a Bible," Andrew says.

I take my Bible back, turn to James 2, and then give it back to Ethan, who looks relieved.

"Thanks," he whispers.

"No problem."

"We'll start in verse 1," Andrew says. "'My brethren, do not hold your faith in our glorious Lord Jesus Christ with an attitude of personal favoritism.'" He stops there. "In the church at this point, there were distinct classes of people. You had the very poor, and you had the very rich. And what the church was doing was putting the rich people, the ones who came in wearing gold rings and nice clothes, in the good seats and the people who were obviously poor in the bad seats."

He points back to the Bible. "Let's pick it back up in verses 9 and 10. 'But if you show partiality, you are committing sin and are convicted by the law as transgressors. For whoever keeps the whole law and yet stumbles in one point, he has become guilty of all.'" Andrew looks up at everyone. "What do you think that means?"

One of the guys sitting toward the front answers. "We need to be fair with people."

"Sort of like not judging a book by its cover?" another girl says.

Andrew squinches up his forehead. "Well. Kind of. But this goes beyond just looking at the 'inner person' or whatever nonsense Disney movies are spouting these days."

I grin. I love all things Disney, but Andrew definitely sees the other side of it. I've sat through a thirty-minute monologue from him about what was theologically wrong with *Beauty and the Beast.*

When he finally took a breath, I said, "Yeah, but it's fiction and a love story, and I think it's adorable."

He just growled a sigh. Sort of like the Beast, actually.

He didn't like when I pointed that out, though.

Andrew closes his Bible, leaving his thumb in James. "Think of it like this, guys," he says. "Actually, one second. Lisa?"

Lisa looks up. "Yes?"

"Do you have any paper clips here?"

Lisa frowns and looks at me. "I'm not sure . . ."

I nod. "I'll get them." There's a pile of them in the very back of the cash register drawer. I'm not sure why they are there or how they got there, but I found them when I put the one check I've ever processed in the five years I've been working here in the drawer a few months ago.

I grab the paper clips, hand them to Andrew, and go sit back down.

Andrew quickly hooks all of them together to make a big chain. "Okay. I'm a visual person," he says, holding the chain from one end. "Let's say this is the Ten Commandments."

I grin.

Andrew sees my expression and narrows his eyes at me. "And no laughing. Just go with me for a minute. This is the Ten Commandments."

The chain is swaying in front of Andrew.

"Now, let's say that this"—he points to the coffee pickup counter—"is heaven." Then he points to the floor. "And that is hell." He bends the first paper clip so it's precariously clinging to the edge of the counter. "And you, my friend, are holding on to the bottom of this chain." He looks around and grabs a red coffee stirrer and weaves it through the paper clip on the end.

Now it looks very precarious. The whole chain is shaking, and the top paper clip keeps moving around.

"The Bible says that the only people who are worthy of getting into heaven are those who have kept the whole law." Andrew points to the chain. "So, you're going along. And let's say that a friend of yours has a really hot girlfriend. You wish she was your girlfriend."

He reaches over and unhooks one of the middle clips. The stirrer and six paper clips fall to the floor. "Bad move." He rehooks the clips back together. "Or, let's say that your mom comes to you wearing an awful puke-colored dress and asks for your opinion of it. You say, 'Yeah, it looks great!'" He unhooks another clip, and again everything falls to the floor. "You can see how it doesn't matter if you've kept nine out of ten command-ments. You still haven't kept the whole law, so you've broken the law. You are not good enough to get into heaven."

He walks back over to the middle of the room. "Which is where we bring in the quality of justice. God is just. He doesn't make excuses for people. He doesn't say, 'Well, but he tried really hard! Okay, let him in.'" Andrew starts shaking his head. "You broke the law. God is just; He can't allow you into heaven."

He picks up his Bible again. "Turn to Romans." There's the gentle hum of people flipping Bible pages, and again I reach over and find Romans for Ethan, who glances at me gratefully.

"Romans is all about the law and why the law exists. Since God is just and He can't let those who have broken the law into heaven, then, friend, you and I are screwed, to put it bluntly. We have no chance at anything other than eternal suffering in the pit of fire. But, there's a reason that God established the law. The law shows us our need for Christ."

Andrew looks down at his Bible. "Romans 5, verses 20 and 21. 'The Law came in so that the transgression would increase; but where sin increased, grace abounded all the more, so that, as sin reigned in death, even so grace would reign through righteousness to eternal life through Jesus Christ our Lord.'"

Andrew finishes up a few minutes later. "God is just. We need to practice justice, not favoritism. I don't care if you think he's the last person on the planet to come to Christ; you preach the gospel to him. Let's pray."

As soon as Andrew says "amen," the low hum of people stretching and talking begins. I look over at Ethan and Lisa, who are both just sitting there, staring at where Andrew was standing.

"Good lesson tonight," I say, trying to get the conversation started.

"Yeah," Ethan says slowly. His expression is unreadable — I can't tell if he's provoked to thought or if he's trying to ignore the message.

Time will tell, I guess.

Lisa blinks and immediately shoots up to go back to work. A few people save their coffee buying for afterward so they can have a warm drink on the drive home. And there's the cleanup.

When I worked Wednesday nights, I hated cleanup. So I always try to help out as much as I can now—at least out on this side of the counter so Lisa and Peter only have to take care of the back.

Peter always disappears to the back to do homework while Andrew's teaching. Someday I hope he'll come listen.

Jack wraps his arm around the back of my chair. "So, good news," he starts.

I look over at him. "What?"

"We're pregnant."

Ethan's head whips around so fast that I swear I hear his neck pop. I'm frowning at Jack.

"Well. Unless God's planning another miraculous conception—"

Jack's giving me a weird look now. "Not *us*, Nutkin."

I'm frowning harder now. "You and your other wife that I'm just finding out about?"

"No. Not me and anyone."

"So the *we* you used right then was not referring to you?"

"Well, not personally."

I cover my face with my hands. I'm so confused. And Ethan is now poking me in the arm.

"I thought you guys were waiting," he hisses at me.

"We *are*," I say firmly to Ethan. "What are you talking about?" I ask Jack.

Jack obviously is not seeing the problem here. "*We* are pregnant," he says. "We, the Hudson Zoo, are pregnant."

I close my eyes.

Aside from the whole causing Ethan to stumble issue, since when did Jack start referring to himself as part of the zoo?

And since when was I supposed to know this?

"You, the Hudson Zoo, are pregnant," I say slowly.

"Well, not me personally," he says again. "But Marco, the hippopotamus, is pregnant. It's her first." Jack says this like a proud dad.

I glance at Ethan, who just raises his eyebrows.

"Seriously," Jack says, "this is a huge deal! Marco is only five years old. And since this is her first baby, we'll have to watch her closely for the next eight months. Did you know that baby hippos weigh between 60 and 110 pounds when they are born?"

I'm hurting for Marco.

"Ouch," Ethan says.

Jack nods. "So, like I said, it's pretty impressive."

Ethan is now agreeing with him, I guess. I'm feeling stuck between them.

"Who's the father?" Ethan asks.

"Randolph," Jack says. "He's not new to this. But the fathers actually have very little to do with the raising of the babies."

So Marco has to carry a hundred-pound baby and gets to be a single mother?

I'm seeing less and less happiness here for Marco. I'm also very thankful that I'm human and that I was only five pounds, seven ounces when I was born.

That is manageable.

"Wow," Ethan says. "How does she give birth? By herself?"

Jack starts talking about the gory details, including that the entire birth is under water, and I'm definitely feeling trapped now. I make some comment about needing to talk to Andrew, and I stand up.

The guys are still talking. I'm pretty sure they don't even notice I'm gone.

I watch Lisa racing around making a few more lattes. Andrew is talking to Liz, so I don't want to interrupt them.

Jen comes over, finishing off her English Breakfast tea in her favorite pink mug. "What's with the pained expression?" she asks.

"Long story and large babies. I'll tell you later."

She makes a funny face but doesn't push it. "Okay," she says slowly.

"Where's your husband?" I ask.

"He's talking to Gavin over there." Jen nods toward Travis and a guy who I guess is Gavin. I have never seen him before.

"Who's Gavin?"

She shrugs. "Some guy who just started coming two weeks ago."

"Oh. Cool."

"Yeah. Ever noticed how awkward it is as a woman to welcome new guys to Bible study?" she says. "I feel like they think I'm coming on to them. So it seems either flirtatious or rude."

"There is no good answer." I nod.

"Well, I opted for rude. Travis can welcome the guys now. I'm just going to be the girl welcomer." She smiles at me. "Welcome."

"Thanks."

"Get anything else done on the wedding?"

I guess Jen has decided she is my Jiminy Cricket for this wedding. If she's not trying to talk me into something for it, she's bugging me about how much more I have to do.

"We set a time," I say.

"Good."

"And we have food picked out."

Jen gets a wary look on her face. "What did you decide on?"

"You don't trust my food-picking ability?"

She picks up on my shocked tone and starts the smoothing over. "Maya, it's not that. It's just that anytime you have to decide something about food, it usually ends up being fortified with saturated fats and has an Italian name," she says soothingly.

"Relax, Jen. I'm not going to serve Bertolli at my wedding," I say.

"Good. Though it would be fitting, I guess." She smiles at me.

"We could have a buffet of every flavor that I like." Now I'm starting to like the genius of this idea.

Jens enthusiasm fades. "Yeah," she says slowly. She's biting her bottom lip now.

"Jen?"

"Yes?"

"I'm kidding."

She lets out her breath. "Good."

"Jack made a special request for mini hot dogs."

I think she's going to cry. Either that, or quit the job of being my matron of honor.

CHAPTER THIRTEEN

It's nine o'clock on Saturday morning. And while I'm usually still snoozing away in my nice warm bed, I am up, dressed, showered, and have my makeup on.

Not necessarily in that order.

Calvin just sits there looking at me as I eat a bowl of Frosted Mini-Wheats. "What?" I say between crunches. "I'm going shopping today."

I even fixed my hair. And contrary to what I read in one issue of *Sophisticated,* wearing my naturally curly hair long does not pull out the curls into beautiful, rich waves.

I poke my hand into my hair and sigh. If anything, it just makes it more frizzy, more out of control, and more annoying.

As soon as this wedding is over, I am chopping it all off again. I'd do it before, but there's just something romantic about having long hair at your wedding.

And mine has almost grown back to right above my bra strap after I cut it short a year ago.

I get a text as I'm putting my bowl in the dishwasher.

Hv U lft yt?

My mother. Her texting abilities never cease to amaze me.

Just about to leave, I text her back. And, yes, I use the complete words. I stick my spoon in the dishwasher, dry off my hands, and find a jacket. It's early September in Southern California, so there's no need for the jacket, really. But it makes me feel more like fall is coming.

I let Calvin out to do his business real quick, and then I find my purse. "Bye, pup," I say, rubbing his silky ears. "Be good."

I give him one of those huge meat-filled bones, and he does a happy-doggy dance. I smile. He won't miss me at all. I run by Jen's apartment to pick her up, and I barely pull into the parking lot before she's tapping on the passenger window.

"Are you excited?!" she squeals, jumping into the car.

You'd think this was her wedding.

"Sure," I say.

"Sure?! Maya, this is the day we find your wedding dress." She says it slowly and mystical like it's Aladdin's lamp. "You should be through the roof!"

I roll back the sunroof and wave a hand out it. "Yay!"

She rolls her eyes. "Sheesh."

I am very excited, but I'm also very nervous. What can I say? This wedding will be the biggest life decision I've ever made next to accepting Christ.

If that doesn't make your stomach twist just a bit, something is very wrong with you.

The drive to San Diego is long most days, and today is no exception, even though traffic isn't too bad. Saturdays can get busy because of all the touristy things to do there.

We get to Mom's house about ten fifteen, and to my shock, Kate's car is in the driveway.

I run up the steps, and Jen starts laughing. "See? That's how you're supposed to be acting!"

I burst through the door. "Mom? Kate?"

They are sitting in the living room, sipping cups of coffee. Kate looks like she's trying to cover up how tired she is. She has more makeup caked under her eyes than I wear in a month. Her smile is exhausted.

But she's here.

"Hey, Maya," she says.

"Hi, honey." Mom is grinning. "Did you forget Jen?"

Jen comes in then. "No, she just ran from me. Hi, Kate, it's so good to see you out and about!" She gives my mom a hug. "Hi, Mary."

"Hi, sweetie. Okay, girls, let me grab my purse, and we can go. Our appointment is at ten thirty."

"Dress shop first?" Kate asks, standing and setting her coffee mug in the kitchen sink.

Mom nods. "Dress shop first, flowers next. And if we haven't run out of steam by that point, we can go by a catering shop I found the other day while I was out grocery shopping."

I squint at her. "You just happened to find it?" I question.

Mom ignores me, which means that she has been out looking for caterers. She picks up her knock-off Coach purse and smiles brightly at me. "Ready, bride-to-be?" Then she starts to tear up. "Oh dear. I promised I wouldn't do this today." She digs in her purse and comes out with a wad of Kleenex that's almost as big as her purse.

I start to get teary myself, but I hold it in. This is a happy day. I'm about to marry the guy who has been my best friend for years.

I give my mom a hug, and we all go into the garage and pile into her Tahoe.

The bridal store is called Jared's, and it's part of an upscale outdoor mall area about ten minutes away from Mom's house.

The architecture of the buildings is beautiful. Lots of stonework and white accents. It looks classy.

We walk in the door, and a lady sitting at a desk in the front looks up at us. "Welcome to Jared's. Did you have an appointment?"

Mom takes charge. "This is Maya Davis. I believe we have an appointment with Samantha?"

The lady looks at the book and nods. "Please come this way," she says, apparently aiming for that low, sexy voice. She leads us past a huge display room full of gowns to a little room in the back. Two couches and a recliner are gathered around a three-way mirror. A tiny changing room is off to the right.

"Samantha will be right with you," the lady says. "And, Maya, please fill out this little card for me real quick. Can I get you ladies anything to drink?"

"Water," everyone says together.

I take the pen and card from her. It's questions about my height and what size bra I wear. I scribble in the numbers.

The lady nods and returns half a second later with four bottles of water. "Take a seat, and please look through our catalog for ideas," she says, exchanging the catalog for the card.

It's heavy. I sit down on the couch, and Mom and Jen take the spots next to me. Kate sits next to Jen.

"Oh, wow," Mom says, breathlessly. "Look at that one!"

She points to one on the first page that, truth be told, I think is overdone to the point of being cheesy. The lace is overwhelming, and there's a huge shoulder bow on the right side.

I'm fairly certain that I am not a bow person.

"Mmm," I say and turn the page.

I get through about ten pages of seeing nothing that looks like me when Samantha comes in. She's a tall, slender, gorgeous black woman, and she's wearing a skirt suit that definitely high-lights her perfect frame.

I'm supposed to try on dresses next to this lady?

I'm almost laughing, but I manage to hold it in. Not only is she everything I'm not—tall, thin, and permanently tanned—but she opens her mouth and has the sweetest southern accent I've ever heard.

"Hi, y'all, I'm Samantha," she drawls.

Well, it's settled. I have officially broken the tenth com-mandment: I am coveting this lady's entire being. The visual of the little red coffee stirrer crashing to the ground with the paper clips is in my head.

Jen pokes me and I jump. "I'm sorry, what?" I ask, realizing that the beautiful Samantha asked me a question.

"Were there any dresses that grabbed your attention?" she says.

I look blankly at her.

She elaborates. "In the catalog?"

"Oh!" I say. "Well, I didn't get too far."

"That's fine. No worries, darlin'. What are some of the styles you think you might like?"

"She liked a lace dress we saw in a bridal magazine," Jen says to Samantha, since I'm having trouble coming up with polite adjectives for "not too big" and "not too ugly."

"Lace? Okay, we have lots of lace."

"It was form fitting and had a fairly short train, and it was strapless," Jen finishes.

"And it wasn't a true white," I add. "It was kind of a pinkish white."

"So like a blush tone? Okay. Well, let me see what I can get for you." She disappears.

Jen settles into the couch and pulls the catalog over to her lap. "I will never, ever get tired of weddings," she sighs.

Mom smiles at her and then pats my leg. "Just remember that your dad has his heart set on dancing the father/daughter dance to 'Come Fly with Me,'" she says. "So you need to be able to move."

I grin. When I was a baby, Dad would put on Frank Sinatra and dance around the living room with me, and he's done that ever since. I danced to that song with Dad when I was six and thought I was Cinderella; we practiced to that song before my first dance in junior high and again before my senior prom.

It's kind of our song.

I nod. "I wouldn't pick anything but that," I say. Now I'm wondering if a strapless dress is a good idea considering the swing-dancing moves Dad and I do.

Samantha returns pushing a tall cart with about seven dresses zipped in plastic bags on it. "Okay, Maya, I have a few for you to choose from," she says. We all stand up and crowd around while she points out the different dresses. "I have a few that are strapless and lace. This one is a halter style just to see if you like that better, same with the one with the straps, and then we have my personal favorite for you." The dress has the slightest pink touch like I liked. "This one is strapless. And you can see the lace." She points to it. The lace covers the dress, but it's not a "big statement" lace.

It's like meek lace.

"It has a little tie around the waist, and there's the faintest hint of sparkle on the bodice," Samantha finishes.

Everyone is *ooing* over the dress. "Let's try on that one first," I say.

"Sounds good." She pulls the dress off the cart and points

to the tiny changing room. "Here are a bra and a slip," she says, giving me what looks more like a corset. "Put those on, and when you're ready, I'll come help you put on the dress."

I nod and go into the changing room. There isn't a mirror in here. I put the slip on no problem, but I'm having trouble with the corset. There are at least fifteen different hooks going down my back. I get the last two near the small of my back and the first two, but I can't reach the other ones.

"How's it goin' in there?" Samantha taps on the door.

"Um. Come in," I say, throwing modesty to the wind.

Samantha nods when I show her the back of the corset. "Don't worry, no one can put these things on alone," she says. She hooks the rest of it for me and then helps me into the dress. There are tiny buttons running all the way up the back of the dress, and she has to button every single one of them.

"Okay, this is a tiny bit big; we would order this dress for you in your size if you decided to get it," she says.

"Could you make it shorter?"

She smiles. "Of course."

I open the door, and my mom bursts into tears.

"It's that bad?" I ask. I walk over to the mirror, and my breath catches.

Wow!

Not only is it a beautiful, beautiful dress, but the pink tone makes my pale "she must have cholera" skin look creamy, like an old Hollywood actress. A thin ribbon goes around my waist, and Samantha tied it so the ribbon falls down the left side of the dress.

The train is fairly short, which is perfect because I'm short and I think a train longer than you are is just not appropriate.

Mom is brushing away tears. "That's the one," she says.

"I've only tried on one," I say.

"I know. But it's just so lovely. And it makes you look beautiful."

I look at Jen and Kate, who are both nodding. "I love it," Jen declares.

"It's very pretty, Maya," Kate says.

I decide that I need to try on at least a few more dresses, but this one is definitely gorgeous. I can't find anything wrong with it.

A few dresses later, I'm sold on the first one.

"Good choice." Samantha grins as I try it on for the second time. "And even better, we're having a sale this week on all of this designer's dresses. I think it's 30 percent off."

"Great!" I say.

Mom nods. "And I have this covered, Maya," she says.

I'm looking in the mirror and smoothing out the dress. Samantha pulls out a veil and combs the holder into my hair. It's a rose-toned veil that matches the dress perfectly.

A few minutes later, I'm dressed in my jeans again. It's amazing how I just don't feel as good as I did in my wedding dress.

We go back out to the front, and Samantha hands the lady we first saw a piece of paper. "So nice to meet y'all," she says sweetly.

"Thanks, Samantha," Mom says.

The lady, who is wearing a name tag that says Julia, looks at the paper Samantha gave her. "Oh, that dress is gorgeous," she says. "And we need to order your size," she says, more to herself. She walks over to a computer and starts clicking around. "Okay, we can have the dress here for pickup in about four weeks. Will that work?"

Mom nods. "That should be fine."

"And you wanted the veil?"

I nod this time. "Yes, please."

She tells Mom the total, and I'm having trouble swallowing. All that for a dress I'll wear for four hours?

"Mom . . ." I start, and Mom waves her hand at me, pulling her credit card out of her purse.

"Hush, Maya. It's your wedding day."

Yeah, but still! The miser in me is screaming for attention, and I try to soothe her. Maybe I'll just wear it around the house afterward. I could do my dishes in it like Monica did on *Friends*.

Then I remember the delicate lace. Maybe doing dishes in that dress is a bad idea.

"All right," Mom says as we all pile back into the car. Kate sits in the passenger seat, and Jen and I are in the back. "How is everyone doing?"

I think she's mostly talking to Kate. Kate nods. "I'm doing good," she says, but she's tired. I can tell.

Having an emergency C-section and a preemie baby takes a lot out of you, I think. I speak up. "Why don't we have an early lunch?" It's not really early, because it's already almost noon, but this way Kate doesn't have to feel bad for needing a break and a pick-me-up.

Jen catches on to my plan. "I think lunch is a good idea," she says.

Mom nods. "Good thought. Well, how about this? The caterer I found has a little café that we can eat at. That way, if the food is disgusting, we don't order anything for the wedding from them."

I grin. "Sounds like a plan!"

Mom drives to a little cabiny type of place with a hand-carved sign out front that says Bread Heaven.

I'm all for eating at a place called Bread Heaven. We walk in, and the smell just about kills me. It's sweet and doughy and savory and yeasty all at the same time, and I stop dead in my tracks.

Jen runs right into the back of me. "Ouch!" she grumbles. "Sheesh, Maya!"

"The smell . . ." I'm whimpering.

There are a couple dozen wooden tables and chairs scattered around a cute shop and a long counter in the back. About twelve or fifteen people are eating soup and sandwiches. A huge plank of wood hangs from the ceiling, and someone has burned the menu onto it.

I think it's unique.

A little corner on the menu promotes their catering services: Bread Heaven at your parties? What a loave-ly idea!

Okay, that's a little corny, I'll admit. But I can take any awful sense of humor if it smells like this place.

There's a hefty man behind the counter wearing a white apron over a hunter green shirt. "Welcome to Bread Heaven, ladies!" His voice booms over the buzz of the café.

"Thanks," Mom says, approaching the counter.

"What can I get for you today?"

I'm staring at the menu: sandwiches and soups, pancakes and waffles, wood-fired pizzas and a few salads.

I inhale again. I can't endure that smell without getting a sandwich. "I want the turkey and cranberry sandwich," I tell the man.

"Sure thing! On what bread?"

There's a whole list of breads on the menu, and I study each one, finally deciding on the honey whole wheat. I pay him for mine, despite my mother's complaining, and get a little red plastic circle that says RYE on it.

"Just have a seat, miss, and we'll get that right out to you." He grins at me and looks expectantly at Kate, who is standing next to me.

"Oh!" she says, scooting over. "I want a bowl of soup, please."

"Okay. What bread with that?"

I find a table for four and stick my little red circle in a holder that's on the table. Kate comes over a minute later holding a blue circle that says WHEAT.

"Interesting way of differentiating customers," she says, taking a seat. Mom gets a green circle that says PUMPER-NICKEL and Jen's is yellow and says SOURDOUGH.

"This place is really cute," Jen whispers as she sits down. "I love the cabin feeling!"

"Let's see how the food tastes," Mom says, all spy-like. She's already examining the silverware bundles for any signs of crusted-on food or water spots.

My mother is a pro at finding water spots on forks. One time, she even went into the back of a restaurant to show them exactly how to wash and dry the silverware so it didn't get spotted.

Dad about had a fit when she did that.

Our soup and sandwiches are brought out a few minutes later, and Mom asks the man for a catering menu.

"Certainly!" he says and comes back with three or four sheets stapled together. "Just let me know if you have any questions."

I fold my hands together. "Let me say a quick blessing," I say. "Lord, thank You for this day, and thank You for these amazing women, and please bless this food. Amen." The smell of the bread was teasing my nose through the whole prayer.

I am going to start praying before we get the food from now on.

The sandwich is amazing. I'm halfway through it before I can even stop to take a breath. Everyone else is chowing down the same way.

Mom's bifocals are perched on her nose as she looks over the catering menu. "Their prices aren't too bad, Maya," she says.

I'm thinking about our plan of having those little smokies and a chocolate fountain. Anything is going to be more expensive than that.

She hands me the menu, and I look at it.

They do a lot more than just soup and sandwiches when they cater. They have all sorts of upscale things on there: bruschetta, caviar, baked Brie.

I flip through the pages. No chocolate fountain though. I sigh.

"What?" Jen says, mouth full.

"There's no chocolate fountain," I say sadly.

Mom rolls her eyes. "So we'll get one and operate it ourselves. This bread is amazing, Maya."

I tuck the menu in my purse. "I'll think about it." It is the best café food I've had in a long, long time.

I get home that night about nine, after dropping Jen off at her apartment. "Thanks for coming with us today," I told her.

She grinned at me. "I wouldn't have missed it. Go home and rest."

I tiredly climb the stairs to my apartment. Poor Calvin has been stuck in the apartment all day; his little bladder is probably ready to pop.

I open the door, and there's no Calvin to greet me. Frowning, I look in the bedroom, because I have a sneaking suspicion that he sleeps on my bed the whole time I'm gone.

He's not there either.

He's not in the kitchen, he's not in the living room, and he's not in the laundry closet. Now, I'm panicking because obviously someone came in here and stole my little beagle.

I grab my phone from my purse.

"Hello?"

"Jack, someone stole Calvin!" I'm almost in hysterics, and I can feel the start of tears in the corners of my eyes. He's only a beagle, but he's my dog—and he's been my baby for almost five years now.

"You didn't get my text, did you?" Jack says calmly.

I rip the phone away from my ear, and, yes, there is the little unopened letter symbol on my phone, which means I have an unread text message.

I push the button and open it. *Love—I brought Cal over here so he could play with Canis and not get lonely or make a mess. Call me when you get back, and I'll bring him over.*

I let out my breath and sit on the couch. "You have him?" I say weakly.

"I've got him. And he's happily attacking one of Canis's bones right now."

I wince. "That sounds painful."

"One of his rawhide bones, Nutkin."

"Not quite as painful then." I rest my head on the back of the couch and rub my forehead. It has been a long, long day. After eating more than my fill at Bread Heaven, we went to three different florists and finally picked a hydrangea and white lily combination for the flowers.

It sounds pretty, but we'll have to see what it looks like in real life.

Then we went to try to find bridesmaid dresses, tuxes, and a photographer.

I was less than impressed with most of the photographers. And I'm still thinking on the bridesmaid dresses. Kate and Jen modeled several for me, but I just didn't see any that made them both look beautiful.

Jack's talking. "I'll go ahead and bring Cal back over. Though I think he'll be sad to leave this bone. It's seriously twice as long as he is."

I smile at that mental picture. "You don't need to bring him back," I say. "I can come get him."

"Well, that's silly. You're already home."

"So are you."

"Yes, but I wasn't gone all day trying on itchy dresses. Speaking of which, did you find one?"

"An itchy dress?"

"A wedding dress."

I grin. "Yes."

Suddenly everything seems more, I don't know, *real.* I've ordered a dress, we're talking about caterers, and there's a church waiting for us.

I'm getting married.

And I just can't help but smile.

CHAPTER FOURTEEN

Sunday morning. Ten o'clock. I'm sitting in one of the chairs in our Sunday school classroom. Jack on one side, Ethan on the other, Lisa beside him.

Something is very déjà vu about this.

When Ethan and Lisa walked through the door—together, nonetheless—I about choked on the delicious cranberry-orange muffin Liz made from scratch.

Now, they are sitting next to me. Lisa is nibbling away at a muffin while Ethan was man enough to chow it down in three bites.

I have issues with men who eat muffins like women. It's a weird issue to have, I know, but it's there.

Liz comes swaying over. "Hi!" she says all bright and friendly like a redheaded angel of welcome. "You guys work at Cool Beans, right?" she says, grinning at Ethan and Lisa.

Lisa, mouth full of muffin, nods. Ethan speaks up, "Yeah, we do."

"It's very good to have you here! Is this your first Sunday visiting?"

Again, Ethan answers, "Yeah, it is."

"Great!" Liz says. "Just let me know if I can get you anything or help you find anything!"

Liz is so cut out to be a pastor's wife.

And what do you know? I just happen to know a pastor who is in love with her.

I look over at Andrew, and he's doing a crappy job of ignoring Liz. He's talking to a bunch of guys, but one eye is always coming back over here.

"Hey, Maya," Liz says, bending over for one of those weird one-person-is-seated hugs. "How are you today?"

I nod. "I'm good. You?"

"Oh, I'm great. How are the wedding plans coming?"

Ah, the ever-present question. "They are coming," I say, holding in the sigh. "Slowly, but coming."

She nods. "Just give me a call if you need me to do anything, okay?"

I smile at her. "You're sweet."

"I mean it. Don't hesitate."

"Okay, peoples, sit your butts in a chair!" Andrew yells. Liz winks at me and takes the seat next to Jack.

Andrew climbs on his squeaky, rickety stool, and I watch him wobble around, trying to even out his weight. Andrew is not a small man. Actually, I imagine that small is a word that has never, ever been used to describe our Viking of a pastor. He's a monster. And he's an ex-hockey star. He does have all of his teeth, though. I think this is a bonus.

Especially for Liz, should anything ever come of their endless flirtation.

Andrew is pushing thirty. You'd think he'd be at the point where flirtation would actually lead somewhere.

He teaches for about forty-five minutes on a passage in James, and then we dismiss. "Bible study Wednesday," he says loudly as everyone is closing their Bibles and the side conversations begin. "And start thinking about fall activities!"

I'm pretty sure no one heard him as everyone is bulldozing for another muffin. Even Ethan and Lisa joined in the mob. I grin broadly at Andrew, and he sighs at me.

"No one listens," he complains, coming over.

"I listened," I say.

"Oh yeah? What did I just say?"

"You said we need to think of falling activities. Though, speaking not as someone from any law type of background, I think it would be kind of a legal liability to take a bunch of singles skydiving or bungee jumping."

Jen is standing behind me, licking muffin remains off her fingers. "And speaking as one who is in the legal field, I would say that's a definite liability. You'll need everyone to sign a waiver stating that you and this church aren't responsible for any accidents."

Andrew is just staring at us. "What?" he asks finally. "I said think of fall activities. As in the season," he says slowly. "Like going to a pumpkin farm or doing a campfire with s'mores or drinking apple cider."

"Oh," I say. "Well, I don't think you'll need a waiver for those."

"Except for maybe the campfire," Jen says thoughtfully. "You never know what a bunch of twentysomething guys will do around a fire."

Jack is laughing.

Andrew just sighs. "Anyway," he says, changing the subject, "Liz, those muffins are the best ones I've ever had."

Liz dimples. "Thanks, Andrew! Fresh oranges. That's the secret."

Then Andrew stands there all awkwardly, picking at his fingers.

This is getting ridiculous. Jack and I are going to have three kids by the time Andrew ever gets around to asking her on a date.

"What are you all doing for lunch today?" Andrew asks, looking at me and Jack hopefully.

I just look at him. I'm not giving him the easy way out again. If he wants to go get lunch with Liz, he's going to have to ask her himself.

"We have lots of stuff to do," I tell Andrew. "Sorry."

Jen is still standing behind me, and I guess she catches what I'm doing. "Yeah, sorry, Andrew. I was gone all day yesterday, and Travis and I need some alone time."

Too many details coming from the newly married, but a good excuse nonetheless.

Now Andrew is even more awkward as he peeks at Liz from behind the finger he's picking on.

Liz is too nice for him. "Well, it looks like we're the only ones who are free for lunch," she says brightly. "Where would you like to go?"

I try really hard not to shake my head. I mean, seriously, Andrew. Man up.

Flustered, he waves a hand around. "Oh, uh, I'm, um, I don't know," he stutters. "Is there somewhere you were wanting to eat?"

Lame. I can't even watch this anymore. I look over at Jack, and he's grinning with a mixture of sheer enjoyment and disbelief.

"How about that sandwich place over by Cool Beans?" Liz suggests.

It's a good suggestion because the tables are spaced far

enough apart that you can have a decent conversation without people overhearing.

"Sounds great," Andrew says, all relieved.

Jack and I leave a few minutes later. He came by the apartment and picked me up for church, which was sweet.

"So," he says, "these plans of ours for today. Do they include watching any of the NFL preseason?"

I grin. Jack and my dad have bonded over football.

"How about we go home and change, then head over to Mom and Dad's, and you can watch football while Mom and I do some more work on the wedding."

"Thanks!" Jack grins. He squeezes my hand as we walk to his car. "You aren't upset that I'm not more involved in the wedding planning, are you?"

"Jack, I don't think any girl is ever upset that the groom doesn't have very many opinions."

He grins again. "Good. Just making sure. As long as you're in a white dress, and we're going on a honeymoon after, I'm very happy."

We get in the car and I start thinking.

"Hey, Jack?"

"Yeah, Nutkin?"

"Honeymoon." I look over at him as he backs out of the parking space.

"What about it?"

"Where should we go?"

He grins at me. "Actually, I was going to surprise you with this, but my parents called and they have a time-share for one of those resorts. We can go anywhere in the United States and a few tropical islands for a week on them."

I'm shocked. "Really?"

"Really. They gave me the website so we can look up the resorts and pick one."

"Wow!" I'm getting really excited. Anywhere in the United States means Hawaii, and despite the SPF 70 I'll be slathering on every thirty minutes, I have always wanted to go to Hawaii.

It's the whole romantic beach getaway. I'm already picturing us—I'll be wearing my swimsuit top and some denim shorts, and he'll be wearing his board shorts and a T-shirt, and we'll be walking hand in hand down the beach, with the waves lightly lapping at our ankles and the sun setting in the background. My hair will be curling in that perfect beachy wave look. And I'll finally, for the first time in my life, have a beautiful tan, and we can eat all the fresh seafood in the world at those infamous luaus.

Jack is still talking. "So, I was thinking, there's this one resort in northern Colorado where it's this whole all-inclusive thing, and we could stay in a cabin in the mountains. There's tons of snow, and people see all these elk and deer and even moose. We could have a big fire every night, and there are some snowboarding places that aren't too far away. And on the days when we can't get out because of the snow, we'll just cuddle together in front of the fire and watch movies."

I think my brain only picked up "northern Colorado," "moose," and "when we can't get out because of the snow."

"What?" I ask incredulously.

"Doesn't it sound amazing? And romantic?" He reaches across the console for my hand and squeezes it tightly. "And we can bundle up and go outside and build a snowman."

Jack has lost his mind.

"I was thinking beach," I say quietly.

"For what?" Jack asks.

"For the honeymoon. I was thinking we could walk along

the beach together and eat seafood and go to luaus and get tan."

His eyebrows go up when I mention the word tan, but he's nice enough not to comment on the fact that I have never, ever tanned.

I have burned on more than one occasion. But never tanned.

He's quiet for a minute. "And go snorkeling?" he asks in a quiet voice.

Okay, here's my thing about snorkeling. I think the whole idea of swimming with the dolphins and whatever sounds like a lot of fun, but I have this deep, unspoken fear that someone will come up behind me while I'm under the water and plug my little breathing tube with their finger.

So, I've never snorkeled.

And the thought of it kind of makes my lungs hurt. "Uh, sure," I say, trying to muscle up some guts.

I mean, surely I would feel the person coming up behind me, right? They would be moving around the water, so I'm sure I would feel them. My worry eases a little bit.

Unless they were in a boat and plugged it from the top.

Fear is back.

Jack is thinking. "We'll keep talking about it," he says finally, as we get to my apartment.

This week Jack was smart and brought a change of clothes with him in a backpack. We take turns changing in the only bathroom. I already had on a comfy sweater, so I just replace my cords with jeans, and I'm good to go. I'm not going to dress too ratty in case we go out to dinner with Mom and Dad.

Then Jack takes his turn. When he finishes, I'm staring in my empty fridge looking for something to hold us over on the drive to San Diego.

"We'll stop somewhere," Jack says after he sees my fridge.

"We eat out a lot."

"And I think we should enjoy it while we can." Jack clips a leash on an ecstatic Calvin. "Someday we'll have kids and no extra income to go out to eat." He looks up at me and grins. "Besides, Bob & Mark's is on the way out of town, and a double-stacked cheeseburger sounds really good right now."

Bob & Mark's is like an upscale Sonic, if you can have one of those. It's a drive-in, but they make gourmet burgers. There's a teriyaki cheeseburger with pineapple on it that is just amazing.

I'm getting hungry just thinking about it. "Okay," I say, shutting my fridge door. "Ready, Calvin?"

"Roo!" Calvin barks, turning in circles.

I wonder why dogs run in circles when they are happy. You'd think they would just get dizzy.

Jack has Calvin, and I grab a jacket and lock the door behind me. We climb down the stairs and into his truck, and Calvin hops in the back excitedly.

"So," Jack says once we're on the road. "Beaches."

"Snow," I say to him. Maybe this is one of those hard parts of marriage where compromise is the best option.

So what's in the middle between a beach and snow? Albuquerque, New Mexico? Or maybe a compromise means you're supposed to combine the two options to get a new one. So, we should go to Seattle?

I rub my head.

"So, this is what my parents were talking about when I was growing up," Jack mutters quietly.

"What?"

"Just learning to mesh with each other and get along. You know, loving each other." He looks over at me and smiles. "My dad used to say, *'A pesar de nuestras diferencias.'*"

I really should have paid more attention in ninth-grade Spanish class. Maybe I would have if I'd known I was going to marry a guy whose dad grew up speaking only Spanish.

Jack's mom has predominately Irish blood. Which is why Jack, for all appearances, doesn't look too Hispanic. He's tall, on the thinner side, and has dark hair and eyes. He gets his natural tan from his dad.

All the Hispanic guys I knew in school were almost as short as I was.

Jack's height comes from his mom. She has one of those weird "I'm taller than my husband" things going on. I find it weird anyway. Probably because I'm five foot two, and in order to marry someone shorter than me, I'd have to start searching the ranks of little people.

I have a sneaking suspicion, though, that they are all on TLC and the Discovery Channel. And the occasional Disney movie.

I blink back to the present. "What does that mean?" I ask Jack.

"Despite our differences," he translates. "We need to love each other despite the fact that we seem to have very little in common in the way of vacationing."

"You really don't like beaches?"

"I like beaches," he says. Then he shrugs. "I guess I just like the idea of snuggling up together and staying warm in front of a fire more. I think it sounds relaxing. A beach is nice, but you've got hundreds of other people there and lots of other men checking out my gorgeous wife in a swimsuit."

I blush. I can't help it. "Oh," I say quietly.

"And I've been to Hawaii before. It's not as romantic as it seems in the commercials and on the postcards. Everything is ridiculously expensive, and those luaus aren't just for you. There are about fifty other people there." He sighs. "Some of whom are so drunk they can't stand up straight."

Hawaii is starting to sound less and less appealing.

"Well, when did you go?" I ask, feeling the need to defend my honeymoon choice.

"When I was in the seventh grade. My dad had a business trip there, and my whole family went."

"Then, of course, it wasn't romantic," I say. "Nothing is romantic when you're in the seventh grade, and you're sitting on the beach with your little brother."

Jack's little brother, Miguel, is about three years younger than Jack and me. He's in school in Minneapolis, studying history, something about as useful as my English degree. I told him that if he continues to major in history, he might want to start applying at coffee shops and restaurants.

I guess a career in the restaurant biz sounds okay to him, because last I heard, he's still majoring in history. Much to the dismay of Jack's dad.

"True," Jack concedes after thinking it over for a minute. "I guess it would be more romantic with you than with Miguel." He grins at me.

I grin back. "But," I say, feeling generous, "the snuggling up by a fire sounds nice too. I don't know."

"Is there something in the middle?"

"Of Hawaii and Colorado? Yeah, the Pacific Ocean. Or, actually maybe even here. We could just stay in our apartment."

Jack rolls his eyes. "Smart aleck. I mean between snow and beach."

"I was trying to think of a place earlier, and I couldn't."

Jack pulls into the drive-through for Bob & Mark's. "What do you want?" he asks, pulling up to the menu with the speaker attached to it.

I lean over to look at the menu, which is pointless because I already know what I want. "A teriyaki cheeseburger, please. With curly fries."

Bob & Mark's makes the best curly fries ever. I don't know what seasonings they use on them, but they are amazing.

Calvin perks up in the backseat when Jack rolls down his window. The dog can smell fries like no one's business.

"Anything to drink?" Jack asks me.

"Lemonade, please."

He nods. He orders my burger and a southwestern burger with guacamole, bacon, and swiss cheese, two orders of curly fries, and two lemonades.

"Can I interest you in an Andes mint brownie for dessert?" the speaker says.

"You probably could, but I'm going to pass for today."

The speaker says the total, and Jack drives forward to the window, pulling his wallet out of his back pocket. "After the nine hundred calories in the burger, I don't think we need a brownie to seal our future heart attack," he says to me.

"Quicker you die, the quicker you're in heaven," I say.

He looks at me. "That just sounds suicidal."

"Not suicidal. Just reasoning for desserts, that's all."

"Did you want the brownie?" he asks me.

I shake my head. After eating the burger and the fries, I usually can't eat again for a good six hours. Bob & Mark's burgers are huge.

Jack pays the lady and gets a paper sack in exchange for his cash. "Thanks," Jack says.

The smell of sweet, tangy pineapple and french fries takes over the vehicle. We both inhale deeply.

"Wow," Jack says. "I'm getting the teriyaki burger next time."

"God, thank You for the food," I say in a quick blessing. "Amen."

I partially unwrap his burger and hand it to him so he can eat and drive. "So," he says, chewing, "what if we went to the opposite side of the country?"

"Like Florida?"

"I was thinking Maine."

I swallow and look over at him. "Maine? What's in Maine?"

He shrugs. "I don't know. Lobsters?"

"Florida has DisneyWorld."

"Okay, you win." He grins. "Or maybe like the North Carolina beach?"

"That's a cold beach," I say, licking teriyaki glaze off my fingers. "We could go to New York."

Jack laughs. "For our honeymoon?"

"Why not? Maybe we'd get cast as extras in a movie." I'm excited now. I've never been to New York. "And we could eat at that hot-dog place like he does in *Fools Rush In*."

Jack is laughing harder. "So, for our honeymoon, you want to visit Times Square, which will probably be covered in a blizzard, and eat hot dogs." He grins over at me. "Sounds romantic."

I smile back. "You don't like it?"

"I like the lodge idea better." He finishes off his burger and wipes his mouth with a napkin. "When do we start premarital counseling?"

I'm trying to remember what Andrew had said. "I think sometime in the next two weeks," I say.

He nods. "Okay. As long as it's after six on a weekday, I'll be fine."

We start to hit San Diego traffic, and he pays more attention to the road. Mom said that she and Dad were planning on just hanging out at the house until tonight, and then they were going by the hospital for a little bit.

Jack pulls up to Mom and Dad's house about twenty minutes later. "Okay, Cal," he says, waking my sleeping dog. "We're here."

Calvin hops up and starts going crazy. He loves Mom and Dad's house.

Mom opens the door before we ring the doorbell. "Hi, guys!" she says, looking cute in fitted jeans and an off-white cable-knit sweater.

I grin at her. "Getting a little excited for winter?" It's only August, and it's San Diego. We don't have cold weather.

She grins. "Maybe." She bends down to rub Calvin's ears, and then he darts into the house to find Dad.

We go in, and I know why Mom has on the sweater. They have the air conditioning cranked so high that it has to be like fifty degrees in the house. I'm glad I brought a jacket.

"Gosh," I say, shivering. "Having hot flashes already?"

Mom rolls her eyes. "No, and thank you for the non-compliment."

Dad comes in and gives me a hug and Jack a handshake. "She talked to your Aunt Carol," he says.

"Ahhh," I say, drawing out the word.

Jack looks at me. "Okay, Carol is married to Jim . . . ?"

"Paul," I correct. "Carol is married to Paul."

He nods. "Right, right. And she lives in . . . ?"

"Minneapolis," Mom sighs. "They got three inches of snow in May." She squints outside at the backyard where the lawn is nice and plush and green. Dad has meticulous taste when it comes to the backyard. There are flowers and vines and palm trees.

And no snow.

Mom sighs again. "I hate Christmas in San Diego. I told your dad we needed a winter house in Minnesota."

"Always a good move in a recession," Dad says, winking at me. "Buying a winter house in a place where it rarely gets above fifty degrees."

"We could wear those cute peacoats and military jackets and more of these sweaters and scarves," Mom says wistfully.

Jack leans over and gives my mother a side hug. "I'm glad someone else in this family likes the cold," he says.

"See, honey?" Mom says to Dad. "Jack will come visit."

"I hope he'll come visit wherever we live," Dad says. We follow Dad and the noise of the football game into the family room, where Calvin is busy playing with a new toy my parents got him.

If this is any indication of how they are going to treat our children, we are going to need to bring in the Super Nanny because of how spoiled rotten our kids will be.

A teakettle starts whistling in the kitchen right as Dad, Jack, and I sit on the couch. Mom starts smiling. "Anyone up for hot chocolate or spiced tea?"

"Maybe you could invest in one of those fake snowmaker things," I say to Dad. "Just fire it up and spray the snow all over the yard. It would definitely be cheaper than a winter house."

"Mmm," Dad says, watching the highlights. "Too much water on the lawn when it melted."

"No one wants hot chocolate?" Mom calls from the kitchen.

"I'll take one," I say, getting up from the couch and going into the kitchen. Mom has got a big tin of mocha powder on the counter beside her.

"You like yours with milk though, right, honey?" she asks me.

I nod. My mother started my love of all things chocolate and coffee right in this very kitchen with that mocha powder. She would make me steaming mochas in a travel mug every morning for my entire junior and senior years. I'd get to school all hyped up on the sugar and caffeine. I thanked Mom for the mochas in my baccalaureate speech since I believe that's the reason I passed chemistry.

Mom starts heating milk in a saucepan on the stove while she makes her spiced tea.

"So, we started talking about honeymoon locations," I say, leaning against the island counter while Mom stirs.

"Oh yeah?"

"Yeah. Where did you and Dad go?"

Mom smiles. "We went to San Francisco. We didn't have a ton of money for a honeymoon, so we stayed pretty close to home. We stayed in this gorgeous suite, ate clam chowder, toured all these places, and drove to the redwood forest." She's still smiling. "It was fun. And relaxing."

Maybe Jack and I are thinking too extravagantly.

Then again, Jen and Travis went on a weeklong cruise to Hawaii. If that's not extravagant, then I don't know what is.

Even if Jack didn't get seasick, I'm not sure I could do a cruise. Sharing a boat with thousands of people and not being able to get off doesn't sound that appealing to me. And then there's the whole thing about *Titanic* being the hit movie of my generation.

I have a feeling that many people in their mid- to late twenties will always have a problem with cruise ships, thanks to that movie.

"Here's your hot chocolate," Mom says. She hands me a big red mug.

"Merry Christmas to all!" I shout. "And to all a good—"

"Maya, they're talking about the Colts game," Dad calls from the living room. I hear the TV crank about six volume levels. "Could you keep it down, please?"

I think we can tell who the Scrooge in my family is.

Mom and I go back in the family room, and it's all Peyton Manning this and Peyton Manning that. Mom sits beside Dad on the love seat and sips her spiced tea.

"Could you turn that down a little?" she asks Dad, who is holding the remote.

He obliges as soon as the story on the Colts is done.

"Dang," Jack says appreciatively, leaning back against the couch cushions. "The Colts are going to be tough to beat this year."

I sit down, cradling my hot chocolate.

"Get a big enough cup there, Maya?" Dad asks.

I sip it and make an *mmm* sound. "Delish!"

Dad laughs. "How's the car running lately, Maya?"

This is Dad code for "How are you doing, Maya?"

"Good," I say. "No problems. Runs very smooth."

"How many miles are you at?"

I study my mug, trying to remember. Why is it that guys always know and care about this stuff? Now, if he asked me what color my car was or how the interior was looking these days, then I would be able to answer him.

Jack looks at me, notices that I'm struggling for an answer, and turns to Dad. "A little over 50,000," he says. "I think 50,200."

Dad nods. "Not too bad. Then again, you two have been bringing your truck here lately, haven't you?"

"Yes, sir. But I figure, it's all the same in two months."

Mom grins over her cup. "That it is! So, Jack, where are you wanting to go for the honeymoon?"

Jack grins at me. "Told her about the debate?"

"No, I just told her we were trying to figure it out."

"Oh." He looks at Mom. "Well, there's this place in Colorado that's an all-inclusive snow lodge," he starts.

Immediately, my mother is on board. "Snow?" she says longingly.

Oh brother. Jack grins at me.

"And I would like to go to Hawaii," I say.

"That's more like it," Dad says. "First week of November you could catch a college game there in Honolulu. And you could probably tour the stadium where they play the Pro Bowl."

My dad and I have very different ideas about what this Hawaii honeymoon should look like.

Jack is getting thoughtful. "I hadn't thought of that," he says.

"What about luaus?" I burst. "And sunsets and lying on the beach and eating shrimp cocktail?"

Dad makes a face. "Shrimp cocktail?"

Jack grins. "And we already covered the whole lying on a beach thing, Maya," he says.

"Curse of the Swedish," Mom says. "Get used to it."

At least my mom and Zach got the blond hair to go with it. My dark hair just makes my complexion look even whiter.

"When are we going to the hospital?" I ask, changing the subject.

Mom glances at the huge decorative clock on the wall. "Probably around five. Zach will be getting off then, and Kate is going to meet him there. I hoped we'd be able to talk them both into coming out to dinner with us. They need a break from the NICU."

I nod. "I can understand why they are always there, but you're right."

Last I heard, one of them has been in the NICU with Ben since Kate got out of the hospital. If she's not there, Zach is.

I think Kate even sleeps in the on-call room. One of those rare privileges the wife of a pediatric doctor gets.

This could explain why she still looks like a truck ran over her.

"They definitely need a break," I say.

We get to the hospital around five fifteen and walk the now-familiar hallways to the NICU. *Familiar* is never a word I like to associate with hospitals.

Our favorite nurse, Brenda, is on duty tonight. She sees us coming and smiles. "Hello, Davis family!" she says brightly. "Dr. Davis and Kate just got here, so you guys must have planned this."

Mom smiles at her. Brenda is probably about forty or forty-five, and she and my mom hit it off right away. Brenda has three kids: two are in college, and one is a senior in high school. She's been working as a nurse since the youngest one was in kindergarten.

"I just always wanted to help people," she told us one time. "So, I see my kids during the day, and I take care of sick babies at night."

Brenda nods to the sinks. "Wash up, and you guys can go in there." Brenda is pretty lax on the two-people-only rule. Especially at night when no one else is here.

We scrub the top layer of skin off our hands and pull on the gloves.

Kate is sitting on the rocker, cradling Ben against her chest and humming to him. He's grown a lot since I saw him last.

"Wow," I say, quietly, walking over. "He's so big now!"

"He's teetering on the edge of four pounds," Zach says proudly. "If he can get those little lungs working 100 percent, we can stop living here."

"They said probably another two weeks, but we'll see," Kate says. She looks so content and happy holding Ben. Somehow, the tiredness and dark circles seem to melt off her face.

I love seeing her like this.

We spend about an hour there with Ben while Mom works her persuasive magic, and before I know it, both Kate and Zach are agreeing to go out to dinner with us.

I must admit, I never thought they would both come.

Zach tells Brenda to page him if anything changes while they are out, and she nods, winking at Mom. "I'll do that, honey. Go have a good dinner."

We decide on my favorite, The Cheesecake Factory, because, wonderful city that San Diego is, there is a Cheesecake Factory less than a mile from the hospital.

I love California.

I'm busy looking over the menu a few minutes later. I'm not sure why I'm looking at the menu, since I always get either the spinach and artichoke dip or the sliders. Both of which are amazing. And, of course, a slice of cheesecake.

"I might get the Steak Diane," Jack says to me. We're all crammed into a booth since the restaurant was so crowded and we didn't want to wait for a table. I think an hour is about as long as Zach and Kate will let Brenda watch over Ben.

So, Dad, Jack, and I are on one side, and Zach, Kate, and Mom are on the other.

"If I had a meal named after me, I wouldn't want it to be a steak," I say.

"I'd want mine to be shrimp scampi," Kate says. "Shrimp Scampi à la Kate."

I'm not the biggest fan of shrimp scampi. Too many noodles, not enough shrimp. But I don't say this. And now that I'm thinking about shrimp, I'm really wanting it.

I decide to branch out and get the popcorn shrimp. Our server comes by and we all order.

"And this is going to be on us," Zach says.

Jack immediately starts shaking his head. "No, no. No, it's not."

"Just accept the dinner, Jack. You guys have given up a lot of time, miles, and gas coming here so often. Let us treat you."

Kate nods. "Please, guys? It would mean a lot to us."

I'm not sure how you can say no to a woman who just gave birth two months prematurely.

Jack sighs.

"Thank you," Zach says. "Now. When are you two going to move to San Diego?"

I laugh. "We're not. I'm very happy in Hudson."

"Yeah, but there's the San Diego Zoo," Zach points out. "I bet they pay a lot better than the Hudson Zoo. And there's the whole 'being close to your nephew' thing."

"We're close to him. He'll be driving down to Hudson for a parent-free weekend before too long." I grin.

"And I bet there's a decent coffeehouse here that is hiring," Zach continues.

Our server comes right then with our food, and I am saved by the sizzling of Jack's steak.

"And I'll leave the dessert menu," the server says.

Dad prays, and we all dig in. The popcorn shrimp is very good, and I'm thinking I have another favorite here.

"So," Dad says, "let's try to think about these next couple of months." He nods to me and Jack. "You guys are getting married November first."

I swallow. "Yes."

"And then you're planning on going to Hawaii to tour the Pro Bowl stadium." Dad winks.

"No," I say.

"And then we've got Thanksgiving. Mom and I were planning on driving to see your grandparents this year."

Grandma and Gramps live about eleven hours away in Redding. It's as far north as you can get and still be in California. But you have to add almost another two hours because you have to drive through tons of traffic to get there. Especially at Thanksgiving.

Dad is still talking. "So, you guys are welcome to come with us, but we understand if you have other plans."

Kate nods. "It will just depend on how Ben is doing."

"I figured," Dad says. "You guys just talk about it. We can figure things out last minute if we need to."

We drop Kate and Zach off at the hospital an hour later. I am completely stuffed with shrimp and the turtle cheesecake.

"Bye, guys. Sleep well," I say, giving Kate a squeeze on the shoulder.

"I'll try." She's back to looking haggard, and I hope she's able to hold Ben again.

"Thanks again for dinner," Jack says to Zach.

"No problem."

Dad drives back to my parents' house, and Jack gets out of the car, yawning. "I think we might need to head back now," he says. "I have an early meeting tomorrow."

I nod. "Okay." I go tear Calvin away from his new toy and give Mom and Dad a hug. "See you guys next weekend."

"Drive safely."

I finally stumble into bed around midnight, and as I curl up under the covers, I squeeze my eyes tight.

Lord, please be with little Ben and help him to keep growing. And please let the few hours of sleep Kate gets tonight count double.

And then I fall asleep.

CHAPTER FIFTEEN

A week passes by in a complete blur. Cool Beans is packed from the time we open until the time we close, thanks to an uncharacteristic cold snap that leaves everyone wanting lattes. And the weekend is gone in a flash since we spend all day on Saturday talking wedding plans and all day on Sunday at the hospital.

It's Monday, and I'm counting the minutes until I am off for the night. Fifty-four minutes to go.

I look back up at the clock as I hand a woman her large cinnamon latte. Fifty-two minutes.

"Will you stop doing that?" Ethan says, handing me another to-go cup. This time it's a decaf vanilla latte.

"Stop doing what?" I ask, frothing the milk.

"Looking at the clock every ten seconds. What is with you? Got a hot date tonight or something?"

I add the espresso, stir it, pile on the whipped cream, and pass it over the counter just as Ethan adds cups number three and four to the stack by the register.

I can't help but sigh. I look back up at the clock.

Forty-nine minutes. At least staying busy helps the time go by faster.

"Jack is taking me to dinner tonight," I say. "He's picking me up here." He'd texted me around lunchtime: *Let's get dinner out tonight. I'll pick you up when your shift is over.*

It's a pretty innocuous text except that Jack's day isn't supposed to end until six, which is an hour after I get off.

Which means he's taking off early. Which means something is up.

Which means I'm trying hard to remember that worrying is a sin.

It's not going well. The remembering, that is.

Ethan is looking at me as I start on the next few lattes. "Isn't that a good thing?" he asks after a minute.

"What?"

"Dinner with your fiancé? I mean, I've never been engaged, but you'd think if you were planning on spending the rest of your life with this person, one dinner wouldn't be that big of a deal." Ethan turns to help the next person in line.

I have decided that I hate cold snaps.

I pass two more lattes over the counter and then make a hot chocolate.

"Dinner's not the big deal," I say when Ethan is done with the customer. "The fact that Jack is taking off work early is the big deal."

"Oh," Ethan says. "Maybe he just had the best day ever, and he's excited to talk to you about it."

"Or maybe he got fired, and he's calling to tell me the wedding is off."

"Maybe he found out he got a raise and a new work schedule," Ethan says, rolling his eyes. "You're depressing to be around today."

"Sorry." I rub my head with the back of my hand. As I finish up the last few drinks, Alisha walks in.

I look at the clock again. Thirty minutes to go. And Alisha is never here this late on a Monday.

"Hey," Ethan says, waving at her, "we were thinking you got lost." He has the stack of time cards ready for her.

She laughs. "Not lost, just busy this time of year. Maya, can I talk to you for a moment?" She points to the back room and heads that way.

Perfect. This will be an awful day if Jack and I both lose our jobs. Maybe dinner out should be at the food kitchen we both serve at occasionally. We can get to know some of our future neighbors.

"Maya?" Ethan says. "She's waiting for you."

I nod sadly and walk in, shoulders low. Maybe if I remind my boss that I'm about to get married, she'll let me keep working. Alisha is sitting at the table, pulling a stack of papers from her purse.

"Have a seat, Maya. How's the wedding planning going?"

I guess there is no need for a reminder. "Okay. Slowly."

She nods. "I hardly got anything planned until the month before our wedding," she says. "It was ridiculous. I was in the middle of finals; Jason was about to graduate from flight school." She shakes her head. "Painful days. Anyway, I wanted to talk with you about something."

Here comes the ax. I brace myself for it. "Okay," I say, trying not to panic quite yet. So, I move back in with Mom and Dad. So Jack and I become that married couple that still lives with the bride's parents.

It's tacky, but it could be done.

"I wanted to talk with you about a promotion," Alisha says.

"Look, I'll be better about . . ." I squint at her. "Wait, what?"

"A promotion?" she says, grinning. "We talked about this a while ago, and I'm just now getting the funds to increase your salary. You'll be the new manager here, and it'll come with a fairly hefty raise because I'll move you to a salaried position instead of hourly." She waves my last time card in front of my face. "No more time cards."

"A manager?" I repeat, stunned.

"Your work hours shouldn't increase too much. I want you to keep working the nine-to-five shift. But you'll have some extra paperwork to do, including collecting the time cards, and I'll make you in charge of this location." Alisha has another café on the other side of town where she spends most of her time.

"In charge?" I can't wrap my brain around the fact that I'm not being fired, I'm being promoted.

Alisha slides one of the papers over. "Here's what your new salary will be," she says.

I blink at the numbers. I think I might be donating to the food kitchen instead of eating there.

"And don't worry about all the particulars yet," Alisha says. "I'll be coming in and training you probably one day a week for the next month so you can get the hang of the little stuff."

I just look at her.

She grins. "Maya? Will you take the job?"

I start nodding. "Yes, please," I say, still stunned. "Wow, Alisha!"

She grins wider. "I'll let it sink in. But don't plan anything for next Monday from five to six, because we'll start your train-ing then." We both stand, and she gives me a hug. "Thank you so much, Maya. This is going to save me so many headaches! Have a good evening, okay? Go celebrate."

She waves at Ethan and leaves. I sit back down in the chair at the table.

A promotion?

Ethan pops his head in. "So, boss, I was just wondering if I should help you clean out your cubbyhole or if you'll finally admit that maybe today isn't going to be as depressing as you thought it would be." There's mockery ringing in his voice, and I glare at him.

"Excuse me, should you be taking a break right now?"

"Should you?"

Valid question. I go back out front, and Ethan is grinning at me.

"Congratulations, Maya!"

"Thanks." I'm rubbing my head, still in shock.

"You know, I've never seen someone take good news quite this way," Ethan says, nodding to the next customer in line.

I watch him take the order, ring it up, and hand me the ceramic mug. "Large caramel latte for here," he says.

I look at the mug in my hand.

Manager?

By the time Jack pulls into the parking lot, I'm still in shock, but it's more of a happier shock. Things have slowed down a little bit, and Ethan is leaning against the counter, waiting not so casually for Lisa.

"Excited to see Peter tonight?" I ask Ethan as he paces behind the counter.

"What?"

"Mm-hmm." I just grin at him as Peter walks in.

Jack climbs out of his truck, and I notice he's not even in his zoo uniform. Apparently, he had time to take a shower and change into straight-cut dark jeans, a collared brown polo shirt, and his aviator glasses. He looks like he should be on a remake of *Top Gun*.

Swell. I'm in a black three-quarter-length T-shirt, jeans that

are frightfully close to tearing at the knee, and my black Sketch-
ers. I spilled coffee down one leg, as is typical at work, so I have
a long brown streak from my right knee to my ankle, and I smell
like an awful mixture of coffee grounds and burnt milk.

"Hi, babe," he says, walking in and grinning at me.

I smile back and wave. "Hi, Jack."

Ethan perks up, too, and I see Lisa walk through the door.
"So sorry I'm late!" she says, nearly growling in frustration. "I
locked my keys in the car at my apartment, and my apartment
manager had to come unlock my apartment so I could get the
spare."

"Wow, I'm sorry," Ethan gushes. "That's awful, Lisa."

Peter is already checking the coffee to see what needs refill-
ing. "Sorry about that, Lisa," he says. "Go ahead and head on
out, guys."

I need no further instruction. I grab my purse from the back,
leave my cherry red apron hanging on the hook, and go around
the counter to meet Jack, who is chatting with Ethan and Lisa.

"So, it's good," he says. He grins at me and takes my hand.
"I'll see you guys later."

"Have fun tonight," Ethan yells as we leave.

Jack leans over and kisses me as we walk to the car. "Hi,
honey," he says. "How about we go to Olive Garden?"

I nod. "That sounds good. You look all spiffy tonight."

He smiles at me. "I had a chance to shower. I didn't figure
you'd want to sit and have dinner with a guy who smelled like
he'd been shoveling elephant dung."

When he puts it like that, my burnt coffee–smelling clothes
aren't so bad anymore.

"Sorry about my coffee-stained jeans," I say, pointing down
at my leg.

He shrugs. "I have those in my closet, too," he says, opening the passenger door for me.

He drives to Olive Garden and talks the whole way there about how Marco the hippo is adjusting to her pregnancy.

I decide to wait to tell him about my promotion until dessert. I'm starting to get more and more excited about it. It will be more work, but the raise will be so nice.

We get seated at Olive Garden a few minutes later. Our server brings our waters to the table and leaves us to peruse the menu.

Jack is still grinning, and I'm not sure what to make of it. He hasn't stopped since he first walked into Cool Beans.

"What?" I finally ask him, setting my menu down. I'm getting the lasagna, like I always do.

"What do you mean, what?" he asks, looking up at me. His eyes are sparkling excitedly, and I'm wondering if he got cut from work early or if he won the lottery and quit his job.

"You haven't stopped smiling," I tell him. "I know you like Olive Garden, but it's not *that* good. What's up?"

He shakes his head. "After we order. I'll tell you after that."

Now I'm searching for the server who has seemed to disappear. This is what I don't like about Olive Garden. In some restaurants, you can see the whole building and you always know where your server is. But Olive Garden is built with like ten different rooms, which just makes it that much harder.

She finally shows up about ten minutes later. "Ready to order?" she asks, clicking her pen.

"Lasagna, please," I say.

"Chicken parmesan," Jack orders. We hand her our menus.

Jack reaches across the table for my hands, and I squeeze his. "Okay, tell me," I say, looking at him expectantly.

He takes a deep breath and squeezes my hands again. "Okay," he says. He's grinning wider than I've ever seen before. "So, I got called into my manager's office today," he starts.

Weird how similar our days were.

"And he sat me down and said I'd been doing a really good job. He said of all the recent hires, I have the best performance rates."

"Wow, Jack!" I say, smiling at him. "That's awesome!"

He grins. "And there's more. He said that since I'd been doing so well, he had a special offer for me." Jack pauses. "There's a zoo in Seattle that is looking for an assistant director in one of their large mammal exhibits."

My brain stops on the word *Seattle*.

"Maya?" Jack says gently, squeezing my hands again.

I blink and focus on his face again. "So your boss is moving to Seattle?"

He shakes his head. "No, honey. He was wanting to put my name in the hat for the job in Seattle. He said that with my qualifications and work ethic and the reference he would write for me I'd have a great shot at getting the job."

Seattle.

Jack wants to move from Hudson?

My chest is feeling tighter and tighter, and I'm wishing that I hadn't ordered the lasagna. Our server sets a bowl of salad and a basket of breadsticks in front of us.

"Parmesan on the salad?" she asks.

When I don't respond, Jack nods. "Yes, please." He watches her for a minute and then nods. "That's enough, thank you."

She leaves.

My stomach is hurting. I'm thinking about Jen, about Andrew and Liz and our church, and about Cool Beans. I'm remembering all the places in Hudson that have a special meaning to me. The park where Jack first said "I love you." The places I always walk Calvin. The bench on campus at Cal-Hudson where I first reconnected with Jack.

And what about my family? We're going to just up and move what . . . like twenty hours away? That's more than a day's drive.

Jack is squeezing my hands again. "Talk to me, Nutkin."

"You want to move?" I can barely get the words past my thickening throat. I feel like I swallowed one of those breadsticks without the help of saliva.

Jack lets go of my hands and sighs. "I don't want to move, per se," he says. "I just don't want to turn down amazing opportunities without thinking about whether or not it could be what God has planned for us."

He thinks God has Seattle planned for us?

"And it's such a great job, Nutkin!" Now the excitement is back. "I'd probably be working with the large Asian animals. And I'd be the site director for that section of the zoo. That's a huge promotion, Maya."

I know he's serious about something when he uses my real name.

"And with that comes a huge pay increase," Jack says. "We'd be able to buy a house, and you wouldn't have to work if you didn't want to. Which will be great when kids come."

Now we're raising children in Seattle? Doesn't it rain like three hundred days out of the year in Seattle?

The only experience I have with Seattle is watching *Sleepless in Seattle* and sighing over young Tom Hanks.

Our server sets our meals in front of us, frowning at the untouched salad plates. "Did you want me to leave these?" she asks.

"Yes, please." Jack nods.

Even the thought of leaving Hudson makes my eyes sting. I look down at my steaming lasagna, and the smell of it—which would normally make my mouth water—is making my stomach turn. I can't wrap my brain around this.

Jack wants to move?

"Let me pray real quick," he says, reaching for my left hand. The diamond sparkles under the soft overhead light, and Jack bows his head. "Lord," he says quietly, rubbing his thumb over my knuckles, "God, just give us wisdom in this. Please. Amen."

I seriously doubt that God wants us to leave our families and our church for some place that is so far away from everything and everyone that we know.

Jack squeezes my hand one more time and then lets go to pick up his fork. "My boss was telling me that Seattle is a great place to live, and there are tons of things to do. Plus, there are lots of neat little suburbs, so you don't have to live in the middle of the city. Sort of like Hudson."

I know people who commute from Hudson to San Diego every day, and I've always thought they were crazy. Why in the world would you drive two hours round trip every single day if you can live by your work?

My stomach is still cramping, and a part of me is seriously hurt that Jack would even consider moving.

"Aren't you going to eat?" Jack says after a few minutes, when I still haven't touched my fork.

"I'm not feeling so good," I tell him. It's true.

Jack looks up at me. "What's wrong?"

"My stomach hurts." And it does. I'm not lying.

Jack immediately reacts. Our server walks past, and he flags her down. "We'll need all of this to go," he says.

"I'm sorry?" she says.

"My fiancée isn't feeling very good. I need probably three or four boxes. And another order of breadsticks, please."

He looks at me when she leaves. "We might as well cash in on some of the never-ending breadsticks."

I nod but my head is pounding. My teeth are clenched, and I rub my forehead.

Moving. To Seattle.

I could possibly accept a move to Los Angeles. Maybe even San Francisco.

But Seattle has an entire state and most of California between me and my family. And what about Zach and Kate and little Ben? Who is still in the hospital, no less.

If we move to Washington, we'll become the absentee aunt and uncle. We'll be those people Ben sees twice a year at Christmastime and in the summer.

Never mind what this would do to my mother.

Our server returns with a stack of to-go boxes and the check. Jack puts all of our food into them and lays a couple of bills on the receipt.

"Okay, honey, let's go," he says, gathering the boxes. "We'll take you back to your car, and I'll follow you home."

I nod, and we leave the restaurant. We drive silently to Cool Beans, and I get out.

"Be careful driving," Jack says. He waits for me to back out and then pulls out behind me to follow me over to my apartment.

I'm almost blinded by tears as I drive. *God, this couldn't possibly be Your will.* I sniffle as I drive, swiping away my tears.

I feel guilty that Jack is so excited and I am so not. I'm shocked that he would even get excited over something that would involve us leaving California. His family lives here too.

I pull into my parking space in front of my apartment, and Jack is right behind me, carrying all the to-go boxes in his hands. I try not to face him since it is very obvious that I have been crying.

Calvin gets all excited when I open the door and he sees Jack and Italian food. "Roo!" he starts howling.

"Maya," Jack says, setting the boxes on the coffee table and grabbing my shoulders, turning me to face him. "Come on. We need to talk about this. I'm not going to say yes unless you're 100 percent on board, Nutkin. You are way more important to me than the job." He pulls me into a hug. "And if you don't want to leave, then we won't leave."

I nod into his shirt, and the tears are back.

"But," Jack says, pushing me away again so he can look at me, "I don't want you to decide this tonight. Okay? Think about it. Pray about it. Try to figure out what you think God's will is. And we'll keep talking about it."

I nod again, sniffling.

"And now, we're going to eat our food while it's still semi-warm." He gently pushes me toward the couch, and I sit. He hands me my to-go box and grabs two forks from the kitchen for us.

We start eating, and the silence is deafening. Even Calvin has gone quiet, sitting by Jack's knee waiting for something to drop.

"Why don't we see what's on TV?" Jack asks, picking up the remote after a few minutes.

The TV is already tuned to the Food Network, and we watch as Guy Fieri waltzes in and out of restaurants, tasting what looks like tantalizing food in his half-entertaining, half-annoying "I get paid to do this" kind of a way.

My dad hates Guy. "I don't understand why I couldn't have

his job," Dad grumbles every time this show is on. "All he does is taste the food and make satisfied faces at the camera."

Jack is apparently of the same mind-set. "This show is ridiculous," he says after ten minutes. "How come we don't have places like that to eat in Hudson?"

I'll confess, I haven't really been watching it. I'm staring in that general direction, but all I hear is *moving to Seattle, moving to Seattle, moving to Seattle* running over and over and over again in my head like that headache-inspiring song on that old show *Lamb Chop's Play-Along.*

I just nod.

The show ends about fifteen minutes later, and Jack looks over at me. I've barely touched my dinner, and he squeezes my arm.

"Talk to me," he says.

I blink at him. "What?"

"What are you thinking about?"

I let out my breath. "Seattle."

He nods. "Just don't make any decisions until you've prayed about it and read your Bible, okay?"

I nod. I can't imagine that God would want us to move, though. Especially when it makes me feel like this. My stomach feels shrunken up, like someone poked it with a needle and it deflated.

"And we still need to pick a honeymoon spot," Jack says.

Honeymoon. My brain can't even move from Seattle to the honeymoon. I don't understand how Jack can be thinking of both things at once.

"Can I talk to my mom about this?" I ask him.

He scoots over and rubs my back. "Honey, of course you can. I want you to talk to as many people as you need to."

I nod.

"Okay." He leans over and kisses my forehead. "Think about it. Sleep on it. And try to eat something, sweetie. I love you."

He leaves a few minutes later. I lock the door after him and just look at Calvin.

Calvin would hate Seattle, especially if it rains three hundred days out of the year. He is definitely a sunny-weather dog. I can't even get him to go outside to go to the bathroom when it rains. He just holds it until it stops.

I don't think he'll be able to hold it for three hundred days.

I sigh at him and go to my bedroom and fall on the bed. I'm still wearing my coffee-stained clothes, and I don't even care. Normally, as soon as I get home from work, I'm longing for a hot shower to rinse away the burnt-coffee smell.

Not today.

I curl up on my side and stare at my closet door.

Lord, You wouldn't want me to move, would You?

There isn't a big booming voice that tells me, "No, Maya, I would never want you to move." I kick off my shoes and pull the covers over myself, dirty clothes and all.

It doesn't occur to me until I'm drifting to sleep that I never told Jack about my promotion.

I close my eyes and don't move for the next twelve hours.

CHAPTER SIXTEEN

"Seriously, Maya, it was a promotion," Ethan says Tuesday morning around eleven. The day is starting out much slower than the last couple of weeks, and Ethan and I are both breathing easier because of it.

I've been staring blankly at the tray of half-iced cinnamon rolls in front of me, and his voice brings me back to reality. "What?" I ask.

Ethan sighs and grabs the knife from my hand, not so gently pushing me out of the way. "What is wrong with you?" he asks, finishing the frosting. "You have been acting weird lately. And today is even worse! I mean, I've never been engaged, but I've always heard that some amount of giddiness goes along with it." He waves the knife at me. "Not depression."

I sigh at him. "Jack got a potential job offer in Seattle." I say it so quietly that Ethan has to lean closer to hear me.

Saying it out loud just makes it that much more real.

Seattle.

I've always wanted to visit Seattle. I've heard it's the coffee capital of the world and that the sights are breathtaking.

But moving there is an entirely different story.

Ethan raises his eyebrows. "Wow."

"Yeah."

"So I'm assuming by the half-iced rolls, three messed-up drinks this morning, and the sad stare that you aren't too excited about this idea." He picks up the tray of cinnamon rolls and slides them into the display case.

"He's really excited," I say dully. "He couldn't stop smiling all through our very short dinner last night." I rub my forehead, pushing back the few wayward curls that have escaped from my ponytail. I barely did anything to myself after my quick shower this morning, so my hair dried frizzy and curly.

I don't even care.

"He told me he'd do whatever I wanted to do, though," I say.

Ethan looks and me. "Well, there you go. Tell him you don't want to move."

I shake my head. "It's not that simple. He's really excited. And I think he's convinced that this is God's will for us."

"Well, did you tell him about your promotion?" Ethan asks, sidestepping the God talk.

I shake my head. "I forgot about it."

Ethan just looks at me. "You are the only person I know who could forget about a big promotion."

"Jack would get a big promotion, too. Enough of one that it makes mine almost obsolete," I say.

"So, what are you going to tell him?"

A customer comes in, and we pause the conversation to make a cinnamon caramel latte and a mocha. I hand the to-go cups across the counter to the lady and look back at Ethan.

"I have no idea."

Jen is not answering her phone. I'm on my lunch break in the back, and I'm picking at the Olive Garden leftovers. I still don't have my appetite back. Which isn't necessarily a bad thing considering my lack of working out lately and the fact that I'll need to fit into a wedding dress soon.

I leave her a voice mail; she'll definitely be able to tell something is up by my voice. "Hey, Jenny. Call me." I hang up. No sense in panicking her.

Moving means leaving Jen. She's been my best friend since we roomed together second semester of freshman year at Cal-Hudson—a huge God thing since we both let the college pick our roommate.

I poke my fork into the lasagna. I really need to eat. Maybe eating will make me perk up a little bit.

Ethan comes into the back and slides a huge mug with a sunflower on it across the table to me. "Drink it," he says.

I take it and sniff. "A caramel macchiato?"

"With three shots."

I raise my eyebrows. That's nearing a heart-pounding amount of caffeine. I start drinking it.

It's really good. "Thanks, Ethan," I say, managing a smile for him.

"And cheer up," he says as he leaves. "All this depression is reminding me of Christmas at my house."

I immediately feel sad—but for Ethan, not for me. Everyone needs a happy Christmas. I always had wonderful Christmases, and I'm immediately stricken with guilt.

Gosh, Lord. I take way too much for granted.

So much for granted. And then I let myself get all down over something that has a likelihood of not happening in the first place.

I down my macchiato in about ten minutes and decide to bypass the lasagna yet again. Maybe tonight for dinner. I close the to-go box, and I'm putting it in the fridge when my phone starts vibrating on the table.

It's Jen. "Hey," I answer, sitting back down in the chair.

"Hey!" she says. "Sorry, I was driving to get some Panda for lunch, and I didn't hear my phone over the radio. What's up? Are you okay?"

I glance at the clock. I have about ten more minutes before my break is up. I decide that the direct approach is best. "Jen, Jack got a potential job offer at a zoo in Seattle," I say quickly.

She pauses. "Seattle?" she says, shock running through her voice. "Why Seattle?"

"His boss found the job for him. I guess he could be a director or something up there." I'm back to rubbing my forehead. I will have no skin there once this decision is made. Really, we shouldn't even be worrying about the increase in a paycheck. Once TLC runs my special, *The Woman Who Rubbed Through Her Skull*, we can just gather royalties off that.

Maybe it would pay for the plastic surgery.

I close my eyes. I'm back to thinking all depressingly again.

"Well, I guess that's cool about the director job," Jen says haltingly. "But, I mean, he couldn't find that in like San Diego or some place a little closer?"

"I don't know."

"I mean, Seattle is like twenty hours away."

"I know."

Jen is quiet for a minute. "So, what did you tell him?"

I think about last night. "Not very much. He told me at Olive Garden, and I couldn't even finish eating after that." I stop talking for a few seconds. "I don't know what to do, Jen. He's so excited about this."

"So, he's going to apply for it?"

"He told me he wouldn't do anything unless I was 100 percent on board with it."

"And what percentage are you at?"

I squint at the clock; I've got three minutes to finish this call. "I don't know, maybe a negative 30 percent?"

She laughs shortly. "I think I'm around a negative 40, but it's really up to you guys. Have you prayed about it?"

"Yes."

"And?"

"And I just keep thinking, surely God wouldn't want us to move right now. Not right after we first get married and right after Ben is born."

"God does do some mysterious things, though."

True. I don't think about that. I look at the clock again. "Jenny, my break is up."

"Okay. Mine is just about to be, so I need to scarf down this orange chicken. Look, I love you, and I'll be praying for you. And talk to Jack about this, okay? Don't just clam up on him."

Jen knows me too well.

"Okay. Love you, too."

I hang up and go out front. We have a few new customers since I went in for break, and two girls are walking in the door.

"Go ahead," I say, smiling shortly at Ethan. "And thanks for the macchiato." I can feel the caffeine starting to work its addictive magic on my brain cells.

"You're welcome. It's not like you to be all moody and troubled like those ridiculous teen dramas on TV."

"I wouldn't have pegged you as someone who watches those teen dramas," I say, surprised.

Ethan sighs. "I have a sister. She thinks they are like the greatest shows on the face of the earth. Anytime I go home, she's curled up on the couch sniffling as some pretty boy contemplates suicide." He shakes his head as he goes into the back. "Really, do we need to be watching that?"

He's gone before I can answer, but, no, I don't think we need to be watching that. That's why I'm a fan of light-hearted comedies. You can laugh and be reminded that everything really will be okay.

I tell myself that as I retie my apron. Everything really will be okay.

The two girls stand in front of the menu for about five minutes, holding up a man in a business suit who doesn't look like he's in the mood to wait. Finally, they make up their minds.

"Can I have an apple cider?" one girl says.

"Ohh! Actually, that sounds better than what I was going to get. I want that too," the other girl pipes up.

"Okay," I say, punching it in the cash register. We sell maybe ten apple ciders a week. They are not a very popular drink, and to be honest, I have never tasted ours.

But I think apple cider is gross anyway. All it is is hot apple juice, and after an unfortunate incident in the second grade where I left my lunch on the playground in the morning, and the chocolate bar my mom packed me melted, my sandwich got all dried out and crusty, and my apple juice got hot, I've never had the taste for it.

"Would you like whipped cream?" I have to ask this, but the combination would make any normal person get queasy.

"Oh," the first girl says, eyes all big. "Yes. Yes, please."

"None for me, thanks," the second girl says. I'm about to applaud her tasting choices when she starts patting her abs. "I need to watch my calorie intake." She looks at me. "I'm getting married in the spring." Diamonds flash in my face.

The spring? And she's already started her dieting? I have less than two months to go, and I'm just now thinking about fitting into my dress.

Sheesh. You'd think she'd at least let herself enjoy the Christmas season. "Congratulations," I say.

"Thanks!" The other girl is looking rather sadly at her, and I remember when Jen got engaged and how excited I was for her and how sad I was that everything was going to be changing.

As you might be able to tell, I don't handle change well.

Like at all.

I make the girls' apple ciders and then help the impatient businessman. "What can I get for you, sir?"

"An americano." He slaps a credit card on the counter and pulls out his cell phone. "Two shots please," he says as he dials. "I have a long day of meetings ahead."

I swipe his card and make the drink, glad that Jack isn't a corporate mogul like this guy. Jack loves what he does, but he's not all about the money.

I hand the man his americano, and he leaves, barking orders to someone on the phone. "Run fifteen copies of the Klein report and thirty of the Waters report."

Ethan comes out then, retying his apron and yawning. "All right," he says through the yawn. "Four hours to go."

I smile at him. "Got a hot date tonight?" I ask, parroting his question from yesterday.

He ignores me.

"Oh wait, that's right," I say, snapping my fingers. "Your date works evenings. Guess there's no date tonight."

He rolls his eyes. "I don't know what you're talking about."

"Oh please. At least admit it. The worst kind of man is someone who won't come out and say when he's smitten."

"Smitten?" Ethan repeats the word, wrinkling his nose. "Who uses a word like *smitten* anymore? You've been watching too many of those English BBC drama things." Then he grins at me and snaps a dish towel at my leg. "Glad to have you back, Davis."

"Ow."

"Please. I barely grazed you."

"So are you guys going to come to Wednesday-night Bible study again?" I ask, rubbing my shin where Ethan got me.

He shrugs noncommittally. "I don't know."

"Because I'll save you seats. You know, if you want to come again."

"You always sit in the very back where no one else wants to sit. Why would you need to save seats?"

"Someday people might wake up and realize that Andrew tends to spit when he's getting excited about what he's preaching on," I say.

"That's gross," Ethan says.

"It happens. Clergy and all that."

He grins. "Back row it is then."

I get home that night and slump on the couch. Calvin hops up next to me, and I rub his silky ears. "Hi, buddy."

He licks my hand.

"Can I ask you something?"

He just looks at me with his big, soulful brown eyes. Beagles have to have the saddest eyes of any dog.

"Why is it that when I come home with Italian food you get

all excited, but when it's me empty-handed you just look at me?"

He sighs and nestles his head on my lap so I'll feel obligated to pet his ears some more. I rub his head for a minute and then push him off so I can go grab my Bible.

It's sitting on my nightstand next to my pad of sticky notes. I carry both back to the couch and grab a pen off the coffee table.

I pull a sticky note off and write on it. *Pros.* I stick that one on the left side of the coffee table.

I write on another one. *Cons.* That one I stick on the right side.

Then I open my Bible and check my concordance. Maybe if I looked up *moving*?

Luke 10:7 is listed, and I flip there: "Do not keep moving from house to house."

I believe I will take that as a con. I write the reference down and put it on the right side of the table.

There aren't very many more results for moving, and all of the rest of them refer to animals and such. So, I flip over to *move* and skim down the list of the Israelites having to move everywhere and find 1 Chronicles 17:9.

"I will appoint a place for My people Israel, and will plant them, so that they may dwell in their own place and not be moved again."

Sounds like another con to me.

There's Psalm 30:6: "Now as for me, I said in my prosperity, 'I will never be moved.'"

Yet another con.

By the time it's nearing seven o'clock, I have about fifteen cons and no pros. And I've looked up *moving, move, leave,* and *cast out.*

I look at the sticky notes in front of me, and I'm not sure

that I could get a better answer from God. Obviously, we are not supposed to go to Seattle.

I set my Bible down and reach for a wedding magazine and the remote. See? Everything is going to be okay. We aren't supposed to move; we are supposed to stay here in Hudson as was always my plan.

Jack could always become a director at the Hudson Zoo. It's not like they'll never need directors here. And with my raise, we'll be fine financially for a while.

The raise that I have yet to tell Jack about.

I pick up the phone to call him and then set it back down. No, tonight is going to be a "me" night. Just me, my wedding magazine, and *Say Yes to the Dress,* which is playing out in front of me on TLC.

I watch snobby brides slap upward of half a year's salary down on a dress they'll wear for six hours at the most and just sigh.

So what if I want to stay in Hudson? At least I'm not all mean and condescending like those girls are. Jack should be happy that he's marrying a lowly coffeehouse worker and not the daughter of some Italian mobster.

It's Wednesday night and I haven't talked to Jack since Monday night before he left my apartment. I have a feeling he's giving me space to think, and I've been taking that space. I have plans to work more on my Pros and Cons list tonight after Bible study, but now with twenty cons I'm not really seeing the point.

I pull into the Cool Beans parking lot and find a spot near the front. Ethan apparently never left after work today because he's still in the same jeans and black polo shirt he was wearing earlier—and the first thing that any of us do when we get home is take a shower and change out of the gross-smelling clothes.

I'm wearing nice jeans and a button-down, western-style shirt with a blue cami underneath it. I look like I need cowboy boots with this outfit, but I'm wearing Crocs, entirely unstylish but incredibly comfy.

I love those shoes. I have this theory that the uglier the shoe, the more comfortable it is. Think about it. Crocs, UGGs, those black arthritic-looking shoes that you have to wear for restaurant jobs. All very comfortable and yet frightfully ugly.

I would be one of those people who Stacy and Clinton would surprise, and I'd say, "I watch your show all the time!" I used to wonder how there could be people in the world who actually watch *What Not to Wear* yet end up on the show, but now I know. It's all UGGs' fault. They created a very expensive, very cushy, very unfashionable shoe, and now women all over the country are going to have Stacy and Clinton show up on their doorsteps to go throw the boots out.

But, hey, I'd take the shopping spree in New York over my Crocs any day.

Andrew is setting up chairs, and Lisa and Peter are preparing for the onslaught of people who will be arriving. Ethan sits on one of the stools at the counter talking while Lisa races around. The only other person from Bible study who is here is Liz, and she's sitting at one of the corner tables, drinking an iced coffee and reading.

I walk over to Andrew, who is muscling a couch into place. "Hey."

"Hi, Maya," he says, grunting. He gets the couch how he wants it and straightens up. "How's it going?"

"Mmm," I say, avoiding a real answer. That would involve

telling him about Seattle, and I want to wait until afterward to talk to him. "How are you?"

"Great. I've got a killer lesson tonight."

"Uh-huh. How come you aren't talking to Liz?"

He glances over at her. "She's reading."

"And?"

"And my mother taught me from a very young age that people who are reading should not be bothered."

I try to nonchalantly read the cover of her book, but she is all the way across the room, and apparently I should have taken my mother up on that trip to the eye doctor a few months back. I squint at her book, but the title is written in very small letters.

Aren't titles supposed to be written in huge bold letters? Maybe it's a sad little book so the publisher thought it needed a sad little title.

"What are you doing?" Andrew asks.

"Trying to see what she's reading," I say, craning my neck further.

"*Jane Erye*. And you shouldn't bend your neck like that. There was a guy on my hockey team who tore some muscle in his neck by twisting it the wrong way."

I frown at him. "You can't do that."

"Do what?" he grunts, lifting a huge upholstered chair and setting it down a few feet away.

"Tear a muscle by twisting your head the wrong way."

"You can when there's another guy slamming you into the wall," Andrew says.

"Well," I say, spreading my hands and looking around, "I don't believe that is happening here, so there was no need to mention it, Mr. Changing the Subject."

"I'm not changing the subject."

"Sure you are. You're trying to avoid talking about why you won't man up and go talk to Liz."

Andrew frowns at me. "Surely, surely, there is some rule somewhere about not telling your pastor to man up."

I grin at him.

He sighs. "Look, I'll talk to her, okay?"

"Yay!"

"Not now," he says quickly, quelling my excitement. "But soon. Sheesh. Asking her out can't be nearly as painful as you bugging me about it all the time."

"We can hope not," I say. I pat his shoulder. "Sorry about the 'man up' comment."

He tries to frown at me again, but a smile sneaks across his face. "Go on," he says, pushing me away. "Find someone else to drive insane."

I smile at him and walk away. There are a few more people here now, and Ethan is still leaning against the counter, chatting away, while Lisa is starting on the boatload of drinks she'll be making.

"Mm-hmm, mm-hmm, mm-hmm," she hums to him as she passes back and forth in front of him. She mans the espresso machine while Peter takes orders. The line is getting longer, and I go lean on the counter next to Ethan.

"So, anyway, I'm thinking my brother isn't going to be getting a psych degree after that little ordeal," Ethan says.

"To what degree?" I ask.

"What?" Ethan says, looking at me.

"Your brother is a psycho to what degree?"

Lisa snorts in the middle of making a cinnamon latte.

Ethan rolls his eyes at me. "He's not getting a psych degree. Gosh, Maya, get a hearing aid or something."

"It's not my fault. You mumble."

"I do not," Ethan protests.

"Yeah, you do. Doesn't he, Lisa?" I look to our pretty co-worker, who is trying painfully hard to focus on the lattes. A blush is rosying up her pale cheeks.

"Uh," she says and then sidesteps the question. "Peter, is this a cinnamon breve or a cinnamon brulee latte?"

Peter squints at his writing on the cup. "Um. Brulee."

"Okay."

Ethan watches Lisa quietly for another minute and then starts a new story. "So, I was on my way to the gym the other day when . . ."

I zone out right about there. I start thinking about Ben again. What if we move and I only get to see him every few months instead of every week? Will he even remember his Auntie Maya?

And what if he has any more complications? I read online that premature babies have a higher risk of childhood health problems. What if he's one of those babies and I'm too far away to help?

I feel a hand on my shoulder blade, and I start.

"Hey," Jack says, smiling one of those *I understand* smiles. "You didn't answer the first couple of times I said hi."

"Sorry." I rub my head and return to that carefree "I'm not going to think about it" mood. "How was your day?"

He nods. "Good. Uneventful. Yours?"

"Good. Pretty uneventful."

Ethan rolls his eyes at me and clears his throat.

"Oh!" I say to Jack. "I forgot to tell you. I got a promotion."

He's genuinely excited for me, which is good. I wasn't sure if he'd see it as a threat to Seattle or not. "Wow!" he says, giving me a hug. "That's awesome, Nutkin!"

"Yeah." I hug him back. "I'm a manager now, and I'm getting a raise."

"Nice!" He rubs my shoulder. "I'm proud of you, Maya."

I immediately feel guilt-stricken. So he can be all supportive and loving even when this promotion conflicts with his plans and dreams, and I can't even finish eating dinner, much less say congratulations.

My mouth feels dried out, like I ate too many of those sour candies. "Thanks," I say quietly.

"Want to find a seat? Or are you waiting for a coffee?"

I nod toward the chairs. "Seat."

I follow him to a few empty chairs and just sigh.

What does God want from me?

CHAPTER SEVENTEEN

We have exactly four weeks and one day until the wedding. It's Friday, October third, and I'm just getting home from my shift at Cool Beans. I've got an hour and fifteen minutes to kill before our premarital counseling with Andrew.

Who, by the way, neglected to tell us that there was homework involved.

I did mine last night. We had to write the answer to the question: What do you think marriage looks like?

I wanted to write cohabitation, but I figured that would get me in premarital-counseling trouble, and you don't mess with the man who is going to be talking at your wedding.

So, I wrote something nice and sweet about it being a relationship between a man and a woman and how I thought it involved cooking dinners together, cleaning house together, doing laundry together, and getting a kiss before leaving for work.

I expect praise for listing chores.

I sit down on the couch and rub Calvin's ears. Mom and I addressed two hundred invitations last weekend, and I mailed them on Monday. We've already gotten one response back.

It was a regrets from an uncle and aunt who I didn't even know I had, so I'm not too disappointed. Two less mouths to feed. And, yes, I realize I sound like the evil warden in an orphanage.

I look over at my coffee table, and the stack of cons is huge. It's edging into the space for pros, and I think God has successfully pointed out His answer. I've looked up every synonym for move I can find.

And I didn't find one pro.

Other than a few random comments, Jack hasn't brought up the subject in the last couple of weeks, and I'm sure not going to. Maybe if we don't talk about it, we won't have to deal with it.

I glance at the clock. I need to hop in the shower before meeting with Jack and Andrew. After I shower and change into clean clothes, I rub some curling gel into my hair and decide it can do what it wills. It's not cold enough yet in Hudson to worry about catching a cold if I go out with wet hair.

And didn't someone prove that was an old wives' tale anyway?

Andrew decided that we would meet at Cool Beans' sister location, Hold the Mayo café. Alisha owns both stores, and she spends most of her time at the café.

Andrew loves their pastrami sandwich. It's almost fascinating to watch him eat it. Sort of like how, no matter how hard you try, you can't pull your eyes away from roadkill.

Now anytime I smell pastrami, I think of counseling. I'm not sure if this is a healthy Pavlovian response or not.

I drive to Hold the Mayo since I'm meeting the guys there as soon as Jack gets off work. Which means I get to experience the smell of pastrami and a mix of hay, sweat, and dirt.

Among other scents that I won't mention. Hazards of working in a zoo, I guess.

At least I smell nice. And I always get the half-salad, half-sandwich combo, so I feel like I'm eating something healthy.

Andrew is there when I walk in, but Jack isn't around. I've got my Bible and the essay I had to write in one hand, and I slide my sunglasses off with the other.

"Hey," he says, staring at the menu.

"Hi."

He glances over at me and sees my wet hair. "You are going to catch a cold."

"It's seventy-three degrees outside and sunny. I passed people sunbathing."

He looks over at me. "In their front yard?"

"Yep."

"Taking lessons from Bathsheba," Andrew tsks. "Maybe you should carry copies of 2 Samuel with you to hand out to the crowds."

"And include a bookmark about skin cancer?"

He grins at me and then looks back at the menu. Which is pointless, because we both know what he's getting.

Alisha is in the back, and she waves to me. I wave back.

Hold the Mayo is set up a lot like Cool Beans, only bigger. The seating is in a split-level arrangement: There are a few tables on the upper level with the front counter, and then the majority of the tables are a few steps down by the fireplace. There's a big back area for food prep and a huge front counter where people can sit and eat while watching sandwiches get created. They also serve Cool Beans coffee, which is why a lot of people I've worked with in the past have somehow ended up here.

Jack walks in two minutes late. "Sorry," he says, taking off his sunglasses and rubbing his eyes. "Long day."

He looks clean, which is more than I can usually say for him.

And he's not wearing his zoo uniform.

"Have a chance to shower?" I ask while he leans over and kisses my cheek.

"Yeah." He raises his eyebrows at me. "You wanted me to shower. I don't even want to tell you what happened while we're at a food establishment."

My stomach turns just thinking about what it could be. "I think I'm okay not knowing," I say.

Andrew looks curiously at Jack. "You can tell me later then, bro. Pick a sandwich."

Jack squints at the menu. "I'm ready whenever you guys are."

Andrew orders his pastrami on rye with three extra slices of swiss. I order half a turkey sandwich on whole wheat and a house salad. Jack gets a meatball sub.

Yuck.

We sit by the fireplace with our number, and Andrew looks at us. "So," he says, grinning all pastorally, "how did the challenge go?"

He has this thing about not calling homework what it is. Instead, he calls it "challenges." I think he should call a spade a spade.

Lyle, one of the guys Jack and I worked with at Cool Beans once upon a time ago, comes over with our food. "Here you go, guys," he says, setting the tray in front of us. "Enjoy. Good seeing you again."

This is our third Friday-night dinner at Hold the Mayo, so I guess they are getting used to us coming.

"Before you answer, let's pray." Andrew ducks his head. "God, bless the food and may the pastrami sit better this time. And be with these two as they are planning to spend the rest of forever with each other. Amen."

"Some things should not be mentioned in prayers," I tell Andrew, sliding a napkin on my lap.

"God knows all. And it's rude to critique prayers." Andrew muscles a huge bite of his pastrami sandwich into his mouth.

Jack is balancing the meatballs on his sandwich, and I dig into my salad.

"So," Andrew says, swallowing. "The challenge. Maya, you go first."

I finish chewing my bite of crunchy lettuce and pull my folded paper out of my Bible. I clear my throat. "Marriage is a relationship between a man and a woman. There is the sharing of chores, like vacuuming, dishes, and laundry. And there's usually some sharing of making the income, especially in the first couple of years. Mostly, I think it's all about loving each other completely."

Andrew wipes his mouth with a napkin. "Now, when you mention loving each other, what does that look like to you?"

"What does love look like?" I repeat.

"Yeah."

How do you explain what love is? I search for the right words. "Uh, well, it's sort of like caring, but a lot more, and you can't, um, imagine living without that person. Is that right?"

Andrew squints at me. "Let's see what Jack wrote," he says, not answering my question.

Jack finishes swallowing half of a meatball and digs a crumpled piece of notebook paper out of his pocket. "I think marriage will be hard," he starts.

I look over at him. Trust Jack to skip the warm and fuzzy parts of marriage.

"I think it will be hard, but I think it will be the best thing that has ever happened to me. I love Maya, and not just for her good qualities—and there are a lot of them—but also for her faults." He winks at me. "And there are a lot of them, too."

Andrew grins.

"I'm excited for this marriage because it means I get to spend the rest of my life with my best friend. And no matter where God takes us, I will always try my best to put Maya's interests ahead of my own."

Andrew nods. "Good answers. Both of you. Maya saw more of the practical side, and, Jack, you saw more of the under-the-surface stuff."

I'm still looking at Jack and thinking about what he said. *I will try my best to put Maya's interests ahead of my own.*

How did I end up with such a sweet guy? I'm filled to over-flowing as I watch his profile as he talks to Andrew. God has been very good to me.

We finish our meeting about seven thirty, and Jack asks if I want to watch a movie. "Let's get that new Adam Sandler movie," he suggests.

After a quick stop at Blockbuster, I drive back to my apart-ment, and Jack follows me. I'm thinking about what Andrew said in closing: "Just remember that the best example of love is always found in Jesus Christ. He said that there is no greater love than someone who lays down his life for a friend. And that, Jack and Maya, is what marriage is all about."

For someone who isn't married, Andrew sure has a lot of wisdom about it. And while I'm super excited to get married to Jack, I have to confess I'm also a little scared.

What if we get married and he discovers that I'm not as cute in the mornings as I am once I've showered and put on some makeup? Or what if my lack of any culinary talent, despite years of watching the Food Network, ends up bugging the daylights out of him after a couple weeks of my Bertolli and instant mac 'n' cheese meals?

Not to mention my worries about the whole "sleeping next to someone" thing. What if I kick? Or talk in my sleep? Or snore? I've never slept in the same room with anyone except Calvin, and he's not too communicative about my sleeping habits.

I pull into my parking space and wait for Jack before I start climbing the stairs.

"Jack?" I say as he walks over, tucking his keys into his pocket.

"Yes, Nutkin?"

"Do you snore?" I keep climbing the metal staircase. He is laughing behind me, and I turn to look at him. "What?" I ask.

"You just have no lead-ins to anything," he says, grinning. "And to be honest, I don't know. I've never shared a room with anyone before."

I unlock my door. So neither of us knows what we're walking into. Somehow, this makes me feel a little better.

"I might kick," I tell him as we go inside.

"Now?" he asks.

"Later. After we're married. When we're sleeping."

He's grinning. "I know later, Nutkin. I was giving you a hard time." He knuckles my head, which kind of hurts. "Well, so you kick. I'll wear protective gear to bed. We'll be fine."

"What if I talk in my sleep?" I ask, sitting on the couch.

"Then I'll answer back." He sits next to me and looks at the coffee table. "What's all this?"

I look over. Crap. I left the Pros and Cons sticky notes there. I totally forgot they were still out when we decided to watch the movie over here.

"Oh. Nothing," I say quickly, ripping the sticky notes off the coffee table.

Jack swipes one of them. "Genesis 44:22," he reads, looking up at me. "Are these for a Bible study or something?"

"Sure," I say, yanking that one from his hand and gathering the rest in a pile. "I'll just stick them in the bedroom so they are out of the way."

Jack pulls his cell phone from his pocket and uses one of those dumb application thingies so he can look up the verse. I hate all these high-tech phones. Whatever happened to just calling someone on your phone? Now it needs to have Internet access, a camera, and a way to instantly order Starbucks delivered to your door.

"But we said to my lord, 'The lad cannot leave his father, for if he should leave his father, his father would die,'" Jack reads off his phone as I'm halfway to my bedroom door. "What in the world, Nutkin? What kind of Bible study is this?"

I'm feeling the need for confession.

I sigh and turn around to face him. "It's about your job in Seattle," I say so quietly that he has to angle his head in my direction in order to hear. Who would have thought I'd be the first one to bring it up again?

"The job in Seattle is going to make a kid's father die?" Jack says, confused.

"No, that is one of the verses I found about leaving." Now it seems silly to have looked all this up.

I frown. It's not silly. It's a very obvious sign from God. I look back up at Jack.

He's just sitting there, frowning slightly. "Wait, so tell me what you were doing," he says.

I sit down next to him, sticky notes covering my lap. "I looked up a bunch of words that had to do with moving in my concordance. You know, to see what God would want us to do about the job."

"Words like . . . ?" Jack prods.

"Like *moving*," I stutter. "*Move, moving, leave* . . ." I let my voice trail off.

Jack just nods. "Get any pros?" he asks after a minute or two of silence.

I shake my head. "No, but I did get thirty-two cons," I say. I definitely think this is enough to convince Jack that we need to stay in Hudson.

"Thirty-two, huh?" he says softly. He reaches for the stack. "Can I take them home and look at them?"

I look at my stack of sticky notes and finally nod. "Okay."

"Okay." He pulls them off my lap and sets them on the armrest beside him. "I'm glad that you're at least thinking about it."

I just nod.

Jack just smiles a flat smile and then reaches over for my hand. "Ready for the movie?"

"You're not a bad fiancée," Jen says at Panda Express on Monday. Cool Beans was as dead as a plastic dinosaur, so Ethan told me, "For goodness' sake, go cheer up someplace and come back when you're happy."

So, I called Jen, and she took an early lunch. I'm poking at my orange chicken and fried rice.

I should have gotten the chow mein. It looked better. The rice today is a little on the dry side. I coat it with more mandarin sauce.

Jen looks stunning and professional in a knee-length pencil skirt and a powder blue, silky long-sleeve top.

"I am too a bad fiancée. I'm not supportive, I'm not excited about his promotion, I'm scared about the wedding and all that goes along with that day . . ." I stab a piece of orange chicken and break my plastic fork.

Jen just looks at me while she chews. "See? You shouldn't take your frustration out on the chicken." She stands and gets another fork from the hair-netted man behind the cash register.

He looks so manly. Not.

She sits back down and hands the fork across the table to me. Then she takes a deep breath. "One at a time. You do need to be more supportive."

I nod pathetically. "I know."

"Because he is going to be the primary breadwinner, and you need to understand that guys appreciate their women affirming their jobs." She's waving her fork at me while she talks.

"Breadwinner?"

"Yeah. Income earner."

I'm trying to decide if I'd rather Jack got paid in bread loaves instead of paychecks. Wouldn't that be the best job ever?

I chew another piece of chicken, careful of the fragileness of my plastic fork, and think about that a little longer.

Nah. Not only would Jack and I weigh nine hundred pounds, but I don't think my landlord would take a loaf of honey wheat bread in exchange for rent.

Jen twirls a string of chow mein on her fork; she was smart and noticed that the chow mein looked fresher than the rice. "And, second, I can understand why you aren't excited about the promotion because I'm not excited about the promotion. But you should at least be excited for Jack."

"So fake it?" I say, shocked. "You want me to lie to him?"

"Yes, Maya, I want you to lie." She rolls her eyes. "No. I mean you can tell him you aren't thrilled about the idea of moving, but you're excited he's doing well enough at work that he's getting promotions."

I scoop a forkful of mandarin-drenched rice and think about that. "I guess that's a good point," I say.

"And about the wedding day," she says and then sighs. "It will all come together perfectly." She smiles at me. "Try not to worry about the details. And about the rest of the wedding day . . ." She reaches over and squeezes my hand. "It will be fine. I promise. Just be yourself."

Whatever that means. I smile at her though. "Thanks for the pep talk, Jen."

"You're welcome. So stop panicking. Jack is an amazing guy, and there are millions of girls out there who wish they could find someone like him." She gives me a sad smile. "You just have to hang on to him, okay?"

I'm curious about the sadness in her expression, but I don't ask. "Okay."

"Good. We need to finish up; I told Wayne I'd be back by twelve thirty." She glances at her watch and then finishes up the last few bites of her chow mein.

We leave at twelve fifteen, and I drive back to Cool Beans. It's just depressing when my car and Ethan's car are the only ones in the parking lot.

I walk in, and Ethan has tuned the radio to the local sports network. Some guy with a nasally voice is shouting numbers over the speakers. "The thirty, the forty, the fifty . . . !"

"Ethan?" I have to yell it because he's not behind the counter.

He appears from the back and holds up a finger, listening to Nasal Man.

"The twenty, the ten . . . touchdown!" the man yells.

Ethan is grinning. "Yeah, baby!" He does one of those dorky

double-fist pumps and then looks at me. "How was lunch, Maya?"

"I don't think you're allowed to change the station," I say loudly over the roar of the crowd.

Ethan sighs, reaches under the counter, and flips the receiver back to the preprogrammed satellite radio station. Alisha built her own song list of fifties and jazz songs.

Elvis is in the middle of crooning "Love Me Tender," and I smile. "Thank you, Ethan. And lunch was great. Go get yours. I can handle the crowd."

Ethan grins. "This is the weirdest place I've ever worked at. There is no telling what the day will be like when you get up."

I nod. "We did more business in the last month than all of last year combined, but today is making our record look bad."

"Maybe the economy caught up to all of our clients," Ethan suggests, taking his apron off. "I won't be long. I'm just going to run and get a hot dog."

I frown at him. "A hot dog? You have your choice of restaurants for lunch, and you choose to go get a hot dog?"

"Football games inspire me." He grins and leaves.

The place is deadly quiet except for Elvis, and I go put my purse in the back room and grab my apron. I come back out hoping to see another car out front, but there's only mine.

I lean against the counter and stare at the nearly full pan of cinnamon rolls. Our weekly Bible study group of retired men didn't even come in this morning.

I bite my lip. I hope that doesn't mean something bad happened. The only other time they canceled Bible study was when one of their wives had a mastectomy. She's now cancer free, but I get worried anytime they aren't here.

We have Internet on the front register, so I log on. I go to

Google and type in *Seattle*.

A bunch of pictures pop up and so does the city of Seattle's website. I click through some of the pictures, most of which are of the famous Space Needle. Which, if you ask me, looks more like a UFO than a Space Needle.

Whatever a space needle is.

There are also pictures of snow-capped mountains, which look just like a postcard. I stare out the windows of Cool Beans and wonder what it would be like to live that close to mountains.

There are lots of mountains in California, but they are a couple-hours drive from Hudson. Hudson is in the hot, flat part of California.

I do a search on Seattle weather, and apparently, they experience all four seasons.

"I'd like a large mocha," someone says right near my face, and I jump, squealing.

"Oh!" I shout.

It's Ethan, and he's laughing. "You are way too jumpy," he grins. "What were you doing? Spying on someone?" He squints at the computer while I gasp for breath. "Seattle, huh? Reconsidering?"

I shrug and close out of the Internet window. "I'm just looking. And, good grief, did you inhale the hot dogs without chewing?"

"I had four of them. And I've been gone for like thirty minutes."

No way. I look up at the clock, and, yes, it's already almost one.

Sheesh. My life is passing before my very eyes.

"Sorry for making you jump."

"Sorry for yelling."

Ethan goes to the back to get his apron and comes back out right as a customer walks in.

It's a lady, and she's carrying the most adorable baby girl I've ever seen in my life. She has the sweetest round cheeks, wispy brown hair, and huge blue eyes.

I can barely pull my gaze away from the baby to look at the mom. She also has blue eyes and brown hair, and she's squinting at the menu. "Can I get a small caramel macchiato, please?"

"Of course," I say, ringing her up while Ethan goes to make the drink. "She is beautiful," I tell her. "How old is she?"

"Eight months," the mom says proudly. "And thank you."

Another lady with another baby walks in then, and in ten minutes, we have six women and eight babies all gathered around the couches and love seats.

There's finally a happy chatter in Cool Beans today, and I'm so glad to hear it. Ethan raises his eyebrows at me as more people come in, and I nod.

"Finally," I say.

He grins.

For the rest of our shift, the traffic is pretty steady.

Lisa walks in and waves to a blushing Ethan.

"Hey, Lisa," I say, trying to hide my smirk.

"Hi, Maya. Hi, Ethan. Good to see that it's business as usual." She goes to the back to deposit her purse and get her apron. Peter walks in the door a minute later.

"I'm out of here," I say to Ethan. "Don't forget to clock out before you talk the rest of the evening away," I say, winking.

"Ha-ha," Ethan says dryly. But he smiles because he knows I'm right.

I grab my purse and head out the door. There's a text message on my phone that I check as I slide into my car.

It's from Jack, and he'd sent it a few hours ago. *Hey, Nutkin, can we go get dinner tonight? I feel like we haven't had a non-premarital-counseling date in a long time. And we still need to finalize honeymoon plans. Love you.*

I text him back. *Sounds good! Let me know when you get off. Love you back.*

I drive home, and Calvin is waiting for me when I walk in the door.

"Roo!" he yodels. "Roo! Roo!"

"What?" I ask, rubbing his ears. I haven't gotten a greeting like this in a long time.

He runs circles around my legs, and I rub any part of his back that is in front of me. Poor dog. He's drawn the short end of the stick lately.

If you can call sleeping twenty hours a day, getting petted every night, getting fed anytime he's hungry, and being given lots of chew toys the short end of the stick.

I pat his head once more and head for the shower. A non-premarital-counseling date. That is a cause to wear something besides jeans, I think. I get out of the shower, wrap the towel around my head, and stand in front of my closet in my robe.

If Jen were here, she'd make me wear a skirt. Because, to quote her, "If the guy is buying, a skirt or dress is the only appropriate thing to wear."

Unfortunately for Jack, I'm not really a skirt or dress kind of girl. Give me a pair of good jeans, and I'm a happy camper. But tonight is going to be special, and I have a feeling it might be our last real date before we get married, so I'm going to dress up a little bit.

I find a black wrap dress with three-quarter-length sleeves that I bought on clearance last year for like $10 in the very back of my closet. It's one of those great pieces that can be either dressed up or dressed down depending on what else you wear with it.

So, I dig out a pair of black heels that I've worn once since I bought them and put on a necklace that my dad gave me my sophomore year of high school.

I call my mom while I'm putting on my makeup and turn on the speakerphone. I've called her every day for the last two weeks to get updates on Ben.

He's still in the NICU, but he's decreasing the amount of oxygen that he needs. We had a slight scare a week or so ago, and they had to increase it again, but he's back down to where he was.

Mom answers on the third ring. "Maya, do you remember your second-grade substitute teacher?"

No hi or hello today. I frown at the mirror.

"Hello, Mother. And what?"

"Hi. Your second-grade substitute teacher? Mrs. Grayson?"

I'm squinting as I put on concealer, but not even the slightest memory of a Mrs. Grayson is coming to my mind. "She was a substitute? For how long?"

"I don't know. A week or so, I guess. Remember? Mr. Miller had bronchitis, so she came in and subbed for him?"

I remember Mr. Miller. He had a moustache that looked like it wished it was a handlebar one. But I'm not even getting a blip as far as Mrs. Grayson is concerned. "Nope. Sorry. Why?"

"Her grandson is in the NICU beside Ben."

"Weird!" I say. I'm feeling the need to burst into a rendition of "It's a Small World After All," but no one really likes that song being sung to them. Probably because it's the gift that keeps on giving since it's stuck in your head for the next week after that.

"Very weird. Anyway, we caught up a little bit."

"Good. How's Ben doing?"

"He's down to 5 percent oxygen. Hopefully they are going to take him off it tomorrow. And Kate's been able to breast-feed him, so he's not on a feeding tube anymore." Mom's voice is filled with gratitude. "I think they'll get to take him home by this weekend."

It's a month later than they were originally hoping for, but they will be taking home a healthy baby, and I don't think anyone is complaining.

I swipe on some eye shadow. "That's so great! We should have a 'welcome home' party for Ben this weekend."

"That would be fun!" Mom's going into party-planner mode, and I can almost see her scrounging for her notepad. "We can have cake and a banner and that cherry limeade punch and—"

I interrupt her. "It will probably be just the family though, don't you think?"

"Oh sure, definitely just the family. Kate probably won't take him out in public for at least three months."

"Then I don't really see a reason to have punch. I mean, we could just have Cokes and stuff."

Mom's voice gets very, very serious. "Maya, there is always a good reason to have cherry limeade punch."

Someone is having a craving. I just nod and then remember Mom's on the speakerphone. "Yes, ma'am."

"Thank you."

My hair is starting to dry in tangled, matted curls, so I need to end this call and address that problem with the help of my blow-dryer.

"I'm going on a date with Jack tonight, Mom, so I need to go fix my hair issues. Just wanted to call and see how Ben was doing."

"Well, you have fun on your date," Mom says. "And don't worry about Ben. I'll call you when I hear more news."

"Okay. Bye."

I push the red button and spend the next twenty minutes trying to get my curls to look halfway decent. I was going for a Kate Hudson curly look when I grew my hair out, but not only is my hair about the color of mud, and hers is this soft, silky golden blond, it's also more on the frizzy side than the silky side.

I'm chopping my hair and going back to the short cut I had a year ago as soon as Andrew says, "I now pronounce you husband and wife." Leave it long for the wedding; chop it short for the marriage. Isn't that the normal trend?

Jack calls at six thirty as I'm sitting on the couch, fully ready to go. I'm watching some nice-looking Canadian guy remodel houses on HGTV. "Hi, Nutkin, are you hungry yet?"

I carefully slide a package of Oreos under the couch cushion so he can't hear the plastic wrapper crackling. "Yes, I am," I say truthfully. If I weren't, the Oreos would not have come out of their little spot in the corner cabinet.

"Great! Well, I'll be at your place in ten minutes. I just need to get dressed real quick."

Suddenly, I worry that Jack is thinking dinner out to In-N-Out or someplace along those casual lines.

You don't wear a black dress and heels to In-N-Out—I don't care how good their burgers are.

"Where are you thinking for dinner?" I ask as casually as I can.

"Does that little steak house on the boardwalk sound good to you? What's the name of it again? Maurey's?"

Oh good. That is black-dress appropriate. It's not too fancy, but it's not fast food. "Yeah, that sounds good," I say.

Hudson is not located near anything that would require a boardwalk, but for some reason, our mayor decided it would bring "old-fashioned charm and a whimsical spot for tourists" to our town.

It is a cute area, but something is definitely missing among all the sand and weathered-looking boards. Like an ocean.

"Okay. See you soon." Jack hangs up, and I unmute the TV.

The Canadian guy has made this couple's basement look like it belongs in a home decorating magazine. He's telling the couple all about how this place is fully ready for a tenant.

And he says *about* like this: aboot.

It's cute. Maybe I could learn to talk like a Canadian.

Jack shows up about fifteen minutes later. "Well, it's aboot time," I say, opening the door.

"What?"

Maybe I'll just stick with the American pronunciation. "You look nice," I say, changing the subject. He's wearing khakis and a green polo. His dark hair is gelled to perfection, and he's grinning at me.

"Not as nice as you look. Have I mentioned how much I love you in a dress?"

"You love me less in sweatpants?"

"Time to go."

I grab my purse and lock the door behind us. The night is not cold at all, so I'm not feeling the need for a jacket.

We get to the restaurant, and they seat us at a cute little table with a lit lantern on it. "Oh, I love lanterns!" I say. "I'm going to decorate our future house in lanterns. Okay?"

Jack shrugs and looks at the menu. "Fine by me. I'm getting the filet mignon."

This place has a steak and salad combo that is the perfect size for me. Not too big, not too little.

Our server comes by and takes our order, leaving us with a basket of hot buttery yeast rolls that smell so amazing. My mouth starts watering.

"So," Jack says.

I look up at him, because I know what he's going to talk about. He probably read through every single one of those sticky notes. I'm already hearing what he's going to say in my brain: *So, Maya, you were right; it does seem like God wants us to stay here in Hudson. I'm going to work hard at the Hudson Zoo and hopefully end up in management there someday.*

"About those sticky notes," he says.

I nod. "Yeah?"

"You obviously put a lot of thought into those," he says slowly, reaching for my hand across the table. "Thought and time."

I nod again.

"But I think you may have missed something," he says quietly.

I look at him, confused. I didn't miss anything—I got New Testament and Old, I found God's words and people's words, and I exhausted my thesaurus looking up synonyms for *moving.*

"What do you mean?" I ask, frowning.

He squeezes my hand, which means he's about to say something I won't necessarily like hearing. "Did you start from the point of not wanting to move when you looked up all those references?" He asks it gently, but I feel it deep in my chest.

I look away from his searching gaze.

"It's not that God doesn't speak to us when our minds are already made up," Jack says. "It's just that I've been doing my own study on whether or not we should go, and I've come up with a few different answers."

My stomach is feeling tight again, and I'm wondering why Jack always has to bring up this conversation at good restaurants. He couldn't do this when we were at Burger King, could he? No, he has to pick the nice ones: Olive Garden. Maurey's Steak House.

He's still holding my hand, and I'd like it back but he's not letting go.

"Maya, I really think we need to keep praying about this opportunity," he says. "I know it will be the hardest thing you've ever had to do, but I just can't escape the feeling that we are supposed to go there."

I can't even look at him. My eyes are starting to sting with tears again. Is this God's sign that maybe Jack isn't the one for me? Maybe I was so caught up in all the emotions of everything that I failed to notice we aren't on the same path here.

I slide my hand out of his clasp and set it in my lap.

I'm not even hungry for the delicious-smelling rolls anymore.

The server comes by with our salads. "Everything turning out okay?" he asks, obviously tuning in to the strained silence at the table.

"We're fine, thanks," Jack tells him, and he leaves.

I stare at my salad. It even has the little grape tomatoes and black olives that I like on my salads. Jack is digging into his with gusto.

"Why?" I suddenly burst.

Jack looks up at me. "What, honey?"

"Why? Why do you want to move? And leave our families

and our friends and our church and our jobs . . ." The list goes on, but I stop there.

"It would be a totally new adventure," Jack says. "Just me and you. It would be like an indefinite honeymoon. We'd get to go sightseeing every weekend and make new friends and find a new church."

"I don't need new friends," I say quietly.

He just smiles kindly at me. "Look, I told you that if you weren't 100 percent on board, then we wouldn't go. So if you're completely sure that this isn't what God's plan for us is, then we won't go. Okay? I won't submit my application."

I nod. There's a little nagging feeling in the back of my throat, and I'm either coming down with something or feeling guilty—or both.

I stab my fork into my salad and crunch on the lettuce. It doesn't taste like blue cheese dressing, but conversations about moving tend to mess with my taste buds.

We finish eating, and for the first time since I started ordering this meal here, I have to get a to-go box for the leftovers. The rest of our conversation feels forced and unnatural.

Jack takes me back to my apartment. "How about we watch *While You Were Sleeping* or something," he suggests.

I nod. A distraction sounds good. We climb the stairs, and I go to the bedroom to change into a pink long-sleeved T-shirt and gray sweatpants. You cannot watch *While You Were Sleeping* in a dress. It's not allowed.

Jack is rubbing Calvin's ears when I come back out, and Calvin is moaning in sheer doggy heaven.

"We still need to solidify honeymoon plans," Jack says when I join them on the couch.

I nod. We've narrowed it down to three choices: northern California, Colorado, or what's becoming my personal favorite—a beautiful, all-inclusive resort in Hawaii. The water is so clear there; it's like you can see all the way to the bottom of the ocean.

Even cold-weather-inclined Jack is liking it.

Still, after our dinner conversation, I almost feel weird discussing a honeymoon. What if we decide that our differences are just too much and we aren't going to get married?

I think Mom would cry after licking two hundred envelopes.

I take a deep breath and try to remember what Jen told me at lunch a few days ago. *Be supportive. Be supportive.*

I mean, surely this wouldn't be a reason to break off the engagement. I love Jack with everything in my heart. I just don't love Seattle the same way. And he's already said that we can stay here if I want to.

Another deep breath.

"I like Hawaii," I say.

Jack nods. "Actually, I'm liking that one more and more, too. I called the resort, and they said that the first week in November is one of the slowest times for them, so that's a plus. We might be some of the only people there."

"That would be nice." I smile.

He grins at me. "Very. I don't want to share you on our honeymoon."

"I don't think you need to worry about that," I say.

But I am worrying about other things. Like where we'll come back to after the honeymoon.

CHAPTER EIGHTEEN

Two weeks until W-Day.

And I still don't know what to do about Seattle. It's Sunday, and I'm driving to see my parents, Zach, Kate, and Ben.

At Zach and Kate's house.

Ben was finally able to go home on Friday, and I'm so incredibly glad. Mom said we were going to have our "welcome home" party today.

And she made the cherry limeade punch.

I get to Zach and Kate's around two-ish and knock lightly on the front door before trying the knob. Mom and Dad's car is already there, and the front door is unlocked.

"Hi!" I call into the house.

"We're in the family room," Mom calls back.

Everyone is gathered around Kate, who is sitting on one of the sofas holding little Ben. It looks like a scene from a movie, with the huge fireplace in the background and Mom, Dad, and Zach all crowded around.

Kate looks up at me. "Hi, Auntie Maya," she says, smiling. She looks so happy and so rested that I almost start to cry.

But I don't. I hold it in. And I reach my arms out for my nephew. "Can I hold him for a minute?"

Kate grins and holds up little Ben so I can take him. He's wearing the cutest little khaki overalls and a collared blue shirt underneath. And the tiniest little loafers.

I can't help but squeal. "Oh, he's such a little man now!"

"Yep," Zach says proudly. "Seven pounds, one ounce. That's my boy."

I hold Ben close and touch his soft baby hair. He has the sweetest little peach fuzz. This kid will be blond like his daddy.

"I love him," I declare to everyone.

"Where's Jack?" Dad asks.

"He had a zoo meeting or something today." I shrug my shoulders like it doesn't matter—but really, he couldn't have taken time off for his soon-to-be nephew's homecoming?

Jack apologized over and over about it last night, saying it was a mandatory meeting and everything. See, this is why I know it's not true what he says about sightseeing every weekend in Seattle. He'll have to go through the same ridiculous amount of training—if not more—that he had to do here, and it will be me, sitting there by myself in a city where I know no one for the first two months.

I've heard of things that sound less fun, but at the moment I can't think of them.

Nor do I want to. I look back down at Ben and trace his chubby baby cheeks with my finger. He is just perfect and a complete miracle.

"If you guys ever decide that you don't want to keep him, you just let me know," I say to Zach and Kate.

"We'll keep that in mind, but we probably won't take you up on it." Zach grins.

"Well, it was worth a shot." I grin at my nephew.

Mom has me help put together the barbecue sauce for the

ribs a few minutes later. "And I've got coleslaw, potato salad, creamed corn, and punch in the fridge," she says, leading the way into Zach and Kate's gourmet kitchen. We leave Zach, Kate, Dad, and Ben in the family room. Zach turned on a football game, and Kate is trying to nurse.

I gladly gave Ben up for that one. His mom can do that job much better than I can.

"Wow," I say, looking at all the food in the fridge. "You thought of everything."

"I even brought a fresh fruit salad," Mom says proudly. "And double-chocolate brownies for dessert."

"Yay!" I say, giving her a hug. "Thanks, Mom!"

She grins. "You are welcome. Now get out that container and the ribs, and let's go ahead and start basting them."

I work on the ribs silently for a few minutes. Mom is busy mixing together the coleslaw and double-checking her list.

"Hey, Mom?"

She looks at me over her bifocals. "Hey, Maya?"

"What are your thoughts on Seattle?" I still haven't mentioned the possible move to my mother.

She shrugs. "I don't know that I have that many, to be honest. Doesn't it rain like three hundred days out of the year there? And it's cold, right?" She shrugs again. "Sounds like good fireplace weather." She looks down at her list and then back up at me. "Why? Thinking about honeymooning there?"

"Jack might have a potential job there." I say it quietly.

Mom just looks at me and finally takes off her glasses. "Oh," she says softly.

"Yeah."

We're quiet for about five minutes. I finish up the ribs. Mom just stands there, looking at the countertop.

"Well," she says after forever, "it's still close to the Pacific."

"Just on the north side of it."

"Yes." She clears her throat and puts her bifocals back on. "I was wondering, honestly, how long you would stay in California."

I jerk my head up. "What? Why?"

She shrugs. "I don't know. I just knew."

I don't think that counts as a valid answer. "What do you mean, you just knew?"

She sighs and looks over her bifocals at me again. "I just always sort of knew that you guys would end up moving away." She starts to get teary now. "I hate it, but I've accepted it. God's been helping me accept it."

"Mom, we're not moving yet," I say.

She nods and blinks quickly, clearing the tears.

"I do not want to move."

"And Jack does," Mom finishes.

I nod miserably.

She's quiet again, and I wrap the ribs in aluminum foil. "Well, honey," she says, "I believe that Jack is the right one for you. And I believe that he's looking to God for his direction. So I have to trust that he'll do the right thing."

"You're saying that you think we should—"

She interrupts me, raising her hand. "I'm saying you should be open to it, honey. Don't be one of those people who tells God her plans."

Later that night, I'm sitting in my bed, propped up on pillows. I've pulled the covers up to my neck, and Calvin is sleeping on his doggy bed in the corner of my room.

The entire apartment is quiet.

I've been staring at my closet for the last two hours. I rub my eyes and look at the clock. It's one fifteen. I've got work in the morning.

And I still can't go to sleep.

My brain is going crazy.

God, have I been telling You my plans?

I look down at my hands and fiddle with my nails.

It's not like I've been a slacker about doing my devotions or praying or stuff like that. I've been reading every night, gathering that list of cons. And I've been praying every day for Jack's heart to change.

I swallow.

But never for *my* heart to change.

I close my eyes and lean my head back against the pillows.

Lord, I don't want to move to Seattle.

I think about everything that I would miss: Jen and Travis having babies. Andrew finally asking Liz out. Ben growing up. Zach and Kate having more kids. My parents retiring and spending more time with us. Summer. Sunshine.

And if we don't move?

I'll miss seeing Jack's face light up when he talks about work. I'll miss out on an adventure—scary or not.

I reach for my Bible on the nightstand and open it up to the book of Psalms. Psalm 121 catches my eye.

"I will lift up my eyes to the mountains; from where shall my help come? My help comes from the LORD, who made heaven and earth" (verses 1-2).

The mountains.

And the Lord.

I set my Bible back on the nightstand and turn off my lamp,

shutting my eyes. It's too much to think about in one night.

It's Monday afternoon at four thirty, and Alisha should be here in thirty minutes for my second-to-last manager training.

I love Alisha, but I'm glad the training is almost over. Half of it I already knew and already did anyway.

I haven't breathed a word about Seattle to Alisha. No sense in getting her all worried about hiring someone else when nothing is said and done for certain.

Ethan looks over at me. There's a slight lull in the crowd, but Cool Beans is pretty full. Lots of kids here studying today.

I love when we have study groups come. It reminds me that I'm not in school and don't have to study anymore. And then I get very happy.

"So," he says.

"So," I say, taking the lull as an opportunity to wipe down the counter in front of the espresso machine.

"Given Jack an answer yet?"

"Asked Lisa out yet?"

He just smiles at me. "Touché."

"Thank you." I swipe at my forehead where an annoying frizzy curl escaped from my ponytail.

"Wedding is almost here," Ethan says. "Did you get my RSVP?"

"How could I miss it?" I ask dryly. Instead of checking either of the two choices—Accepts with Pleasure and Declines with Regret—he drew another box, wrote Accepts with Regret next to it, and checked it.

"Why do you regret going to my wedding?" I ask, snapping the towel at his pant leg.

"I regret going to any wedding. I regretted my sister's; I regretted my cousin's. When I was four, I had to be the ring bearer in my uncle's wedding, and I really regretted that one." He rubs his forehead, wincing.

"What happened?"

"I had to borrow a tux from my older cousin, who was the ring bearer in my mom's wedding, but Bradley was six when he was ring bearer. So the tux was huge, and we had those little elastic suspenders to keep it up."

I can see where this is going, and now I'm joining him in a sympathetic wince.

"The clasp broke, my pants fell down halfway down the aisle, I tripped on them, and the rings went flying." He sighs. "It took us twenty minutes to find them both."

"Sorry. Well, hopefully you won't regret your own wedding."

"I'm not the marrying kind," Ethan says, shaking his head.

"You're the lonely miser kind?"

He rolls his eyes. "No, I just don't believe that a piece of paper dictating that I have to stay with that person is very romantic."

Just when I think he might be getting closer to becoming a Christian . . .

I hiss the steam out of the espresso wand, running the cleaning cycle on the machine.

"So you think it's more romantic to have no commitment?"

He nods. "Yeah. No commitments. I like that."

"Yeah. Prepare for a lonely, miserly life."

"Why?"

I rub a clean cloth over the machine. "Because. No girl in her right mind is going to go for a guy who has zero intentions for her. Every girl wants a gorgeous wedding; every girl wants the security of knowing that her guy will never leave her," I say.

Ethan shrugs. "Maybe Christian girls."

"All girls, Ethan."

"Whatever."

Alisha walks in then, sliding her sunglasses up into her hair. "Hey, guys. Maya, are you ready to start? Perry has a band concert thing tonight at six, so we'll have to make tonight's training a short one."

I finish the espresso machine and nod. "Ready when you are."

Lisa and Peter come in then, and Alisha nods. "Let's go ahead and start."

Tuesday, I get home from work at five fifteen, and there are four boxes stacked neatly by my apartment door. I grin. I picked up the mail on my way in, and there were about fifteen of those little RSVP cards in there.

I unlock the door, push Calvin out of the way, and slide the boxes into my living room. Some of them are heavy, and I don't remember registering for heavy things.

Registering was fun. Jack lasted for about two hours before he'd had his fun with the little scanner gun and was ready to go.

And I still had about six pages of things to register for.

So, Mom and I went back the next day and did the rest of it. She was more informative than Jack anyway. With Jack, I would hold up a cheese grater and ask if he thought it was nice, and he'd say, "Uh. I don't know. Sure, if you like it."

Mom actually had advice. "I don't know if I would get a handheld one, Maya. After grating a pound of cheese, your wrist is going to be killing you."

Jack calls as I'm poised with the knife over the first box.

"Hey, Nutkin. What are you doing?"

I squint at the box. "Um, nothing."

"Nothing?"

"Nope." I carefully slide the knife through the tape, trying to be as quiet as I can. Jack always thinks I'm going to cut off my finger and have to wear my wedding ring around my neck whenever I open boxes.

"Did we get any more RSVPs today?" he asks.

"Fifteen or so."

"Yays or nays?"

"I haven't opened them yet." I grimace as soon as the words leave my mouth.

"That's the first thing you do when you get the mail," Jack says. "Wait a second!"

"What?" I say, trying to sound all innocent.

"You are opening a package! Without me! And you're probably using a knife, which I already told you makes me nervous."

"Which is why I didn't tell you I was using one," I say, opening the first box. It's our sheet set, from my aunt and uncle.

"You could at least wait for me. You'll get to open all of the presents at the shower. I mean, I didn't get to pick stuff out, so you'd think the polite thing to do would be to let me open it."

"That was your fault," I say, pulling the sheets out and setting them on the growing pile of marriage stuff in the corner of my living room.

There is no way me, Jack, all this stuff, and our two dogs are going to fit in this little apartment. And we haven't even had our shower yet. Jen has it planned for Saturday early afternoon and then a lingerie shower with just the girls our age later that night.

I'm already trying to work on my keep-from-blushing face. It's not going well.

He laughs. "I guess so."

The second box has a speaker system in it with a dock for an iPod. It's from a sweet couple at our church, and it has a note attached to it: "We registered for this same speaker, and we love it!"

I did not register for a speaker system. Or a dock. Whatever that is.

"Jack?" I ask.

"Yes, Maya?"

"We just got a speaker system."

"Sweet, we got that? Awesome!" Jack says.

"You registered for it?"

"It looked cool."

"Do you even have an iPod?" I sure don't. I am about as electronically handicapped as you can be; a TV remote is the only thing I know how to work. Plus, I hear music all day long at Cool Beans, so when I'm home, I want quiet.

Quiet, or the soothing sounds of chefs cooking on the Food Network, Stacy and Clinton ragging on someone about her hideous wardrobe, or the Style Network telling me whose wedding it really is.

Jack just laughs.

I open the next box, and yes, Jack does have an iPod.

"I cannot believe you registered for this stuff!" I say.

"Did I get the iPod? Way cool!"

"We will never use this!"

"We might," Jack says. "We could use it to set a romantic mood when we're making dinner. Or we could use it on long car trips. Or I could wake up to Aerosmith in the shower."

Aerosmith. I do not, nor will I ever, want the first thing I hear in the morning to be "Walk This Way" or "Dude (Looks Like a Lady)."

Really, I can't think of a worse way to wake up in the morning. Jack is very odd.

I just sigh and add the speakers and the iPod to the stack. There's one more package, and it's an assortment of spatulas and spoons.

Since both Jack and I have been living on our own for so long, we really didn't need that much. I only registered for a few of the kitchen items that Jen took when she moved, new bath towels, and some new bedding, since I figured I could safely assume that Jack didn't want to sleep on gerber daisy sheets.

However, when you don't register for much, it looks like people just guess at what to buy you. So, we've gotten a lot of things that I don't foresee us using or even needing.

Example: A chip and dip plate that has little mice wearing ponchos and sombreros painted on it in bright, obnoxious colors like teal, lime green, and mustard yellow.

Not only am I not a fan of anything involving rodents, but rodents on a chip plate are even more disturbing.

"What are you up to tonight?" Jack asks.

"I have to do my premarital homework before Thursday. That's about it." We moved our last premarital counseling up a day. Mom is driving over Friday morning, I'm taking the day off, and we're finishing up all the details that still need to be taken care of. We're finalizing everything with the caterer, DJ, florist, and church and making sure that we have everything for decorations.

"Let's go get a hamburger and watch a movie or something. Something not wedding related."

I smile. "Sounds good."

Jack shows up thirty minutes later holding a paper sack dotted with grease stains and a copy of *Braveheart*. He's grinning.

"Hello, beautiful bride," he says, kissing me. "And how does this sound? Hamburgers and William Wallace." He says it with flourish and starts to go get plates.

I just look at him, hands on my hips. "I'm sorry, doesn't William Wallace get married in *Braveheart*?"

Jack pauses halfway to the kitchen. "Uh . . . yes."

"Guess we can't watch it then," I say, smiling cheekily. "But don't you worry. I found the perfect movie that doesn't even have the thought of a wedding in it." I pull the movie out of my stack of DVDs.

"*Hairspray*?" Jack reads the title dully. "Seriously, Nutkin?"

"Nothing to do with weddings in this one," I say, patting the DVD. "Just good old-fashioned fun, music, and an awesome soundtrack."

"Isn't it a musical?"

"I'm sorry?" I hedge the question.

"No. Sorry, Nutkin."

"It was worth a shot."

He looks at my DVD collection. "How about *Spider-Man*?"

The one superhero movie I have. And it's not even mine. I borrowed it from Zach two or three months ago, and I've forgotten to give it back.

Considering all the distractions Zach has had, though, I think I'm off the hook on this one.

"*National Treasure*?" I bargain.

"Mmm. Okay." Jack is starting to dig in the paper sack for french fries.

After suggesting it, however, I change my mind. "I mean, how about *Little Giants*?"

Is there really a better movie from the past than one of those infamous kids sports movies that all came out when I was around ten?

Jack agrees. "Sounds great. And I'm starving, so let's eat."

I push the DVD into the player, and we settle on the couch, surrounded by napkins to catch all the extra grease.

I'm thinking I'm not doing such a fabulous job being proactive about fitting into my wedding dress.

Jack got me a cheeseburger and my favorite fries. They are crunchy on the outside, soft on the inside, and have this amazing seasoning salt on them. So good!

The movie ends about nine o'clock, and Jack kisses me good-bye. "Have a good day tomorrow, love. Just think. A week and a half, and we'll be on our honeymoon."

I smile dreamily. "In Hawaii." I've already started buying sunscreen.

He grins. He hasn't brought up the Seattle thing this week, and since I'm teetering on the edge of a decision, I don't want to say anything until God and I have completely sorted this out.

He leaves with another kiss, and I pick up my Bible from the kitchen table. Instead of focusing solely on the words *move* and *leave*, I've been trying to also include *go* and *send*.

It reminds me of a song I learned in Sunday school when I was a little girl. "Children, go where I send thee. How shall I send thee?"

Is it sad that I can still remember all of the motions to that song? I guess our five-year-old Sunday school teacher loved that song.

It's amazing how many times in the Bible God sends someone somewhere.

I'm starting to see where God is going to have us end up, and I'm trying my hardest to be okay with it and to stop all this mindless worrying.

Thursday night and our last premarital meeting. I'm the first one to get to Hold the Mayo, and I'm standing in the entrance, staring at the menu.

I always get the half turkey sandwich and a half salad. Today I will be different.

It is our last meeting, after all.

I almost feel sad that we're done. It seems so final. There's still so much about marriage that I don't know, and we're basically being given a pound of bacon and thrown to the wolves.

The bacon only acts as a distraction for those wolves for so long.

Jack gets there a few minutes later and wraps me up in a hug. "Nine days," he whispers in my ear.

I grin.

Then again, I'm really glad this is our last meeting because it means we are finally, finally getting married.

Andrew comes in about five minutes late. He's basically growling as he looks at me, Jack, and then the menu. "Women drivers," he mutters.

I can't wait until Andrew marries Liz and they have all girls. That's always what happens to big, overgrown Vikings like Andrew. They marry a prissy woman, who then produces prissy girls.

It will be fun to watch.

"Ready then?" Andrew says and doesn't wait for our answer. He places his order with a new kid I haven't seen before. "I want the pastrami sandwich."

Surprise, surprise.

I branch out and order the club sandwich with a side of fresh fruit.

We sit at the table, and Andrew slaps his hands on it. "It is

Thursday and your last appointment, so be prepared for a go-forth-and-conquer message."

"What does Thursday have to do with it?" I ask.

"Because Thursdays are go-forth-and-conquer days. You still have to make it through one more day before the weekend, and while all of your willpower does not want you to get out of bed in the morning, you still have to."

The new kid brings all of our food over. Jack got a corned beef sandwich, which looks more like a tower than a sandwich.

"I'll pray," Andrew says. "God, bless the food. Bless Jack and Maya as they are about to get married, and, Lord, please keep Your hand on the women driving all over these streets. Give them eyes to see and ears to hear. Amen."

I wasn't aware that you could use the "eyes to see" verse to apply to driving skills, but Andrew is a pastor and I guess he can do whatever he wants.

I take a bite. It's okay, but not as good as the turkey.

I don't like change.

"Challenges, folks. Who wants to go first?" Andrew swallows and looks expectantly toward me and Jack.

This week we had to write down the top three things we thought could be problem areas in our marriage. I've been praying about this one all week, and even though He didn't write the answer on my front windows with a Sharpie, I definitely know what God's answer is.

"Jack can go first," I say. Mine needs to be last.

Jack shrugs and nods. "Okay." He grabs a piece of paper from his pocket and clears his throat. "I think we'll probably struggle with who will do some of the stuff we've each been accustomed to doing ourselves. Like finances and stuff like that."

Andrew nods. "Good point. You'll have to work out a system."

"And I think we might have some minor issues with dinner stuff," Jack says, grinning at me.

"Hey. You knew I didn't cook before you asked me out, much less proposed," I say, smiling back at him.

"Takeout." Andrew nods.

"And lastly, I think we might have some problems as it relates to future kids."

I frown at that one. "What problems?"

Jack smiles at me. "I think you'll want to wait longer to have them than I will."

"Oh," I say. Actually, I could have guessed this. Jack loves kids. Always has, always will. It's a sweet trait, but he's right.

I can wait a year. Or five.

Andrew is nodding. "All good things to discuss. And as far as the kid thing goes, it's a great thing to pray about. Kids will change everything. Don't forget that."

Jack nods.

"Your turn, Maya." Andrew takes another monster bite of his pastrami.

I unfold my list nervously, swallowing, breathing another quick prayer.

This is Your will, right?

It's His will.

I take a deep breath. "I'm worried about how we'll adjust to living in a new place surrounded by people we don't know."

Jack's head snaps up.

"I think we might have issues with him working too much and me missing my family and friends back here. And lastly, I'm a little concerned about the whole getting married and moving thing. Too many emotions at one time." I swallow and take another deep breath, waiting for the reaction.

"What?" Jack says so quietly that I barely hear the question.

"We need to move," I answer, just as quietly.

"To Seattle?"

I nod. "To Seattle. I'm not saying it's going to be easy," I warn him.

"I know, honey."

"But I'll try to adjust."

Andrew is just looking back and forth at both of us. Jack is grinning so wide that I can see his back molars, and I feel a weird mix of relief and sadness.

"Well," Andrew says. "This is a surprise twist to our last counseling meeting."

"It may not be the last," I tell him. "You will probably get a bunch of long-distance calls in the near future."

"Just as long as you call the church line," Andrew jokes.

"It's not for certain yet," Jack says to me. "I still have to get the job."

I just shrug. It's a formality. I know he's going to get the job because I know God has us moving to Seattle.

What I don't know is why.

And I'm trying not to think about my family and friends here, and how I'll do without them.

Anytime I do think about it, I immediately get teary eyed.

Andrew finishes one half of his sandwich. "Well, let's talk about the whole 'moving away' thing then, okay?"

We spend the next hour discussing the hows and whens and whys, and at the end of the hour, I feel a little calmer than I did at the beginning.

Jack is still ecstatic.

"You're sure?" he asks me as he walks me to my car. We've already waved good-bye to Andrew and wished him luck with all the women drivers out there.

I open my door and look up at Jack. It's dark outside now, and the only lights around are creepy, dingy streetlights.

"I'm sure," I tell him.

"Positive?" he asks. "Because we can stay in Hudson. I don't want you to think that we can't stay here, that we have to move."

I nod. "I know."

"Because I don't have to put my résumé in," he continues. "I mean, nothing has been done yet, so we don't have to do anything still."

It's like he's trying to talk me out of it now. I look up at him. "I thought you wanted to move," I say.

"I do. I just want to be sure that you are 100 percent on board with this."

I take a deep breath. "Look, Jack, I'm not saying that I won't have a hard time with this. You'll probably witness a lot of tears over the next few months because change is not something that I handle very well."

"I know," Jack says gently.

"But I really do believe that this is where God is taking us. I don't know why, and I'll probably not react well to it sometimes, but I really do know it's God leading us there."

Jack is quiet for a minute, just looking at my face. "Okay," he says finally, "I'll put my application in."

"Okay," I say.

He leans down and gives me a kiss. "It will be an adventure, you know."

I nod. "I know."

He holds the car door open for me. "Have fun with your mom tomorrow."

I grin. "I will." I haven't told Mom about my decision yet.

I'll tell her tomorrow. And I need to let Alisha know that she will want to promote Lisa instead.

Which will be fine with Ethan, since then she'll work the day shift with him.

"I love you," he says gently, leaning in for another kiss.

"I love you back. See you tomorrow, Jack," I say, smiling and starting my car.

He watches me leave the parking lot.

Mom gets to my apartment at eight o'clock the next morning.

Eight o'clock.

On my day off.

I stumble to the door straight from bed. I'm wearing my pink-striped pajama pants, a black cami, and no socks. I fell asleep last night watching *What Not to Wear* and dragged myself into the bed at two.

I open the door and just squint at her.

"Well, this is a welcome sight to see after driving for an hour," Mom says, rolling her eyes. "Nice hair."

"Mmm," I moan, rubbing my out-of-control curls. "What time is it?"

"Eight o'clock. We've got lots to do today, Maya! Go take a shower."

There is no question in her voice. I nod. "Yes, ma'am." I start drifting toward the direction of the bathroom. Calvin is all excited that Mom is here, and she's looking around my trashed apartment, tsking.

"What is all this?" she asks, pointing to our stack of gifts.

"Presents," I say.

"You aren't going to put them away?"

I shake my head. "I have to write thank-you notes."

Mom reaches in her purse and hands me a cute little note-book. "Here. Happy week before the wedding."

"Thanks. What's it for?"

"To write down what gifts you get," Mom says in a *duh* tone of voice.

"Oh."

"Please go shower so you can have some coffee and wake up."

I nod. "On my way."

Twenty minutes later, I'm showered, have makeup on, and there's curling cream in my still-wet hair.

Mom is sorting through the presents and writing each one down.

"You don't have to do it, Mom," I say.

"I know. I want to." She points to the speakers. "Did you register for that?"

"Apparently. Jack wandered off for about ten minutes when the two of us were registering, and I now know where he went."

Mom just shakes her head and smiles.

We take my car, and I make a quick stop by Cool Beans. Lisa took my shift today, and she waves as I run in. "Hey, Maya!"

"Hi, Lisa." I smile at Ethan. "Can I get a mocha to go please? Large. And a small regular dark roast."

Lisa rings me up, and Ethan makes the mocha and pours Mom's coffee.

I pay and leave. The florist, the caterer, and the bridal store are in San Diego. The DJ and the church are here. We decide to do the San Diego stops first.

I decide to tell Mom about Seattle on the hour-long drive.

"So, Mom," I start.

She looks over at me and just smiles a sad smile. "I figured."

"What?"

"I figured," she says. She pats my leg. "And I think it's a good thing. Or at least I will. Someday. Maybe."

I glance over at her, and she's sipping her coffee slowly. "I don't like it too much," I say quietly.

"Me neither. But it's life. And I've always wanted to spend some time in Seattle. So, you might see a lot of us there."

"Good," I say. "You guys have to come visit. A lot. Okay?"

I see a tear slip down her cheek, but she bats it away quickly and straightens up.

Good. Because crying and driving on the interstate are not good activities to do at the same time. As I can attest to from past experiences. And anytime my mother cries, I cry.

So I try very hard to pretend that I didn't see anything and stare straight ahead through the windshield.

"So, bridal store first?" Mom asks as we start to hit the San Diego traffic.

I nod. "Sure. Why not?"

We get to Jared's and walk inside. Samantha, the beautiful woman who helped me try on dresses, is standing behind a desk near the front.

"Maya!" she says warmly, and I'm immediately impressed that she remembers me. "We got your dress in last week; let me go get it. Want to head on back to dressing room four?"

I nod. After much debating, I finally chose the bridesmaid dresses from here, too. I'm picking Jen's up for her, and Kate is coming by to get hers tonight after Zach gets home.

Mom and I go into the dressing room, and Samantha pushes a huge bag at me a few minutes later. "The bra and the slip are both in there; so is the veil. If you ladies need help, just let me know."

Mom helps me with the bra and with the millions of buttons running up the back. "Goodness!" she exclaims halfway up my back. "The people who designed this were not thinking of the mother of the bride's fingers."

I laugh.

I get the dress on, and it fits perfectly. As I come out of the dressing room, Samantha is nodding and smiling. "Wow, that looks even better than I remember!" she says sweetly.

It does. They took about a foot off the bottom of the dress and cinched it in more around the waist and the top so I don't have to worry about a Janet Jackson wardrobe malfunction at my own wedding.

I'm thinking that would be bad.

I bought shoes last week, and I brought them today. Mom digs them out of my purse and brings them over.

They match perfectly.

I grin. "Yay!"

Samantha and Mom both laugh. "I love my job," Samantha says.

We load the dresses into the car and start driving toward the florist. They are delivering the flowers to the church on the wedding day but told Mom they would have a sample of the centerpieces for the reception when we came today.

We walk in and find a gorgeous—I mean, *gorgeous*—display of blue hydrangeas, tiny pink button flowers, white lilies, and greenery sitting on a table near the front of the store.

I'm not a florist or a typical girl or Leopold from *Kate and Leopold*. I wasn't even sure what a hydrangea was before we came the first time.

A lady is in the back. "Can I help you?" she asks me and Mom.

"Yes, we're here to see a sample for my daughter's wedding next week. It's Maya Davis," Mom says.

The lady checks a note in the back and then nods to the beautiful display. "That's it."

"Wow," I whisper. I poke at the hydrangea, and the lady has quite the fit.

"Don't, don't, don't touch the flowers," she stutters, running over. "Those were put together with care and precision, and I don't want you to mar their beauty."

Mom and I both squint at her. "They aren't anchored in?" Mom asks.

"They can't be touched?" I ask at the same time.

"They are anchored in," the lady says, breathing hard. "But they are only a sample, so they may not be as firmly placed as the finished product will be."

Okay, so I'm not going to be able to touch it. We look at it for a few more minutes, make sure we're on the schedule for next Saturday, and leave.

"Well, that was weird," Mom says as we climb in my car.

"Very."

"Beautiful arrangement though."

"Maybe it's because she's so nitpicky?" I ask. Still, I have little cousins coming to this wedding. There's no way that at least one of the arrangements isn't going to be touched.

"Maybe." Mom shrugs. "Let's go to the caterer and get a sandwich. I didn't sleep in like someone else, so I'm hungry."

I grin.

We decided to go with Bread Heaven for the catering. I'm pretty sure I couldn't have gone with anyone else.

We double-check our order with them, and Mom makes the final payment. "We'll be at the church about an hour before to set up," the man says.

I nod. We ordered a bunch of appetizers just because they sounded so good. And the wedding cake, of course.

I think we're set on food for this afternoon wedding.

Mom gets a sandwich, and I give in and get the same turkey and cranberry sandwich I got last time. Only this time, we get them to go.

Mom's in question mode on the drive back to Hudson.

"So, if Jack gets the job, when will you find out?" she asks, munching on her sandwich.

I'm having a hard time unwrapping mine and holding the steering wheel, so Mom takes it from me and pulls off the wrapper. "Thanks. He told me it would be about a month after we got back from the honeymoon."

Mom nods. "Okay. And when would you guys move then?"

"I think he'd have to report there by the fifteenth of January," I say. Jack told me all of this last night.

Somehow it makes me feel better, because at least we'd get to stay here for Christmas. I can't imagine moving around Christmas.

And missing out on Ben's first one.

Mom just nods. "Good. Then you guys can come for Christmas at our house."

"Good. Because that's the plan. We want to stay at your house Christmas Eve, if that's okay."

"Just as long as you don't interrupt Santa Claus. I think Zach and Kate might stay with us, too. They haven't decided yet."

We get back to Hudson and head straight to meet the DJ. Jen recommended the guy she used. I guess he works as a DJ for a local Christian station that I never listen to.

They play the same songs over and over and over.

Unless Elvis is singing them, repetition gets old fast.

The radio station looks like any other storefront on Walker Street, but the inside is a lot different. There's a wall almost directly in front of us and a lady sitting at a desk. "Can I help you?"

"We have a meeting with Little D," I say, feeling slightly stupid.

Seriously, who goes by Little D?

The most I've done is talk to this guy on the phone, and he said he was available that weekend and would give us a terrific deal.

The lady at the desk nods and sends us to an office buried in the very back. The recording light is off above the door, and I knock lightly.

"Come in!"

I open the door and figure out how Little D got his name. It is not too often that I'm eye level with guys, considering I'm five foot two, but this guy is most definitely my height.

Maybe shorter.

Poor Little D.

He reaches over and shakes my hand. "Maya?" he asks me.

"Yes. This is my mom, Mary."

"Nice to meet you," Mom says.

"Same to you. Have a seat," Little D says, waving to his disaster of an office. There are two chairs free of the stacks of papers littering his desk, so Mom and I sit there.

He sits down behind the desk. He's maybe in his late twenties or early thirties and has a deep radio voice that doesn't seem like it belongs to his tiny frame.

"So, eight days," he says, grinning. "Are you excited?"

"Very," I nod, smiling back.

"Did you bring the song list?"

I nod and pull the paper from my purse. He asked me to write all the songs we wanted for the first dance, father/daughter dance, mother/son dance, and the entrance and exit. He also asked for a list of songs I hated, so he wouldn't play those.

He looks over my list and just nods. "Good choices. I really like Frank Sinatra."

"So does my dad," I say with a smile.

"Well, I'll be there to set up pretty much when the wedding starts, so everything will be all ready when you guys walk in," Little D says.

I nod.

We finish up with him, and by the time we leave, it's almost three o'clock. I look at Mom, starting to feel the busyness of the day.

"How are you doing?" I ask.

She nods. "One more stop."

We drive to Bethany Church. My mom still hasn't seen it yet.

"Oh wow!" she says appreciatively as we pull into the parking lot. "This is beautiful!"

"Isn't it great? Wait until you see the inside."

"You should definitely get some pictures of you two on the front lawn," Mom says.

We finally booked a photographer two weeks ago: Lila Harris. She came recommended from another couple at church, and after looking at her work, we checked to see if she was available. And lucky for us, she was.

We walk into the church, and I find Pastor Mark again. "Is it okay if I show my mom around?" I ask after we say our greetings.

"Sure, sure!" he says. "Go right ahead. And if you have any questions at all, you just let me know. Okay?"

"Thanks!" I show Mom the sanctuary and then the adorable reception room.

"The decorations will definitely work here," Mom says. "And we can use all of those tables?"

"I think so," I say.

Mom is checking things off on her fingers. "So, we have lights, we have tables, we have flowers, we have food, we have napkins and utensils . . ." She keeps mumbling to herself as she walks around the room.

I'm pretty sure we have everything, and if I forgot something, I don't even care anymore. We will do without it.

"I think we've got it all!" she says brightly. She looks at me. "So, all the guests will come in here after the wedding while we take pictures."

I nod. "Right. And then Little D will announce us when Jack and I walk in."

"What a name, right?" Mom grins. "I guess we could start calling you Little M."

"How about Lil' M?" I say. "We'll get the whole rapper thing going."

Mom rolls her eyes. "Oh boy."

"Yo, yo, yo," I start, making the motions of spinning a record.

"Here we go."

"Yo, I'm here with my ma in the weddin' chapel," I continue. "And we're trying to figure out the details so the peeps won't . . ." I can't think of a word that rhymes with *chapel*.

"Grapple?" Mom suggests.

I hate that word. It sounds like a bad word. I'm not sure why, but I always blush whenever anyone says it.

"Eh," I say, rolling my shoulders. "I wasn't cut out to be a rapper."

"You can say that again," Mom says. "The Christmas presents from you live in infamy."

"Not *wrapper*, Mother. But thank you for the upbeat and encouraging comment. See if you ever get the Maya brand of Christmas wrapping paper again."

"Thank you, I would prefer not to," Mom says, grinning at me. "And just so you know, wrapping a jewelry box in leftover corn husks does not count as paper."

"It did in the olden days."

"Did not."

"Did too. People wrote on corn husks."

"People wrote on papyrus, Maya Davis. And let's leave. I feel weird arguing with my twenty-five-year-old daughter about paper in a church."

I just laugh.

CHAPTER NINETEEN

After two showers on Saturday, I get home and feel the insatiable need to take a bath.

Just for a little bit of variety.

Jack, Jen, and Travis came to help unload the presents, and after we finish stacking everything in the living room—with the exception of the lingerie gifts, which are quickly hidden in my room—they all decide we're getting pizza and watching a movie.

I guess my bath will have to wait.

"I'm voting for *Count of Monte Cristo*," Travis says.

"I don't have that movie," I say.

"I have it in my car."

"You keep it in there just in case?" I ask.

He grins.

"Well, I don't second the motion," Jen says, flipping her blond hair over her shoulder. "I think we should watch a romantic movie. You guys are about to get married. If that's not a good reason to watch a romance, then I don't know what is."

Jack comes into the living room from the kitchen where he was calling in our pizza order. "Twenty minutes," he announces.

"Good. That will give us time to eat before we decide what movie we're watching." I roll my eyes.

Jen, Jack, and I sit on the couch, and Travis sits on the floor, where Calvin immediately hustles into his lap.

"So," Jen says, grinning at me. "One week."

"I know," I say, shaking my head. In retrospect, the last three months have flown by. During the day to day, it seemed like forever, but not anymore.

Even the days when Ben was in the hospital seem to have gone by fast, now that he's growing and healthy.

"One week of blissful singleness left," Travis proclaims, and Jen immediately chucks a throw pillow at his head.

"What does that mean?" she demands, barely disguising her smile.

Travis ducks, and the pillow crashes into the presents behind him. I watch the tower teeter for a minute before it finally rights itself.

I really need to start putting those away.

Jack wraps an arm around my shoulders. "Time for my stuff to move on in," he says. "I've already been boxing things up."

Jen nods. "Good."

I look at Jack, and he nods. "Jen," I say quietly.

"Yeah?" she looks over at me and then nods. "Sure, definitely, feel free to use some of the boxes I collected. Where did we put those, honey?" she asks Travis.

"That's sweet, Jen, but I need to tell you something."

She looks down at her hands before she looks at me. "Oh," she says dully.

"What?" Travis asks, oblivious.

"I've applied for a job in Seattle," Jack says. "It's not a definite that I'll get it, but my boss seems to think there's a really good chance I will."

"Wow," Travis says. "Seattle."

Jen is still looking at her hands. "Seattle," she mumbles.

I reach for her shoulder. "But it will be okay," I say. "We'll e-mail and call and text still. And we'll be coming back here every couple of months anyway to see everyone."

She nods and takes a deep breath. "How long before you'll have to move?"

"The earliest will be January fifteenth," Jack tells her.

I can see her immediate relief. January still seems like light-years away. It's only the last week of October right now.

"Okay," she says quietly. "Okay." She's still not looking at us, and I have a feeling she's blinking back tears.

I look away. Tears just get me going.

The doorbell rings, and I stand to get the pizza. Travis hands Jack a $10 bill, and Jack brings over the cash.

A pimple-afflicted kid is standing there with the insulated pizza carrier. "I've got a pepperoni and sausage and a pineapple and bacon," he squeaks.

"That's right," Jack says, handing him a wad of cash. "Thanks."

"Have a good night."

We put the pizzas on the coffee table, and I grab paper plates and a bunch of napkins.

By the time everyone leaves, it's almost midnight, and we never watched a movie.

"Sweet dreams, love," Jack says, kissing me goodnight. "Just think, one week from today and I don't have to leave." He grins, hugs me tight, kisses me again, and goes down the metal stairs, leaving me alone with my beagle in an apartment that smells like grease.

"One week," I tell Calvin. "Weird, weird, weird." I'm pretty sure it will go by extremely slow since I'm so excited about the wedding.

The week flies by. I tell Alisha on Monday that I will most likely be moving sometime in the middle of January. Andrew calls on Tuesday to double-check the rehearsal time, and Ethan shows up on Friday with a present that looks like it was wrapped by a dog.

"Happy last day of work for two weeks," he says awkwardly, handing me the present.

"Awww, Ethan!" I say, making a big deal about it since I know he doesn't want me to. "Thank you!"

"Don't say that until you open it," he says.

I pull the wrapping paper off, and it's my favorite mug from Cool Beans—an extra-large blue mug with big sunflowers painted on it. "Ethan!"

"I know how much you like it, so I asked Alisha where she bought it." Now he's acting very shy. "I just wanted to give it to you today so it doesn't get broken in the middle of all the wedding gifts tomorrow."

I give him a hug. "Thanks, Ethan."

"Mm-hmm," he says, hugging me quickly. "Now, seriously, we need to get to work."

I'm only working until noon, and Lisa is going to take the rest of my shift. The rehearsal starts at five, and the rehearsal dinner will be at six thirty at a Mexican restaurant here in town.

I jump in my car at noon after getting a hug from Lisa. "Happy start to the wedding!" she shouts.

I drive straight to the church, coffee-smelling clothes and all. Mom and Dad are meeting me there with all the decorations, and we'll get those put up before the rehearsal, hopefully with enough time for me to change into the dress Jen insisted I wear tonight.

Mom and Dad are going to stay at a hotel tonight so they aren't driving the hour back and forth today and tomorrow. And

Zach, Kate, and Ben will be staying in the room next to them, but they aren't driving up until the rehearsal.

Mom and Dad's car is already in the parking lot, and I go inside and find the decorations are halfway done.

"Hey, honey," Dad grins, giving me a hug. "Last day of singleness. What do you think?" He waves to the decorations.

They look beautiful. Mom and I bought tons of little twinkle lights, and they are draped elegantly over the black curtains. When the lights are off in here, it will look like a fairyland. All the tables are set up, and Mom is just now pulling out the tablecloths.

"We got an early start," Mom says, waving at me. "I want you to have plenty of time to get ready for tonight."

"Wow, it looks awesome!" The lights were going to take the most time. Now, we just need to get the tablecloths and chairs set up. The florist is coming in the morning to set up the sanctuary and put the centerpieces on all the tables.

It's beginning to sink in a little bit.

"I'm getting married!" I yell, jumping up and down.

Dad starts laughing. "Good time to finally recognize it."

The night goes by so fast, even though I try my hardest to make it slow down. The rehearsal passes in a blink. Dinner is over and done with before I feel like I've even appreciated the excellent Mexican food. Jack's mom is hugging me and saying how excited she is that I'm going to be in her family. Jack is passionately kissing me goodnight as we leave the restaurant.

Then it's time to go home and get a good night's sleep before the wedding.

Right.

I step into my apartment, which is quickly becoming not just mine. Jack's stuff is now piled around the gifts, and it's impossible to walk through the apartment without hitting or kicking something.

Calvin is sitting in the middle of the living room, looking depressed.

"I agree," I tell him.

Between the two of us—with me doing most of the work and Calvin doing most of the sitting there aimlessly—we get the gifts put away and most of Jack's stuff shoved into a closet. We can organize it when we get back from the honeymoon.

It's almost one in the morning before I finish. And I'm still too jittery to go to sleep. So, I grab my Bible and flounce onto the bed.

I flip to 1 John, remembering one of the passages we went over in premarital counseling.

"Beloved, if God so loved us, we also ought to love one another. No one has seen God at any time; if we love one another, God abides in us, and His love is perfected in us. By this we know that we abide in Him and He in us, because He has given us of His Spirit" (4:11-13).

I think about that.

God, help me to always love Jack. Regardless of what happens, whether it's Seattle or here or somewhere else entirely, Lord, help me to remember that this is the man You've chosen for me. Please help us to follow You above everyone and everything else, Lord.

I pull the covers up to my chin and close my eyes. I do need sleep.

My wedding, after all, is tomorrow. I look at my clock once more, the LED lights glowing in the dark room.

Actually, it's today.

I get to the church at ten o'clock. The florist is already here, and so is my mom.

"No, no, that arrangement goes here," Mom is telling the lady. She's already in her dress, hair done, and looking gorgeous.

"Sorry, sorry. We'll fix it."

I grin.

I did my hair and makeup at home, and I think it looks pretty good, all things considered. My hair is actually curling like I hoped it would.

"Hey," Jen says from behind me.

"Hi, Jen." I give her a hug.

"Maya?" Mom peers from the stage to the back where I'm standing. "What are you doing? We need to get you into your dress; you have pictures in an hour!"

I don't try to tell her that it only takes about ten minutes to get me into my dress.

I find the room where all the girls are supposed to be getting ready. Mom brought my dress with her.

"Well, why don't we go ahead and just fix your hair and makeup," Jen says, pulling a curling iron and makeup bag from her purse.

I thought I already had, but I don't push it.

An hour later, I'm curled, hairsprayed, and dressed. And nervous. I can feel my heartbeat in my hands.

I'm not sure that's a good thing.

The photographer sticks her head in. "Everyone ready?" she asks, grinning. Dad is right behind her, and I think he gets a little teary at the sight of me in my gown.

Pictures seem to take forever, and by the time we're done, my cheeks hurt. And I'm ready to just get going with it already!

One o'clock takes forever to get here.

Zach knocks on the door to our room and pokes his head in. "All ready?" he asks, grinning.

"Yes, can we please just start?" I ask. "Find Andrew and tell him to get this party started."

He laughs. "Patience was never really your strong suit." Then he grins big-brotherly at me. "Love you, sister. You look beautiful."

I grin.

Finally, we get the cue from the photographer, and everyone files to the closed sanctuary door. Dad is standing with me in the back, Jen is right in front of me, and Kate is before her. Zach and Ben are going to lead the procession, since Ben is our ring bearer.

And a very alert one. He's fast asleep in his daddy's arms.

Kate looks back at me and grins. "Happy wedding day, Maya."

The music starts, Zach and Ben walk in, and the girls follow. Dad looks at me.

"Love you." He grins and squeezes my hand super hard.

"Love you," I say back to him, smiling.

The doors open, the bridal march begins, and we're walking down the aisle.

Jack is standing at the bottom of the stage, waiting. And oh my, is he a sight to behold today. His hair is gelled to perfection, and that tux looks amazing on him.

So does the huge grin splitting his face.

Andrew is standing next to Jack. "Who gives this woman?" he asks as Dad and I stop in front of the two of them.

"Her mom and I do," he says, kissing my cheek.

I take Jack's hand, and he helps me up the stairs.

"You look gorgeous," he whispers in my ear.

"You don't look so bad yourself." I grin.

"Dearly beloved," Andrew starts.

I can't keep my eyes off Jack. He's smiling so sweetly at me. I feel treasured and beautiful just looking at him.

We repeat our vows, and I get a new ring, one that is equally as gorgeous as the first one he gave me.

"You may now kiss the bride."

Jack leans in, and even my toes are tingling once he pulls away. He grins at me, eyes shining.

"It is with great joy that I get the pleasure of presenting Mr. and Mrs. Dominguez," Andrew says with gusto.

The audience applauds, and I see my mom crying.

"Shall we, Mrs. Dominguez?" Jack grins at me, tucking my hand over his arm.

"We shall, Mr. Dominguez." I nod.

We run down the aisle and out the doors toward . . .

Toward what? Seattle? Hudson? Somewhere completely different? I look at Jack, who is laughing and grinning and just glowing.

And I know it doesn't matter.

God matters. Jack matters.

And the rest will work itself out.

For now? I just want some cake.

ABOUT THE AUTHOR

ERYNN MANGUM plans her life around caffeine, but when she's not tipping the coffee mug, she's spending time with her husband, Jon O'Brien, or hanging out with family and friends. She's the author of the LAUREN HOLBROOK series and the MAYA DAVIS series. Learn more at www.erynnmangum.com.